MW01533633

Edith and
the Mysterious Stranger

Also by Linda Weaver Clarke

Melinda and the Wild West

Edith and
the Mysterious Stranger

A Family Saga in
Bear Lake, Idaho

Linda Weaver Clarke

Bedside Books
An imprint of American Book Publishing
5442 So. 900 East, #146
Salt Lake City, UT 84117-7204
www.american-book.com
Printed in the United States of America on acid-free paper.

Edith and the Mysterious Stranger

Artwork designed by George Clarke, design@american-book.com

Publisher's Note: This is a work of fiction. Names, characters, places, and incidents either are the product of the author's imagination, or are used fictitiously, and any resemblance to actual persons, living or dead, events, or locales is entirely coincidental.

ISBN-13: 978-1-58982-469-0
ISBN-10: 1-58982-469-5

Clarke, Linda Weaver, Edith and the Mysterious Stranger

Special Sales

These books are available at special discounts for bulk purchases. Special editions, including personalized covers, excerpts of existing books, and corporate imprints, can be created in large quantities for special needs. For more information e-mail info@american-book.com.

In memory of my parents:
Marcus Gilbert Weaver (1914–2005),
my father, a man of dignity
Florence Milred Weaver (1917– 1978),
my mother, who was determined to wait
for the man of her dreams

Foreword

Linda Weaver Clarke has a talent for weaving fact and fiction into a satisfying story. Her research and dedication to accuracy give readers a taste of the true Wild West. Also, her ability to create realistic and likable characters gives readers a chance to experience the West, as it must have been, through the eyes of characters we grow to love and admire.

In this tender love story, *Edith and the Mysterious Stranger*, Clarke introduces her readers to the world of outlaws and cattle rustlers. Our eyes are opened to the problems caused by lawlessness on the open frontier.

In addition to the knowledge gained about the Wild West, readers are also given some insights into human nature. Edith sets her sights high and is determined that her dreams will come true. It is important to look for the best in others and demand the best from ourselves. I think readers of all ages will enjoy this new installment in the Roberts family saga.

Betsy Brannon Green
Best-selling mystery author

Chapter 1
A Sneaky Husband

Melinda listened carefully as the door squeaked shut. She heard footsteps walk across the porch and disappear in the distance. She sighed with relief. Finally, he was gone and she was alone now. This was what she was waiting for, a chance to escape. She felt like a prisoner in her own home. She had been bedridden for two whole months, and was sick and tired of her bed, her walls, her books, and especially looking at her wardrobe full of clothes that no longer fit. How she wished she could snatch one of her favorite dresses and go out for a stroll!

Melinda looked down at her swollen belly and tenderly stroked it with her hand. She knew she was bedridden for the sake of her unborn child, and was resigned to staying in bed, but toward the end of the day boredom set in. She needed something more to do, some way to bide her time, a way to fight off the depression.

Already she had spent two months in bed and had another five months to go. How could she do it and remain sane? It was as if her life was on hold for nine whole months.

All she wanted to do was just get up and walk into the kitchen for a snack, but her overly protective husband forbade it. He was such a worrywart. Gilbert had offered to get her something to eat before he left again, but she had refused in a most indignant manner. She had refused because she was feeling a bit ornery.

Melinda had looked up into her husband's eyes and said adamantly, "I'm not hungry, Gilbert."

"But you've just got to eat something to ward off the morning sickness."

"Nothing sounds good to me. I just don't know what I want right now."

"Are you sure?"

"Just go! All right?" she snapped.

That was all Melinda had said and then she turned toward the window and stared off toward the Wasatch Mountains, avoiding his accusatory look.

She figured her ornery attitude had stemmed from being helpless. Her husband had been pampering her, waiting on her, but she wanted to be independent. She wanted to go out and dig in the soil, plant a few flowers, hoe a few weeds. She would also like to tidy up the house a bit and make it clean and neat. Since she was down in bed, Jenny, her stepdaughter, had been keeping the house clean and doing a good job, too.

This was frustrating because Melinda enjoyed her independence. Now she was dependent upon others for her every need. This was completely against her grain. In the past, she never had enough hours in the day to play the piano or have some quiet time to herself to read. And now that she had all the time in the world, she couldn't pick up another book if she tried. She was all read out.

Melinda shook her head with irritation. What was wrong with her? She loved reading. Perhaps her orneriness was affecting her attitude about everything.

When her sixteen-year-old stepdaughter, Jenny, and her six-year-old son, John, were out of school they sometimes headed for Aunt Martha's to visit and that was where they were today. Melinda was alone now, and she decided that it was time to rise and take control of her life. After all, she could take a little stroll into the kitchen and get a snack all by herself with no one hovering over her. What harm would that do?

Melinda placed the book she had been reading on the bed, pushed the covers aside, and slid her feet to the cool wooden floor. She looked down at her small, round belly and stroked it once again. She was only four months along and was barely showing. She had not felt any movement of life yet, but she couldn't wait. She was feeling pretty good and had not had any cramping now for over two weeks and was very much relieved.

Two months ago, she began to have cramps five minutes apart. When they wouldn't stop and became stronger and unbearably painful, Gilbert ran for the doctor. Melinda was put in bed indefinitely. Since she was bedridden, she hadn't had any problems and what cramps she did have were very minor. Surely, it would be all right to get out of bed for a few minutes.

Melinda slowly rose to her feet and walked over to the wardrobe, pulled her robe out, and slipped it on. She grabbed a brush, looked critically at herself in the mirror, and began to brush her dark auburn hair. Her thick tresses had a natural curl, and when the sunlight shown through the window, they shimmered with a reddish glow.

Melinda was a strikingly beautiful woman with a smooth, velvety complexion and fine, delicate features. She was thirty-four years of age and was unusually tall. She had beautiful green eyes that twinkled when she smiled. Gilbert had told her that her eyes were the color of shamrocks, and they brightened when she was happy.

With a smile of satisfaction, she laid the brush on her dresser and walked down the hall. Just as she entered the living room, she heard a deep warm voice, as if chiding a small child.

"Ah, ah, ah!"

Melinda was startled. She quickly jerked her head around and saw her husband sitting on the sofa with his arms folded across his chest, with a broad grin on his face. He had the look of a parent catching a child with her hand in the cookie jar, and he was enjoying the shocked expression on his wife's face.

At the age of thirty-eight, Gilbert was ruggedly handsome, had expressive dark brown eyes, and his strong jaw gave the look of authority, but his soft eyes betrayed him. He was as mellow as a cuddly kitten, good-humored, and tolerant. And the love and devotion he had for his wife shown in his eyes. His dark brown hair was thick and wavy. He was a cattle rancher with broad shoulders and was an imposing figure. He stood six-foot-two inches, every inch of him muscle. It was impossible to ignore especially when he folded his arms across his chest so he could look stern when making his decisions.

That was the expression he had at this very moment. His arms were folded, accentuating his biceps. His face was stern, but his eyes glistened with amusement that he had caught Melinda out of bed.

Inside, he was suppressing a grin, hoping to look like a stern parent as he asked, "Melinda, what are you doing out of bed?"

"I…" Her mind feverishly searched for an answer.

"Yes? I'm listening."

"I…uh…you see." She took a deep breath and plunged in. "Gilbert, I'm sick of my bed. I'm sick of reading. I'm sick of being waited on. And I'm sick of the pictures on my wall."

Gilbert chuckled. "All right, I'll buy you new pictures."

Melinda placed her hands on her hips with indignation and stared at his broad grin. He was amused at catching her out of bed. This irritated her to no end. How did he know that she would sneak out of bed after he left the house?

Looking at his amused expression, she asked soberly, "How did you know?"

"Know what?"

"I heard you walk outside. I heard the door shut. How did you know I would get out of bed?"

Grinning even wider, he rose to his feet and walked over to her, took her by the shoulders, and looked into her large green eyes. "Do you think I don't know you? When I asked you if you needed anything, you got a little impatient with me, snapped a bit. Then when I leaned over to kiss you goodbye, I could see it in your eyes. I knew what was on your mind. So, I just turned around and snuck back into the house."

Melinda slumped and dropped her hands to her sides. She wanted to defend herself but knew she would lose even if she tried. She looked at him and said softly, "I'm feeling better, though. I haven't had any cramps now for two weeks."

It sounded lame, and she knew it. She even knew his answer even before he spoke.

"That's because you've been in bed. There's no need getting out when I'm here."

At that moment, Melinda felt ashamed. She realized that Gilbert was trying to help. He was the most unselfish man she knew, and she should never take his helpfulness for granted. Not every man was this supportive, and she knew it. She needed to be more patient and tolerant.

Melinda knew that she could never love a man as much as she did Gilbert, and the love she had for her husband was deep. She had been so absorbed with self-pity that she had taken her frustrations out on her dearest possession: her husband. She was not thinking of anyone but herself, and she did not like who she was at that very moment.

Why had she taken her frustrations out on the one she loved most? Tears welled up in the corners of her eyes as she admitted her failings to herself. She wiped them away with the back of her hand as they trickled down her face.

With a quivering voice, she said, "I'm sorry. Please forgive me."

Gilbert smiled as he pulled her into his arms and held her lovingly, listening to her sobs of regret. As she quieted down, he pulled back and looked at her tear-stained face.

He took a handkerchief from his pocket and gently dabbed her cheeks as he said, "Don't worry, my Love. Everything will be all right. I've got Joe doing most of the chores on the ranch for me so I can be close to home and check on you from time to time."

"I know, Gilbert. I just don't like being dependent on others. I'm not used to it."

Melinda's eyes lowered with humility. A few small strands of hair had fallen appealingly about her face, and being with child had caused her countenance to glow, giving her a radiant look. Her expression was so enchanting that it had an effect on Gilbert, making his heart swell. He slightly lifted her chin and gazed into her eyes and the message he communicated was one of devotion and adoring love.

He tucked his finger under her chin, lifted it toward him, and kissed her tenderly. Her lips were warm and sweet as he gave her a lingering kiss, one of tenderness and longing. A warm glow filled his heart at the touch of her lips, and his heart picked up speed. How he loved this woman!

As he stroked her silky hair that had cascaded around her shoulders, he let it slide through his fingers. Then he wrapped his arms around her. He held her close to his chest and she melted into his arms.

As Melinda felt his strong and protective arms tighten around her, she gave in to the delicious warmth spreading through her as she returned his kiss with just as much longing, turning her senses to mush. Lost in the wonder of his kisses, all her depression and concerns began to fade away. She marveled at what a delightful pleasure it was to be in love.

Gilbert snuggled his face into her tresses and whispered, "I love the way you melt into my arms when I hold you."

The way Melinda responded to his hugs always had an effect on Gilbert. She had responded like this from the very first day he held her in his arms, and he had never had anyone react to his hugs like that before. Gilbert pulled back and gazed into her eyes with affection.

"I just worry about you, Melinda. I don't want any harm to come to you. Besides, you have miscarried several times before. If you won't stay in bed, then we'll have to do what the doctor suggested."

Melinda instantly jerked back and looked into his eyes with shock. "No, Gilbert. I won't take alcohol to stop the cramping. It's against my beliefs. You know that. Besides, what would it do to the baby? I can't risk hurting her."

Gilbert grinned at her spunk. "I know how you feel about it, Honey. But we need to do whatever it takes to protect our baby. So, you'll go to bed then?"

Melinda nodded. She was defeated and she knew he was right. She could not fight it. She didn't want to lose another baby, and Gilbert was only trying to protect her and their unborn child.

Then with a jolt of surprise, Gilbert's eyes widened as he asked, "Did you just say 'her'?"

Melinda nodded.

"How do you know?"

"Just a feeling. Don't bet on it, though."

Gilbert chuckled with delight. "How about if I make a bed on the sofa for you, and you can watch me fix supper?"

Melinda nodded. "I'd like that."

The living room and the kitchen were situated in one large room with the kitchen and dining room on the left side of the room and the living room and fireplace on the right side of the room. Against one wall was her pride and joy. Gilbert had bought her an upright piano when they were first married. He enjoyed spoiling her with gifts, and a piano brought her great pleasure. She hadn't had a chance to play since the morning sickness set in about three months ago.

Gilbert took her hand and led her to the sofa. Before she sat down, he placed his hand on her round belly and asked, "Any movement yet?"

Melinda smiled. He was just as eager as she was and it pleased her beyond words. "No. But I'll tell you when I do."

The concern and worry in Gilbert's eyes was obvious, and he had every reason to be. As he protectively took her in his arms without saying a word, he leaned his head against hers and took a deep ragged breath. As he let it out slowly, he tried to put aside his uneasiness, his apprehension.

Melinda could feel something was bothering him and suspected what it might be. She felt his arms tighten around her and heard him breathe in deeply.

"Gilbert, what's wrong?"

He shook his head.

"What is it?"

Melinda leaned back to look into his face and his eyes had misted.

"Melinda, I couldn't bear it if something happened to you, too. Please listen to the doctor's advice. Do you understand what I'm trying to say?"

Melinda realized why he had become emotional and held her so protectively in his arms. She had married Gilbert just seven years ago. Jenny was Gilbert's daughter from a previous marriage. After nine months of marriage, his former wife died while giving birth to Jenny. He had blamed himself for years because he had brought her to Paris, Idaho, in 1887, when the west was quite wild and good doctors were few. That was sixteen years ago, but the memory of it was still vivid in his mind, and he was worrying that the same thing would happen to Melinda.

Feeling remorse for being impatient, Melinda gazed into his eyes and knew the anxiety he felt at that moment. "Gilbert …" She hesitated as she bit her lip, and then said softly, "I'm sorry I was ornery with you." She wiped his unruly hair back from his forehead, noticing the concern in his eyes. "I love you and will be more careful from now on."

Gilbert pulled her close to him again, held her tightly against his chest, and whispered in her ear, "Be as ornery as you like, but just stay in bed. Please? You've only got five months to go."

"Five months?" Melinda groaned in despair.

Chapter 2
The New Ranch Hand

David was standing in line at the Cozy J to be interviewed for the cattle drive by Gilbert Roberts. As he waited, twisting his hat in his hands, he turned toward the porch of the large ranch house and saw an attractive young woman. She had hair that was the color of wheat and large blue eyes, the color of the bluest lake he had ever seen. She was tall and slender with fine and delicate features. She wore a light blue flowered dress that fit snug to her waist, and her hair was pulled away from her face, allowing him to see her youthfulness and innocence. The afternoon sun accentuated the silkiness of her hair as it hung over her shoulders, and this young teenage woman intrigued David.

As his eyes swept over her, he realized, in all of his eighteen years, he had never seen a young woman this tall before, nor this attractive. As he watched her intently, she happened to turn in his direction and their eyes met. He smiled at her and gave a nod. She smiled back and quickly looked down at the ground, fiddling with her skirt. She acted quite shy, which he had not seen in a female for a long time. And that intrigued him all the more.

When she looked up again, their eyes met, she smiled shyly, and then turned away once again. Her smile and mannerisms gave her a sort of ethereal beauty, and he grinned as he noticed her coy manner. He wondered who this sweet young lady was.

When her eyes found his once again, he smiled; she flushed a rosy color and quickly averted her gaze. David chuckled with amusement. This distant flirtatiousness was sort of fun. He knew she had noticed him just as he had noticed her. This young woman's curiosity seemed to be just as piqued as his was.

Gunplay nudged him playfully and said, "What game are you two playin'? I've been watchin' ya'll." Then he grinned. "She's sure a perty one. Ain't she, David?"

David shook his head adamantly. "I don't know what you're talking about."

"She's a shy one but I reckon you could do something about it. Don't know if she'll give ya the time of day, but no harm in tryin'. Maybe after the interview, ya'll can meander over and introduce yourself. It doesn't hurt to get to know the boss's daughter."

"The boss's daughter?"

"Yup. I overheard the other hands talking about her. They said the boss has one daughter and one son. I just figured she was the one."

David nodded as he watched her from a distance. He was not really interested in helping with the cattle drive. He and Gunplay were here as part of a scheme, as part of a plan that had been set up. He was new to this cattle-rustling business, but he was not new to cattle ranches. He was young, but he was used to hard work and had been well trained on a few ranches.

David was a tall muscular young man. He had blond hair that touched the top of his shirt and light blue eyes with a distinct dimple in his chin, which made him attractive to most young women. And he knew it, too. His shoulders were broad, his arms were tan, and his eyes sparkled with mischief.

Why he chose this destination, he was not sure. He knew he wanted excitement in his life, and maybe this was the answer. He was a handsome young man with a touch of rebellion. Why he chose to be contrary, he was not sure, either. His father had been hard on him and pushed too much. Perhaps that was the reason. He knew of his father's love, but David felt rebellious. His mother was a soft-spoken woman and tried to help alleviate the tension that sprang up between David and his father. For some reason, they clashed. Now, here he was learning to be a cattle rustler. He knew his father would not approve, but this was *his* life and this was how he chose to live it.

Yes, this was going to be exciting. The adrenaline rushed through his veins as he thought about it. This was the life he had chosen, and he did not regret it one bit. He felt lucky that he had come upon the Tall Texan, one of Cassidy's Wild Bunch. He seemed like a good leader, and he had a well-planned scheme that he knew would work. Many had said the Tall Texan couldn't make it without Cassidy, but now he would prove them wrong.

David had to chuckle to himself as he thought how his own life had paralleled to Butch Cassidy's. They each came from religious backgrounds and loving parents, went to church regularly, and were taught correct principles of right and wrong. They both worked on ranches as teenagers, and a cattle rustler had befriended them both. David's mentor happened to be the Tall Texan. He often wondered if he would follow the same path and become another "Butch Cassidy." With the help of the Texan, perhaps he could be.

Gunplay nudged him. "It's your turn."

David turned and nervously walked inside the bunkhouse for his interview, hoping all would go well and that he would be hired.

Jenny was standing on the porch when the door of the house slammed shut. She turned around and saw her little six-year-old brother John walk outside. She gave him a wink as John looked up at his big sister.

"Jenny, where's Pa?"

"He's still interviewing men for the cattle drive."

"Oh. How come?"

"We don't have enough men to make the drive. We have twenty–five hundred head to take and we don't have enough men."

"Oh. When will he be done? I need to talk to him."

"Pretty soon. He's interviewing the last man now."

"Oh. I just have a question to ask him."

John's tone was low and soft with a touch of hope, and Jenny noticed it right away.

"What do you have on your mind, John?"

"I was just thinkin' about asking him…" He hesitated. "Well, if I could go along this year. I'm older now and bigger. And I've been working hard helping Pa. I've got a muscle, too. Wanna see?"

Jenny tried to suppress a giggle, knelt down beside her brother, and wrapped her arm around him. "'Fraid you can't go this year, buddy. He doesn't take greenhorns on a cattle drive."

John looked puzzled. "I don't have no green horns, Jenny."

She laughed softly. "No, you're the greenhorn. That means you don't have any experience."

"Oh."

John's voice was a little saddened as he looked down at the ground. Jenny took his face in her hands and turned it towards her. Then she looked into his beautiful dark brown eyes and pushed a few strands of brown hair out of his face. He was the spitting image of his father.

"John. It's not bad to be a greenhorn. But in a few years you'll get experience and then you can go with Pa. I've gone with him every year now since I was eight and that's because I know what to do. I'm going this year, too."

"Is it fun?"

Jenny's eyes brightened at the memory of it. Her father had taken her at such a young age because she had coaxed him every day until the day of the cattle drive. Not only that, Melinda encouraged it, not only to strengthen their relationship, but also to give her confidence in herself.

She was about to answer John's question when she saw an image move out of the corner of her eyes. She turned and saw the same young man walk out of the bunkhouse with a smile on his face. He looked too happy to have been turned down. She wished she knew what had happened. The young man was having an earnest conversation with the fellow beside him. Then the man pounded the younger one's back and laughed out loud. The older one climbed upon his horse and then waved to the younger one and rode off. Then the man with the adorable dimple turned and began walking toward her, smiling.

"Oh, my!"

"What, Jenny?"

She sucked in her breath, and her eyes widened. "Oh, my!"

"What?"

"He's coming this way."

John acted completely confused with his sister's actions. What had come over her?

Jenny had just turned sixteen and young men were beginning to notice her. This was new to her, and she was not sure how to handle it. She had been such a tomboy for so long that her parents finally insisted on her acting like a young lady. She was supposed to wear dresses more often instead of men's pants, and help around the house instead of doing the chores outside. Life was becoming quite interesting now that she was considered a young woman.

Jenny sensed that she had life in the palm of her hands, but at times she was not sure if she was ready for it. Her parents treated her like an adult, and she even took care of John when her stepmother wasn't feeling well. In fact, she never thought of her stepmother in any other way but her very own mother.

Melinda had treated her with unconditional love since the day she became her new teacher eight years ago. It was then that Melinda helped her in a most difficult time of her life, when her peers were rude and said unkind things, shunning her because she was different. When her father proposed to Melinda, Jenny was ecstatic with joy. At the age of eight, she would have a mother of her own choice.

David had a broad grin on his face as he walked up to Jenny and stood before her. He took off his hat and held it in his hands, twisting it as he looked into her eyes. The dimple in his chin deepened as he grinned, making him even more charming.

"I'm David Walker. I was just hired by your pa. He told me to take a note to you."

Jenny could not take her eyes off him and could not find any words to say. She noticed that he had a pleasant sounding voice and he was so good looking that she wondered if she should pinch herself to see if she was still awake.

David stuffed his hand in his pocket, pulled out a piece of paper, and then stretched forth his hand to give her the note, smiling the whole time. Jenny reached for it, and when his hand brushed against hers, she blushed. Why was this young man's smile having an effect on her? For all she knew, he could not be trusted. He could be a vagrant or something.

When she didn't say a word, David wondered what was wrong. He had never met anyone so shy before, or so lovely. No, shy was not the correct word. She wasn't necessarily shy, but was more reserved, aloof perhaps.

David grinned. "Cat got your tongue?"

She shook her head.

David cleared his throat and said, "The man that interviewed me is your pa, isn't he?"

Jenny nodded.

Then David pointed to the note in her hand and said, "I think your pa wants you to read that, if I'm not mistaken."

He waited for her to open the note and when she read it, her eyes widened. She looked up at David and asked, "What did you say to him?"

"What do you mean?"

"Pa usually doesn't do this."

Her voice was firm with a touch of bewilderment.

"Do what?"

"Well, he said you'll be staying with us until the roundup. He usually has the men come back in September, just the day

17

before. But for some reason, he's hired you on the spot and he says that you'll stay on until the roundup is over."

"That's right."

"I'm confused."

"Well, I've had a bunch of experience on other ranches, so maybe that was it. He's really nice. We talked for a long time."

"I noticed. He's usually done in half the time he spent with you."

She was baffled by this new information. Her father was never this trusting with someone he didn't know.

"So, what else did the note say?"

"That you'll be having supper with us and to set an extra plate."

David smiled. "Is that all right with you? You seem a little put out by all this."

Jenny shook her head vigorously. "No, just confused. That's all."

Gilbert called out to David, interrupting their conversation, and said he would show him his sleeping quarters in the bunkhouse. After telling him what time he was expected for supper, Gilbert headed back to the house.

As he dished up the baked potatoes, Jenny was spreading a tablecloth out on the table.

"Pa? Why did you hire a total stranger for the next couple months? I haven't seen you do that before."

"Don't know, Jen. He's had lots of experience even though he's only eighteen. I sort of felt sorry for him. Besides that, I just felt good about this young man, so I went with my gut feeling and asked him to stay."

"Oh." Jenny went to the cupboard, pulled out some plates, and then looked over her shoulder at her father. "I'm looking forward to this roundup, you know. I like being out in the open stars and hearing the cattle lowing in the background. It's my favorite time of year."

Gilbert turned toward his daughter with a sober look and said, "Uhm...Jen?"

"Yes, Pa?"

"I've been talking with your mother and we both feel that since you just turned sixteen you shouldn't go out on roundups any longer."

Jenny's face fell and her eyes widened. "What?"

"Well, you're now a young lady and it's about time that you..." Gilbert hesitated. "Well, acted like one. Young ladies don't go on roundups and trail drives."

Jenny became defensive and her voice was firm. "Pa, I've done this every year since I was eight. You have taken me on every roundup. This just isn't fair."

"Fair or not, you're now sixteen."

"Pa, listen to me. There are plenty of women who do this sort of thing. How about Jane Mason?"

"Who?"

"Jane Mason. She's been Idaho's Calamity Jane ever since 1899."

"But Jenny, she's a cattle and horse rustler. You can't compare yourself to a rustler. She's an outlaw."

"Sorry Pa. All right. How about Kittie Wilkins?"

Gilbert laughed out loud. "Now, she's one you can look up to. She's the Horse Queen of Idaho. She started her own business in 1885 and is still going strong. I heard that she had 4,000 head one time, and she exported them by train to the East Coast and sold them all to the United States Army."

With a look of despair, she begged, "Just let me go this last time for old time's sake and then I'll be a lady, Pa. Please?

You can't do this to me. I've been looking forward to this all year. If this is what being a woman is all about, then I don't like it one bit. Do women have to fight for everything we get?"

Melinda walked in at that moment, and with a touch of tenderness said, "Jenny, we just want the best for you. You shouldn't be in that sort of atmosphere any longer. These are rough and rugged men, and it's not what your father and I want for you. When you were younger, you needed your father desperately, and we both thought it was best. But now we want you to act like a young lady. That's why we chose this decision together, not to be mean or hurtful."

With frustration, Jenny responded readily. "Did you know that because women are being told what they can and can't do, they're rebelling and doing something about it?"

Melinda slowly sat down at the table and answered, "Yes, I know, dear."

"How about Miss Monaghan? She worked as a gold miner. She was a cowboy and she served on many juries during the past thirty years. She wasn't about to let men tell her how to live her life."

Gilbert looked astonished. "How could this be, Jen? You know that women are never called on juries, let alone allowed to work in gold mines. Besides that, a woman can't be a cowboy."

Jenny had a broad grin on her face, and with an air of satisfaction, said, "Well, Pa, she lived as a man for thirty years without anyone knowing it. She went by the name of Joe Monaghan and has been living in Idaho up until recently."

"Recently?"

"Yes, she died this year."

"All right, Jen. Where did you find this information and if she pretended to be a man, how was she found out?"

Jenny giggled as she touched her hand to her mouth. "Pa, can't you figure that out? The undertaker discovered it after she died. I read all about it in a magazine." Then she got a sly smile on her face and looked at her parents. "Now if you don't want this to happen to me, we have to make a compromise."

Jenny looked at her mother for support; if her mother agreed, then her father would, too. She knew how to play this game. If she could get one on her side, then the other would collapse and support the other one. It was as simple as that.

Jenny walked up to her mother with begging eyes and said, "Please, Mama? Just one last time? Let's compromise."

Melinda smiled. "Gilbert, she's got a point. It sounds like she's done her homework. What do you think about a compromise?"

Gilbert had a look of concern as he said, "I want her to be a lady, Melinda."

Jenny jumped in quickly. "Pa, I promise I won't beg to go after this year. Let this be my last time. Mama's been teaching me a lot about being a lady and I don't think there's going to be a problem."

Jenny and her father were always able to talk things through. He tried to listen and understand her point of view many times, but for some reason he was being a little more stubborn than usual. And Jenny was not sure why. Was acting like a lady that important to him?

Just then David knocked on the screen door, interrupting their discussion.

Gilbert called out, "Come in, David." When he opened the door and poked his head in, Gilbert gestured to the sofa.

"Come in and sit down. We're just having a family discussion. Maybe we can get your opinion on the subject."

"I'd be glad to."

David closed the door behind him. Then he meandered over to the sofa, sat down, and watched the family.

"Melinda, this is my new helper, David. He'll be staying on until September."

Melinda nodded. "Glad to meet you, David."

David smiled back and then turned to Gilbert. "So, what's up?"

"Is it all right if I ask his opinion, Jen?"

"Sure, Pa."

"All right. David, what's your opinion about a woman going on a cattle drive?"

David was amused by the subject and chuckled. "Well, I haven't heard of it before. But it's not very ladylike if you ask me. It's ridiculous."

Jenny glared at David, giving him a look that could kill. Gilbert chuckled. Melinda did not say a word. And David was quite uncomfortable by the look Jenny was giving him. Feeling uneasy, he adjusted himself on the sofa and listened.

Gilbert gloated. "You see, Jen?"

Just as Jenny was feeling completely defeated, her mother instantly came to her rescue. "Being outnumbered isn't very fun, is it, Jen?" She turned toward Gilbert and said, "Personally, I've noticed that Jenny has been quite the lady recently. She's been more polite and helpful, even more patient to her brother. In fact, I think that if Jenny promises to continue such behavior, then going on a cattle drive doesn't hurt one bit. She's done it for years. Perhaps this can be her last one and we can celebrate it by giving her the best experience on this cattle drive, sort of like one that she'll never forget. What do you say?"

Jenny jerked her head around and stared at her mother. "Really, Mama?"

Melinda nodded.

Jenny turned to her father with begging eyes. "Please, Pa?"

Gilbert shook his head in dismay, turned to David and said, "For some reason, women seem to argue better than men. They can bring out points that a man never thinks about and many times I wonder what it has to do with the subject in the first place." Turning back to Jenny, he smiled. "All right, you win. You can go on this cattle drive. But remember, it'll be the last one. Deal?"

Jenny's eyes widened with joy as she strode over to her father and wrapped her arms around him, hugging him tightly. "Thanks, Pa. I really appreciate it. And it's a deal." Then she whirled around to face her mother and said, "Thanks, Mama."

Jenny was elated…ecstatic…overjoyed. They had worked it all out. But when she looked at David, she was surprised at his expression.

He had turned pale and was staring at Jenny in disbelief. He was speechless, or in shock, almost stunned by what he had just heard.

David quickly turned toward Gilbert and asked, "Do you think that's wise, sir?"

Gilbert smiled. "She's gone with me for the past eight years. She knows what she's doing."

"But, sir…"

David's voice had a touch of concern and his eyes were wide. What was happening here, he thought to himself. This can't be.

23

This was unexpected. It would not be safe for a young girl to go on this drive, especially with what was being planned by the Tall Texan. She could get hurt. Did her mother say, "One that she'll never forget?"

He had to discourage her. When he looked at Gilbert, he realized that he might alert him and he could become suspicious. David cleared his throat and quickly changed the subject.

"Whoa, am I starved! Do you need any help?"

Jenny looked into David's eyes as if she could see something, but David tried to hide it by being cheerful and soon the subject was changed to food and questions about the ranch and where David was from.

Chapter 3
Edith, Melinda's Cousin

"Is he going to be all right? Is he still improving?"

Edith heard the worried voice of a mother as she quietly closed the door to the bedroom so her patient would not be disturbed.

Sarah's voice had an anxious edge to it. Her son was on the mend, but each day she feared he would have a relapse. And each day, Edith would say the same thing, "He's still improving. Don't worry so much, Sarah."

As Edith turned around, she saw the worried and concerned look in Sarah's face. Her stress and worry for the past month had formed dark circles under her eyes and she looked weary as if she hadn't slept for days.

"Tell me the truth, Edith. I need to know. He's not regressing, is he?"

Edith knew that her sister had faith in her. That was why she immediately called her for assistance.

"Don't worry, Sarah. Your son is still improving."

"How can you tell?"

Sarah was seated on the sofa nervously twisting a handkerchief in her hands, and the stress was showing at the corners of her eyes and mouth.

"I didn't go to college and graduate with a degree in nursing for nothing. I know what I'm doing and he's improving. Trust me."

"But you know what the doctor said last month. Tommy has diphtheria and he said he had done all that he could to save his life and could do no more. He even consulted with other doctors and they agreed. They all gave up on Tommy. They said it was now in God's hands."

"Now, Sarah! Listen to me. Everything is going to be all right." Edith chided with soberness. "Isn't that why you sent for me? Because they gave up and you have faith in me, right? Not because I was the last resort?"

Sarah gave Edith a sheepish look and answered softly, "Yes, that's why I sent for you. I believe in you. But I do have to admit that you were the last resort."

Edith suppressed a smile, sat down beside her sister, put her arm around her, and squeezed her tightly. "Don't worry so much. Tommy has come a long way since I arrived and he's definitely getting better, I can assure you. You must have more faith in God."

Sarah sat quietly listening to every word, still twisting her handkerchief. She was known as the worrywart of the family and it was always Edith who came to the rescue.

When this consolation did not seem to work, an idea flashed into Edith's mind. "Sarah, here it is, July of 1904, and do you know what? Last year, a couple of brothers named Wilbur and Orville Wright made a contraption that flies off the ground."

Sarah's eyes widened with disbelief.

"Yes, it's the truth. They call it an aeroplane. They say that it won't be long until they have it perfected." She quickly opened her bag that was lying next to the sofa, pulled out a newspaper clipping, and read, "Wilbur and Orville Wright have invented the world's first power-driven machine. It was flown at Kitty Hawk, North Carolina, December 17, 1903. The Wright Brothers flew four times that day, taking turns with one another. The final flight of the day was 852 feet in 59 seconds. The Wright brothers have discovered the principle of human flight."

Edith folded the newspaper and looked into her sister's eyes intently. "Sarah, my point is this. I believe the Wright brothers not only used their knowledge, but they had to have faith in what they were doing. Sarah, I believe they might have been inspired by God." Taking Sarah's hand in hers, she continued. "That's what we're doing here. I'm using all my knowledge the best I can, but at the same time I have to have faith in God that he's guiding me. He can inspire us and help us know what to do in life."

Sarah nodded hopefully. "Do you really think the Wright brothers were inspired of God? Do you think this aeroplane will do us any good?"

"Possibly."

"So, Tommy's not regressing?"

Edith affectionately wiped a loose curl from her sister's brow and tucked it behind her ear. "When I first arrived last month, it was touch and go. Ever since then, he's been improving daily, and I'm not saying that because I know what a worrywart you are. I can see it and I can feel it in my heart. It's been a month now and I can see a vast improvement. He's out of danger."

Sarah laid her head against her sister's shoulder. "Thank you, Edith. That means a lot to me. I needed you, not just for Tommy's sake but for your support."

Edith never gave up. That was her nature. She had the gift of sympathy, and knew how to aid and comfort the sick. Many times she acted as a midwife during the birth of babies. One reason why she was such a successful nurse was because of her faith. She always relied on the Lord to help her as she cared for her patients.

Sarah sat up straight and smiled as she pulled an envelope out of her pocket and waved it teasingly in front of Edith's face. "By the way, you got a letter from Mama."

"Really?"

"Really."

Edith grabbed it from her sister's hand and immediately broke out in a grin as she tore the envelope open and began to read.

Edith was a beautiful, elegant woman and her natural olive complexion enhanced her beauty. Her lips were full and shapely. She was tall with hauntingly dark brown eyes, so dark that one could barely see her pupils. They were large and expressive and it was as if she could speak through her eyes, something she inherited from her Welsh ancestors. It was difficult to hide her emotions from those who knew her best. Her eyes seemed to show her every mood, her sadness or joy, her frustrations or elation, her worry and fears.

She always believed that actions spoke louder than words. Most people knew of her sincerity and love for them without even saying a word.

Her thick dark hair was naturally curly, and it was so dark that most were tempted to call it black. It was long and rich looking, but she always kept it in a loose, soft chignon. She would twist her hair into a large smooth roll and pin it at the nape of her neck. Sometimes she wore a small silk flower or some sort of ornament pinned to her hair.

Edith knew that she was a very picky and independent person when it came to romance. The right man had to have certain qualities and she was not about to back down. Some told her that her expectations were too high and that such a man did not exist, and was only in the figment of her imagination. But she was stubborn and would not let go of her dream. It didn't matter that she was called a "spinster." What mattered to her was choosing a man to live and grow old with for the rest of her life. Being picky was worth all that to her.

Many men had courted Edith, but she inevitably found fault with each one. Either he was too shy or too bold, too ignorant or too proud, too arrogant or too quiet, too short or too tall, too old or too young. One good-looking gentleman turned out to be so arrogant and egotistical that she never encouraged him to return. She was not about to waste her valuable time with someone she was not interested in.

Usually after a gentleman's first call, she would always find some excuse to avoid another. First impressions were important to her and that was when she made her judgment. Her mother had often told her to look beyond that and give a man a second chance or she might pass up the perfect man. But Edith was strong-minded and did as she pleased.

She was looking for someone who had similar beliefs, interests, and personality traits as herself. So she tried to remain patient as her loved ones introduced her to this man and that. Besides, she knew they loved her and meant well. They just wanted her to be happy. Edith knew deep down inside herself there was a very special person waiting for her, but she had not found him yet.

Edith looked up from reading her letter and said, "Sarah, I know that you're constantly worrying about your son but Tommy is steadily improving. He's out of danger now and there isn't much more that I can do. You can easily do what I've been doing. I see no need to stay any longer."

"I don't understand," Sarah said with a creased brow.

"Right now Mama needs me desperately."

"But I need you, too." Then realizing what she had said, she looked at her sister and asked softly, "What's wrong?"

"Well, do you remember our cousin, Melinda?"

"Yes. She married that rancher. As I remember, she was quite smitten by him. He was quite a catch."

"Yes. He's not only good-looking but the Cozy J is a pretty nice-sized ranch."

"What does the J stand for?"

"Before he married Melinda, it was just Gilbert and his young daughter Jenny. So he named it after her."

Sarah smiled. "What a sweet gesture. So, what about Melinda?"

"Well, she's been married now for seven years and has only been able to have one child who is now six years old. She has had a few miscarriages, and they usually happen within the first five months. She's with child and is having problems again. She had terrible morning sickness but now it's pretty much gone. She's four months along and she's been cramping regularly. She just might miscarry again and needs my help, Sarah."

"But can't she go to the doctor so you can stay here with me?" Sarah asked pleadingly.

"The doctor has demanded that she stay in bed until the baby's born. He keeps telling her that she should take a few glasses of wine or whiskey each day to take her cramping away. But Melinda won't have any of it."

"Oh, no."

"Yes, it's true. I've heard many a doctor recommend it. When the expectant mother takes it, the poor baby doesn't move around much afterwards for several days and that's a scary thing. Mama says the doctor is quite upset at her for not listening to him. He told her that she should take it like medicine." Edith slowly shook her head with disgust. "I don't think it's healthy for the baby, personally. Herbs are the best remedy. I'm glad that she's sticking to her beliefs and won't have it."

Sarah sighed in resignation. "When do you think you'll leave?"

Edith stuffed the newspaper and letter into her bag. "You don't need me any longer, Sarah."

Sarah nodded reluctantly, not wanting her sister to leave.

"I think I'll leave tomorrow if it's all right with you."

"Tomorrow?"

"Yes. It's quite a ways to travel from Salt Lake Valley to Paris, Idaho. Mama says that as long as Melinda stays in bed, she won't have any more problems, but I need to get some herbs down that lady before it's too late. Mama's been helping a lot by watching their little six-year-old, but she thinks I should come and help."

"As I remember, that little boy of hers really took to you."

"Yes." Edith smiled at the memory of the young child. "He's really adorable. When I went home last Christmas, young John sat on my lap the whole time. He was so cuddly and sweet."

31

Edith doted on her little nephews and nieces, and her cousin's little boy was no exception. She was thirty years of age, and had accomplished much in her life. She took a Nurses Training Course at the Hospital in Salt Lake City, and attended college at the same time, receiving a bachelor's degree in education; not only that, Edith had sung professionally and had a trained, rich contralto voice.

Edith had accomplished a lot during a time when the United States had not recognized women's rights, let alone the higher education of a woman. The four surrounding states that had accepted women's rights were Wyoming, Colorado, Utah, and Idaho. She had chosen Utah to get her education. It had become a state in January of 1896 and had immediately introduced women's suffrage. Utah was the third state and Idaho was the fourth state to give women the right to vote and to encourage equality. And for this, Edith decided to live in a state where equality was recognized.

Edith was excited about going back home to Bear Lake Valley to see her mother and relatives. Southern Idaho was her beloved home, and she loved it. She had seen a little of the world, traveling throughout the United States, singing here and there, giving a part of herself to others. Now she just wanted to settle down, do a little nursing, find a home with a white picket fence, and plant flowers like her mother.

Chapter 4
The Challenge

That evening, a twinkle came into Melinda's eyes as she smiled. She covered her legs with a lap blanket and leaned back on the sofa. Looking at Gilbert seated in his overstuffed chair and reading contentedly, she commented with a nonchalant air, "You know what? I think I'd like to introduce Edith to Henry. They would make a lovely couple."

Gilbert looked up from his book with a look of surprise. "How did you come to that conclusion?"

"She's an educated woman with a degree, and she sings professionally, to boot."

"What does that have to do with anything?"

"Well, Henry's educated, too. He's the superintendent of schools in this whole county."

"You mean to tell me that an educated woman would not be interested in someone like…say Joseph? He's a successful farmer and works part-time for me as a ranch hand."

Joseph was Gilbert's dear friend. He was dependable and realized their situation, so he volunteered to help out whenever possible. He was one in a million.

Melinda's brow creased as she thought for a moment. "Joseph? I don't believe so. Besides that, she's an accomplished musician."

"So is Joseph. He plays the guitar."

Melinda snickered. "That's not the same thing, Gilbert."

"But how about me? I didn't go to college and I don't know one thing about music, and you married me. And you had a degree as a teacher."

"But that's different."

"How?"

Gilbert grinned. Closing his book and laying it aside, he wondered how she was going to get out of this one. He had her, and she knew it.

Jenny was seated on the sofa beside her stepmother, writing in her journal when she heard this little bit of banter. She grinned as she listened to their discussion, wondering how her stepmother was going to answer her father's question.

Melinda was trying to think of some good reasons why Gilbert was different from other men, but her mind had gone blank. She could not think of one reason he was so different. There was something special about Gilbert. But how could she put it into words?

"Well? How is it different?" Gilbert persisted.

Melinda's eyes lit up and she held up her hand triumphantly and began naming five fingers worth of reasons. They were lame reasons, but they were reasons, nonetheless.

"You were very intelligent...and read many books...and so smart financially that you had your own ranch...you were self-educated..." She hesitated and then grinned with amusement. "And muscular."

Gilbert burst into laughter. Was that the best she could do? After settling down, he said curiously, "Muscular? Now let's not change the subject here. We're talking about educated versus uneducated. Remember?"

"All right. So I was infatuated with your build. I couldn't help it."

Gilbert grinned with a look of satisfaction.

"All right, Gilbert. Uneducated men seem to feel insecure with a woman who has too much education or experience behind her. That's what I think."

Gilbert chuckled in a warm and deep voice. His chuckle always warmed up a room. It was like a warm breeze on a summer's day, and it made one feel comfortable inside.

Gilbert loved a challenge, and Melinda always invited competition to fulfill that need. So he sobered a bit and said softly, "Melinda, I didn't feel that way about you. In fact, that intrigued me. I liked what you were and what you represented."

"Well, you were different."

"Now, there's that word again: different. I'm not much different from other men."

"Sorry, but the fact still remains that you were self-educated."

"All right, I'll accept that. Now, how do you know if Joe is or not? You don't know him well enough."

"But, Gilbert, he doesn't seem like her type."

Gilbert chuckled again and it brought a smile to her lips.

"Well, he doesn't, Gilbert."

"What is her type, if I may ask?"

Melinda hesitated. "I'm not sure."

"All right, Melinda. How about this? We both introduce Edith to a man we feel is perfect and see what happens. What do you think?"

Melinda's eyes widened with excitement. This would be quite interesting, not to mention fun. She didn't even have to think about her answer.

"Agreed."

"But, Melinda, there's one stipulation. You can't help her make a choice. You can't influence her at all. All right?"

"Influence her? There's no problem there. I already know who she'll choose."

Gilbert laughed once again as he combed his fingers through his hair. "Oh, you do? How do you know?"

"I know how a woman thinks."

Gilbert slowly shook his head. That was one thing he could never figure out. How a woman thinks was one of the great challenges of life, he thought. Women were a great puzzlement to men, and Gilbert was still surprised at the things Melinda said and did, even after seven years of marriage.

Chapter 5
Edith's Spunk

Edith looked out the window of the train. As it rapidly passed miles and miles of open plains, she noticed the tall mountains that surrounded this lush green valley on every side.

Bear Lake Valley was situated in the tops of the Rocky Mountains with pine trees and white quaking aspen covering the mountainside. This mountainous region was full of jagged cliffs, steep terrain, rolling hills, and rapid flowing rivers noisily cascading over the rocks. The lakes among these mountains were clear like mirrors, just the perfect invitation for swimming. In the valley below, the deep aqua color of Bear Lake could be seen from a distance as each wave rippled toward the sandy beach. Farther north were yellow buttercups spread out like a beautiful carpet, and cattle were grazing in verdant meadows.

The wispy clouds formed lacy designs in the sky and made Edith yearn to be in an open field, feeling the breeze sift through her hair and across her cheeks once again. It was a hot summer day, and she could see the golden wheat gently waving in the breeze. The alfalfa had just been cut. She knew if she was outside at that very moment, she could smell the familiar fragrance of fresh cut alfalfa.

As she stared out the window at the beloved land she knew so well, she saw herds of cattle roaming about in pasture after pasture. In September, they would take these cattle to market and sell them for a good price. How she loved this place!

Southern Idaho was where she grew up and had many wonderful memories of times gone by. And now she was home again. The memories came flooding back as she saw the town of Montpelier come into view, making her heart pick up speed and causing an aching feeling in her chest.

As the train began to slow down, she leaned forward and pressed her nose to the window so she could see if her parents were there, waiting for her. Paris was only ten miles south of Montpelier and soon she would be home. As the train came to a stop, she quickly got to her feet, grabbed her bag, and headed for the entrance of the train.

Edith stood at the steps of the train, lifted her fluffy dark blue skirts that were lined with petticoats, and carefully stepped down to the ground and looked around. The long-sleeved white blouse had soft ruffles just above the bodice that continued around her shoulder to the back of the blouse. It buttoned at the neck and was tucked inside her skirt, giving her the look of a suffragette.

She put her hand on her hip and shaded her eyes from the sun as she searched. Her parents were nowhere in sight.

This surprised her. They had to be as excited about her arrival as she was. After all, it had been a while since she had been home and every letter she had received from her mother was begging her to come home for a visit.

The train conductor walked toward her and she handed him her ticket so he could get her luggage. When she heard her name called out, Edith snapped her head around and there was her mother, running toward her.

Martha was a small-boned attractive woman of medium height. Her silver-gray hair was placed attractively on her head in a loose bun. Martha's high cheekbones were flushed from running and she had a broad smile on her face. Martha wore a casual brown dress that she held with one hand so she could run easily, as she waved the other high above her head.

"Edith!" came the loving voice of her mother once again. "I'm here, Edith."

Edith dropped her bag and ran into her mother's arms. As they held one another in a loving embrace, tears welled up in her eyes, and her heart was throbbing like no other. It felt so good to be in her mother's arms once again.

After a few seconds, she wiped her eyes with her sleeve and looked around. "Where's Papa?"

"He's been feeling a little under the weather, lately. I put him in bed and said that our favorite nurse would be home to take care of him personally. He was none too happy about being left home in bed."

Edith smiled. She knew her father, and he would be waiting impatiently for her return. "Then let's go, Mama."

When a couple baggage men dropped two large trunks beside Edith's bag, Martha pointed toward them. "Are those yours?"

Edith nodded. "They're nice, aren't they? I got them for this trip since I would be staying here for a few months. I'll get a porter to help us load them up."

As she turned to leave, Martha took her arm and said, "I've already got someone. I wouldn't dare come all this way without someone to help out."

Edith looked into her mother's face and saw a twinkle in her eyes and a sly grin on her lips. She wondered if her mother was up to her old tricks again. Martha was a romantic; therefore, she was a matchmaker. She was known throughout the towns of Paris and Montpelier as the local cupid and no one was safe with Martha around.

"Here he comes now, Edith."

Her voice had a lightness and excitement about it. Martha's enthusiasm had given her away, and now Edith knew for sure what was on her mother's mind. She remembered how Martha had invited Gilbert over time and time again so Melinda would become interested. He was a widower, and Martha took pity on him, hoping to make a good match. Her delicious Sunday meals each week helped her cousin to get to know Gilbert much better. That was a match that was "heaven sent" for Gilbert. He needed someone like Melinda in his life.

Edith rolled her eyes, and quickly decided to meet this man and get it all over with in a hurry. Martha pointed to a lean gentleman briskly walking toward them. He looked about her age, was a tall, good-looking man with dark blond hair and blue eyes. He had a broad smile on his face and a sparkle in his eyes. After he came to a halt, Martha put her hand on his shoulder and introduced them.

"Henry, this is my daughter, Edith." Looking at her daughter and patting the man's shoulder affectionately, she continued. "Henry knew that your father was sick and so he volunteered to help me. He's the superintendent of schools in our county and has come to love our little community."

Edith extended her hand for a handshake. One thing she could not handle was a weak handshake, and to her, a handshake told quite a bit. That was usually what she went by when getting to know people. A man's firm handshake meant confidence and security, plus he was not only secure in his convictions but he was secure with himself. The very idea of a "dead" handshake was not satisfying at all, and she based her first meeting on that one handshake.

Instead of shaking her hand, Henry bowed slightly at the waist, squeezed her fingers tenderly, and gave her hand a kiss.

This kind of greeting startled her greatly, and she pulled her hand free, feeling self-conscious. She knew this sort of greeting was done, but she had never been comfortable with it, not one bit.

Henry looked at Martha with teasing eyes and winked. Then he smiled as he flirtatiously said, "I'm glad to meet you at last, Miss Edith. I've heard a lot about you. All your mother ever talks about is her daughter and how talented she is and how many lives she has saved. But I must say that she was not all together truthful in her description of you. She left out how absolutely lovely you are, my dear."

Edith was taken aback by his flirtatious compliment, not to mention the kiss on her hand. And did he just say, *my dear*? She was not used to such boldness. And from a stranger, no less! How dare he assume that she was so taken with him that he could say anything he pleased. What bravado!

Henry pointed toward the luggage and asked, "Are those your trunks?"

She felt like a suffragette, fighting for her rights, as she retorted, "I must disagree with you, sir. My mother is always truthful, and flattery will get you nowhere." She turned toward her luggage and grabbed her bag. "And yes, these are my trunks."

When Edith looked at her mother, she noticed that she was aghast at her daughter's conduct; disapproval was written all over her face. Her mother never liked how blunt she was. In fact, Martha had taught her refinement and ladylike behavior, to be polite to others at all times. When Edith turned toward Henry to see his disapproval, what she saw surprised her greatly. Henry was grinning from ear to ear at her retort. He was amused by her feistiness.

Henry rubbed his chin thoughtfully and then replied with eloquence, "But, Miss Edith, I couldn't lie about how I felt when I first saw you. It would be totally unfair to limit my feelings. Personally, I was not flattering you. I meant what I said. You're a stunning woman, and it's the truth, not flattery."

Edith was surprised by his frank reply. He had such audacity. "Do you dish out compliments so freely to every woman you meet?"

"Only the ones I'm impressed with. And your mother has talked about you so lavishly, that after having seen you, I was quite impressed."

Henry grabbed a trunk and carried it towards the buggy. Edith looked at her mother and could see her mother's disapproval. She had gone a little too far with her spunk. This was something that her mother had always talked to her about, and she had not learned to curb her tongue. Martha had always told her that she was too feisty for her own good.

She wanted to immediately defend herself but could see the look in her mother's eyes. It was a look that meant, "We'll talk later."

Edith gave a deep sigh. As she watched Henry heft her trunk into the buggy, she wondered if maybe she was too hasty in her judgment, but at the same time he had been much too bold for his own good. More so than what she was use to, anyway.

Edith knew that she was very picky when it came to men. She took courtship and marriage seriously and she knew what she wanted in a husband. In fact, that was why she hadn't found the right one yet, because she didn't want to lower her standards.

She was looking for someone that was sincere but had a fun sense of humor, was confident but not overbearing, intelligent but a down-to-earth straight-thinking fellow. He had to be polite and mannerly but at the same time have a touch of romance in the way he spoke to her.

These things were imperative in a relationship. Edith was picky, but she wanted to be happy in marriage and these attributes were important to her.

Chapter 6
Joseph, the Ranch Hand

Joseph was sitting on an old tree stump on the Cozy J mending a saddle for Gilbert. The shadow of the barn protected him from the heat of the sun and a cool breeze gently ruffled his hair.

He was bent over the saddle and was studiously working when an inanimate object hit his neck and interrupted him. He unconsciously swatted his neck as if it were a pesky insect and continued working on his project. After a few moments, he felt another object hit him on his shoulder, and he swatted at it, mumbling, "Pesky insects!"

When he heard giggling from around the corner of the barn, he straightened his broad shoulders and narrowed his eyes. He would recognize that laugh anywhere. He continued repairing the saddle as if he had not heard the cheerful laughter of young John, knowing that it would not be the end of the little boy's pranks and teasing.

When he felt something hit his back and then his head, he jumped up, dropping his saddle to the ground, and said loud enough for his tormentor to hear. "That does it! You're gonna get a whoopin', little man."

As Joseph turned around, he saw John peeking around the barn, laughing uncontrollably. When their eyes met, John screamed at the top of his high-pitched voice, the tension building up as they stared at one another.

Joseph grinned as he took large strides toward the little culprit, and John quickly turned on his heels and ran as fast as his little legs would go, giggling and screaming intermittently.

Joseph knew exactly where he was going, the same place he always went when they played this game of chase. John dodged inside the barn, ran for the haystack, and burrowed his little body into a pile of hay. Not making a sound, he lay quietly waiting to be found.

Joseph strode into the barn mumbling, "Where is that little mischief-maker? If I get a hold of him, he's gettin' a whoopin'."

John put his hand over his mouth, but it didn't work as the giggle burbled from his lips.

"Ah-ha!" Joseph said in triumph as he grabbed the giggling boy by the leg.

A scream pierced the air with uncontrollable laughter as Joseph pulled the boy out of the hay and began tickling his mid-section.

"I'll teach you a thing or two," he said with a grin as John doubled up with laughter.

"Stop! Stop!" he screamed.

Joseph grabbed John's knee and continued tickling him as he said, "What's the magic words?"

"You can't make me say it."

Joseph stopped, picked the giggling boy up, and threw him over his muscular shoulder. He turned on his heels and headed out the barn door toward the trough, with a broad grin on his face. His sky-blue eyes were laughing as he came upon Gilbert.

When John saw his father, he yelled "No! No! Help, Pa! Joseph's got me. Help!"

Joseph chuckled. "This little culprit has it comin', Gil. It's about time I taught him a lesson. He's gonna take a little swim."

John looked at the trough with widened eyes and sobered as he begged, "I'll say it. I'll say it."

"All right. I'm waitin'."

"Joseph is the best bronco rider on the ranch."

"Only the ranch?" Joseph said in feigned disappointment. "Is that the best you can do?"

"Joseph's the best bronco rider in town."

"Just our town?" he said as he stopped in front of the trough.

"No, no! Don't do it," John screamed as he eyed the water in the trough. "The best in the country!"

"Now that's better." Joseph laughed as he lowered John to the ground, kneeling beside him. "All right, little man. Now what? I'm waitin'."

John smiled and swung his little arms around Joseph's neck and hugged him tightly. Joseph picked him up and held him, grinning the whole time.

Gilbert was shaking his head with wonder. "The things you do just to get a little praise."

"Hey! I'll take what I can get."

Gilbert chuckled. "You already know you're the best bronco rider in the valley."

Joseph smiled approvingly. "Thanks, boss. By the way, I've got some extra tomatoes in my garden. Want some?"

Gilbert nodded, wondering if it was good timing to ask him about meeting Melinda's cousin. Would he be good for Edith? She was a wonderful woman with great qualities, but she never gave a guy a chance. First impressions were important to her. Would she look twice at Joseph, a farmer? Gilbert wasn't sure. Perhaps he would give it a day or two before springing it on him.

"I think a nice ripe tomato sounds delectable. Ours aren't on yet."

"Follow me!" Joseph said as he swung John onto his shoulders and headed toward his farm.

John leaned down and kissed Joseph on the top of the head and then wrapped his little arms around his forehead.

As they walked toward the west, Joseph noticed the sun was setting over the mountains, leaving a pinkish glow in the wispy clouds above. A couple swallows circled a tree, protecting their young, and the gentle lowing of cattle could be heard in the distance. What a beautiful day! Joseph felt lucky to live in such a blessed little community as this.

Chapter 7
Henry's Visit

It was Sunday and the family was seated around the table all except for William who was still feeling under the weather. He was still in bed recuperating.

"Please pass the roast beef, Martha," Henry said with a smile.

As Martha passed the platter, she hoped that inviting Henry over was a good idea. This way her daughter could learn more about him. She had tried it once with Melinda and Gilbert, so why not with her own daughter?

As Henry dished a portion of meat on his plate, he said, "Edith, your mother told me that you did all the cooking tonight. I'm really impressed with your skills as a homemaker."

Then he looked at her apparel and smiled. Her white muslin dress was gathered at the waist and fit snuggly to the bodice. It was buttoned at the neck with a small ruffled trim, complementing her long slender neck. The off-white color contrasted with her olive complexion and she looked absolutely lovely.

He cleared his throat and added, "By the way, did I tell you how nice you look this evening?"

"Yes, Henry, you have. Several times." Looking at her mother and seeing her disapproval, Edith quickly changed her attitude and forced a smile. "Thank you very much for your compliment, though. You're very sweet, Henry."

When Henry touched her hand affectionately and smiled, Edith gently pulled her hand free, feeling uncomfortable with his boldness. Why didn't her mother understand that she needed to do this herself without any help whatsoever? She would eventually find the right man without anyone's help. But no, this was too much to expect from the Matchmaker.

As a child, she used to be amused by her mother's efforts as she watched her pair up couples. She had made many couples happy, not to mention Melinda and Gilbert. In fact, Edith used to think it was quite romantic. But tonight, it was far from romantic.

"So, you'll sing for me tonight, of course," Henry said as if it was an order, instead of a request.

Edith was appalled at his attitude, and she quickly shook her head. She sang when she wanted to and not because she was ordered to. Besides that, she was not in the mood. Why she was feeling so rebellious, she was not sure. She had sung for her parents' friends many a time. This was not an unusual request. Perhaps it was Henry's attitude. He had been such a know-it-all during the whole evening, like some intellectual snob who was always right.

Martha gently rested her hand on hers and said, "Of course she will, Henry."

And then she smiled at Edith as if she had no other choice. Edith tried to smile back at her mother, but it was another forced smile.

After the table was cleared and dishes were done, they settled down in the living room to talk for a while and let the food settle. As she listened to the intellectual jabber of this educated man, she wondered what her mother saw in him. Aside from not having the same opinions about men, she and her mother got along terrifically. They could talk about most anything; they went shopping together, and ate out every now and then.

That evening, before their guest had arrived, they had talked and laughed together. She had told her mother what was happening in her life, and her mother was supportive of her interests. Then after dinner that night, just before they walked into the living room, her mother had given her a definite plea. Her last words were, "Please, don't embarrass me."

Edith snapped back to reality and tried to listen to what Henry was saying, but not be bored at the same time.

"So, you see," Henry labored on. "Women should have the right to vote in the East. I believe in the equality of the sexes, as long as the women can cook well and have a meal ready on time without delay, keep the house clean, and take care of the children. That's not a man's duty or responsibility. When we get home from work, that's our time to sit and relax after a long hard day. We all have our duties, and if women do theirs and we men do ours, then we'll all get along much better. We all have our place in society. It's going to take time for the eastern states to accept equality, but they'll come around."

Equality? Was that his definition of equality? Did he actually say that it was not a man's responsibility to take care of his own children and to not help around the house? That was it. Edith had had enough.

She took a deep breath and exploded, "That's your definition of equality? So, we have our duties and you have yours?"

"Of course."

"How about Melinda? Her husband cooks for her when she's busy with the children. Right now she needs the help because of her condition."

"Edith, don't get me wrong," he said patronizingly. "In times of emergency, one needs to make exceptions. But women should never take advantage of a man's good heart or good nature."

"Advantage?" she snapped impatiently. "Gilbert helps her because he wants to, not because she demands it."

Just then, Martha quickly interrupted, as if trying to save her daughter's face. "My dear, I think you misunderstood. He doesn't mean to insult women, but he's only stating his opinion. That's all."

"Well," Edith huffed. "Then I'll state my opinion, as well." She stood on her feet and took a deep breath as she clenched her fists tightly. "Women need help with the household chores at times. Do you think we have enough hours in the day to get it all done, especially with children and other outside responsibilities? Besides that, what's wrong with a man tending and taking care of his own children? With a father's helping hand, a child can make the right decisions in life. You underestimate a husband's role in marriage. If you want me to describe true equality to you, I will. Equality is Gilbert helping Melinda with cooking and cleaning and with the children, whether she needs it or not, simply because he wants to help. By the end of the day, a woman's exhausted and needs her husband's help."

The whole time Edith was talking, Martha was holding her breath, waiting for what was coming next.

Edith pointed an accusing finger at Henry and said, "How many times has a woman given up the idea of pursuing her talents simply because her husband could not help with the household chores and encourage her to work on her own talents so she could better herself?"

The whole sentence came out in one long breath. After she was done, Edith waited for a response.

Henry was speechless. He drew in a breath of air and said softly, "I see what you mean. I never thought of it that way before. I didn't mean to offend you." Hoping to change the subject and the wrath of this woman, he took a deep breath and asked politely, "Would you mind singing for me?"

At that request, she abruptly excused herself by saying she had a full-blown headache.

Later that night, Martha walked into her bedroom, sat down on the bed beside her, and apologized. "I'm so very sorry for what I did. I shouldn't have invited him over. I can see now that it was a mistake. I didn't realize you were so annoyed with him until tonight. Please forgive me."

Edith touched her mother's hand. "It's all right, Mama. I understand that you're concerned about me."

"Sweetheart, we need to talk."

Edith knew that meant a serious talk, so she took a deep breath and sighed. "All right, Mama. What is it?"

"Edith, you never gave him a chance. You're not looking at the inner person."

"The inner person?"

"You know, his heart or the spiritual side of him. Henry has a good heart, and that's why I invited him over. But

Edith, you're not allowing yourself to see beyond your own prejudices."

"Prejudices?" Edith said impatiently.

"Just let me finish what I have to say. Please?"

Edith nodded reluctantly, not sure if she really wanted to hear this.

"I know that differences of opinion between couples are common. Your father and I didn't always agree on issues at first, but with time we gradually helped one another to understand our own point of view. We learned to respect the other's opinion. No one couple has everything in common at first. That would be impossible. What you need is to get to know a man deep inside first, not his outward appearance but his heart, his spiritual side."

Martha tapped her chest with her fingers for emphasis. "Inside here, Edith. Do you understand? Don't challenge men so readily."

Martha smiled as she affectionately placed her hand on her daughter's face and repeated, "Get to know a man's heart, Edith. That's what you have to look for."

Then she leaned over, kissed her daughter on the cheek, and then left her with her thoughts.

Edith snuggled into bed but didn't go to sleep right away. She was too wound up. Was her mother right? Was she truly that hard on men, judging them and passing sentence all in one evening?

She had been told by many a friend that she wasn't giving men a chance. Was it because she had not looked at a man's heart, the spiritual side of him? But how was she to do this? She was so used to judging men by first appearances.

As a tear trickled down her cheek, she pulled her knees up to her chest and prayed. She prayed that some day she would learn what her mother was saying, that she would understand and look at the inner person, for the goodness deep inside.

Edith swiped at her tears as they rolled down her cheeks and onto her pillow. Perhaps her mother was right. She needed to try harder. As she gradually relaxed, calmness came over her and she gradually fell into a deep sleep.

Chapter 8
The Mysterious Stranger

David was carrying a large bag of feed toward the corral. When he saw little six-year-old John split into a run and come to a halt right in front of him, he laughed. He noticed that John had become like a little puppy dog, following him around the ranch and chattering all the time. He also realized John's admiration for him and David relished in it.

With eagerness, John looked up at David and asked, "Can I help?"

David stopped, looked down at John, and smiled. "Don't know. Are you strong enough?"

"Sure am." John pushed his sleeve up and flexed his arm. "See? I'm strong."

David tried hard to suppress a chuckle. He dropped the sack to the ground, knelt beside him, and felt the small muscle in John's arm.

"Wow! You've got something there. I think it might be the beginnings of a muscle, young man."

John grinned. "You see?"

Jenny had tied her mare to a post and was brushing her down when she was distracted by their conversation. She turned around and looked down at the two of them. When she giggled, David instantly turned and faced Jenny. When their eyes met, he stood and nonchalantly walked over to her.

"He's got the makings of a real muscle there, I believe."

"Oh?"

David grinned, his eyes flirting with hers as he spoke. "I've got a little brother just a year older than John. I love this age. They're so eager to help out."

Jenny smiled. "Especially when they have a hero."

"Hero?"

"Haven't you noticed that he trails you around?"

David hadn't thought of being a hero to a kid before. He turned around and looked down at John who was struggling with the bag of feed, trying to pull it to the corral.

David chuckled. "But a hero is someone you look up to. I'm not anyone to look up to."

"Sure you are. You make John feel as though he was someone special, and that means a lot to a little boy. He seems to have more life when he's around you. I've noticed you've got great qualities, David." Then Jenny blushed and instantly looked down at the mare to avoid his eyes, as she brushed its side with faster strokes. "Anyway, you're a hero to John."

This took David by surprise. She had blushed right in front of him. She liked him and he knew it. No girl blushes unless she likes someone, and that much he knew about females. Besides, he enjoyed flirting with Jenny. It was fun. He felt it was harmless flirting and she responded so readily. Of course, he realized he was just using her to get close to her father, but at the same time he was enjoying this harmless flirtation.

David watched her brush the mare vigorously. "Jenny, you are a puzzlement to me. You have a knack of building me up when you don't even know me. And then in the same instant, you become coy and reserved."

She glanced up shyly and back to the mare, not saying a word.

"I have two sisters and one is reserved and the other is so talkative that you can't shut her up. The reserved one reminds me of you. She loves to read and work with her hands. And she's very pretty, too…like you."

Jenny's face flushed a rosy color as she moved the brush across the back of the mare even faster. Had he just given her a roundabout compliment? How does one react to that? She looked up at David, and he smiled at her as if amused. The intensity of his gaze surprised her and she quickly averted her eyes as she continued brushing. All this attention from a boy was new to her, and she was not sure how to respond.

Taking a deep breath, she asked, "How old are your sisters?"

"One is sixteen and the other is fourteen. I miss them a lot."

Jenny looked up from her brushing and rested her hand on the back of the mare. "You've been here for a week and this is the first time you've spoken of your family. What are your parents like?"

"Ma is a good woman, gentle and soft-spoken. Pa is quite the opposite. He's a banker."

Jenny giggled. "A banker? You just don't seem like a banker's son to me."

David laughed along with her, and Jenny could see the faintest amusement in his eyes.

"To tell you the truth, Jenny, I'm not. I'm my mother's son."

"Oh, that explains a lot."

David placed his hand on the back of the mare next to hers, and looked into Jenny's eyes. His eyes held hers for a long moment before he spoke. "Well, I've got to get back to work or your pa will fire me because I'm letting John do it all."

He chuckled as he peered down at John, who was still struggling with the large bag of feed. David slipped his hand on top of hers and smiled.

Jenny's heart fluttered at the touch of his hand. It was warm and gentle, and Jenny felt a little tingle of excitement inside. This young man was having an effect on her, and she was not sure why. Could it be all the attention that he was giving her?

She was a young woman now and noticed that young men were looking at her in a different way than before. Her heart beat erratically, and warmth crept into her cheeks as he slid his hand off hers.

David winked at her and then meandered toward John. "Hey, young man, let me help you with that bag. Whoa, look at this. You've pulled it several feet from where it was."

John beamed with pride.

***

Melinda was seated on the porch, rocking back and forth in her rocking chair, feeling relaxed and happy. The herbs that her cousin had given her last week had worked, and she was so relieved. Edith would be arriving anytime to check on her, so she thought she would wait outside.

As she peered out in the distance, she could see her husband splitting wood for the winter months to come. He stopped, pulled a handkerchief out of his pocket and wiped his brow. After stuffing it back, he turned around and smiled.

He waved to Melinda and called out, "How are you doing?"

"Just fine. I'm enjoying the fresh air."

"Good."

He turned back to his work, and then Melinda's eyes focused on Jenny. She was brushing her mare down. She always took great pride in her mare and took good care of her. She had tied her to a post near the barn and was humming to herself as she stroked her mare with the brush. She was extra happy today.

Melinda had watched a little of the interaction between her daughter and David, and she was concerned. She was not sure why, but for some reason she felt a strong need to protect her daughter. But from what? From David? He was harmless enough.

The rattling of a buggy brought Melinda's attention to the road and all thoughts of Jenny disappeared when she saw Edith approaching. She stood and met her at the bottom of the porch.

After Edith reined in the horse, she picked up her skirts and stepped out of the buggy. "Melinda, how are you doing?"

"Much better. The herbs are working, Edith."

"Good. I knew they would. Have you been taking the raspberry tea everyday?"

"Yes, twice a day like you said. I put the raspberry leaves in boiling water and let them bubble for ten minutes. Then I put a tablespoon of honey in my glass to sweeten it." She pulled a face. "It tastes horrible without honey."

"I know. And how about the cayenne pepper?"

Melinda wrinkled up her nose. "Now that was a tough one. I tried putting honey with it but it stung my mouth, so I just put an eighth of a teaspoon on the back of my tongue and quickly followed it with water. That way it's done and over with."

Melinda pulled a face in disgust and Edith laughed with delight.

"Edith, why is it so important that I take it daily? I can handle the herb tea, but the cayenne?"

Edith instantly became sober. She needed to let Melinda know the seriousness and importance of following her instructions. "Listen to me, it's very important, Melinda. Cayenne will prevent you from hemorrhaging. It will protect you during pregnancy and while giving birth. The cayenne will strengthen your system and prevent any problems during childbirth. Do you understand the importance of it?"

Melinda nodded. "I understand. The catnip tea is what really surprises me, though."

"What happened?"

"Well, a couple days ago I woke up with severe cramping. They were three minutes apart. It was so bad that I rolled into a ball, holding my stomach. It was the worst I've had."

"Oh, no!"

"Gilbert woke up when he heard me groaning in pain. He immediately went to the kitchen, put some catnip leaves in some water, and began boiling them for ten minutes. Then he put some honey with it to sweeten it. He knows how I gag with herb tea unless it's sweetened."

"I'm the same way."

"Well, he rushed back into the bedroom with it, blowing on it all the while so I could drink it. He told me to sit up but

I couldn't. I hurt so badly. So, he helped me up and handed the tea to me. As I sipped, I just knew it wouldn't help. It didn't make any sense to me. How could a simple herb tea take away such serious cramping?"

"It really does. I've seen it work, Melinda."

"Well, you were right. After twenty minutes, they began to subside and after thirty minutes they were completely gone. The following day in the afternoon, the same thing happened again. But this time Gilbert had some tea already made in case of another emergency. He quickly ran down the hall and brought it back. The cramps were gone within twenty minutes. It works. It really works."

Edith nodded. "I told you it would. You just have to trust me."

"Thank you." Melinda took Edith's arm, led her into the house, and then sat down on the sofa. "So, how are you feeling? You look a little despondent today."

"Oh, Melinda, I am. I'm a little confused."

"Confused? That doesn't sound like the cousin I know. You're usually self-confident and sure of yourself."

"Well, I've only been here for one week and last weekend Mama invited Henry over for Sunday dinner. She's quite the matchmaker, you know. Well, I tried my best to talk to him and be civil, but everything he said and did seemed to irritate me. He was so self-assured, so know-it-all, as if he knew all the answers. Well, anyway, Mama was embarrassed by my behavior, and Henry was amused by it."

When Melinda lovingly touched her hand, Edith shook her head and sighed. "Maybe it's me. What if I'm picking Henry apart just because Mama likes him? Could I be such a rebellious spirit?"

"You? Rebellious?" Melinda laughed. "No, I think it's more of a reaction to others trying to be cupid. You know, like your friends, your mother, and even me. Maybe we try too hard because we want you to have the same happiness that we have."

Edith nodded, understanding the reasoning behind it. She knew they all loved her. They were just trying too hard. That was all.

She squeezed Melinda's hand and smiled. "I finally told Mama in the gentlest way, that I could find the right man all by myself."

"Good for you."

"You know something? I should give Henry another chance. He's got great qualities. He's intelligent, friendly, educated, and polite. But then...he's also a little arrogant, overly self-confident, very opinionated, and quite bold. Not to mention flirtatious. Did you know that he actually kissed my hand the first time that we met?"

Melinda nodded with amusement, not saying a word but listening intently.

Edith shook her head in dismay. "You see, there I go again. Picking Henry apart, judging him without even knowing him." She placed her hands over her face and moaned, "Oooh, what am I to do?"

Melinda laughed at her cousin's plight. "You're so funny, Edith. Henry's not so bad when you get to know him."

"Yeah, probably not. That is, if you enjoy being lectured to about the equality of the sexes."

"The equality of what?"

"Never mind. I'll tell you later. Well, anyway, something else came up. A couple days ago Mama handed me a letter."

Edith pulled the letter out of her bag, and the corners of her lips turned up into a slight smile. "Mama said that we truly don't know men until we're married because we never get to know the inner person."

Melinda's brows lifted. "The inner person?"

Edith placed her hand on her chest and tapped her fingers. "You know, the heart, his spiritual side. We're so busy courting and trying to impress one another that we never get to know the soul of the person."

"That's true. I believe that."

"So, after Mama handed me this letter, she said that she couldn't answer any questions because she had given her word."

"Her word?"

"Uh-huh. Her word." Edith's eyes lit up. "I've never read a letter like this before in my whole life. It's a letter of sincerity. It has heart. I brought the letter with me so I could share it with you and see what you thought."

"But there's one thing that confuses me and that was what your mother said. Why did she say she could not answer any questions?"

"That's one thing I haven't told you, yet. It's because the letter isn't signed. He's remaining anonymous, so to speak. Either Mama doesn't want me to know who he is, or he doesn't."

Melinda stared into her eyes with curiosity and excitement. "I'm ready. Read it or I'll burst."

The softness in Edith's eyes was evident as she read:

Dear Edith,

A kind friend has asked me to write to you, for it is through letters that one may learn the deepest thoughts and feelings of another. Too many times we see what's on the surface of another person, but never get to know the soul. Many times we hold back our inner feelings and never express them for fear of ridicule or nonacceptance, or perhaps because we would be embarrassed.

Therefore, we never see into the deepest recesses of another person's soul. We seem to guard ourselves so we don't get hurt, but at the same time we won't let that person see who we truly are. At one time I read that it is better to have loved and lost than to have never loved at all. But at the same time, we don't want to get hurt so we protect ourselves. I believe sometime in our life, we must take a chance.

To let you know a little about me, I moved here several years ago from across the mountain. It's a small community that is surrounded by mountains on every side. The land is lush and green and is a beautiful little valley. But something tugged at me and told me to move to Bear Lake Valley, so I heeded the feeling.

As you, I also love music and thrive on every note I hear. Music uplifts me when I feel let down. It seems to bring a spirit of peace and joy into my soul. Life would truly be dull without music. I feel that man can become closer to God through music. I have no real talent as you do, but I can play the harmonica.

If you are interested in writing in response to my letter, then give it to Martha, and she'll know what to do with it.

Most sincerely,
A Friend

"Oh my, Edith!" Melinda put her hand on her chest. "A person's soul? That's something I haven't thought of before. A person's inner soul...I like it. He truly sounds wonderful."

Edith's eyes were bright and alive as she answered, "I know. That's the reason I'm here. I've been mulling this over for a couple days, trying to figure out what I should do. I need your opinion, Melinda."

"All right. First things first! Do you think it's Henry? Do you think your mother realized you needed to get to know the inner Henry first?"

"No. I don't believe he's anyone I've ever met. You can tell what a person is like by their mannerisms and words they use. This definitely does not sound like Henry, Melinda."

"Has Gilbert introduced you to Joseph?"

"No. Who's he?"

"He's a farmer that lives here in Paris and he works part-time for Gilbert. He's a nice enough fellow, but he's sort of quiet. He's polite but he keeps to himself." Melinda looked a little sheepish as she continued. "I was going to invite Henry over to meet you myself."

Edith giggled with amusement. "So, if Mama wouldn't have introduced us, you would have?"

Melinda nodded. "Sorry. Well, anyway, maybe Gilbert gave up and decided not to introduce the two of you. Perhaps he could see what was happening with your mother. He's quite perceptive, you know."

Edith shrugged. "Well, since all's well with you. I'm going home but I'll come over tomorrow to check up on you again. Have you felt any movement yet?"

Melinda shook her head. "Not yet. That seems to be Gilbert's first question each night when we get ready for bed. He's so cute. He's just as excited as I am, if not more so." Then she looked at the letter and asked, "Are you going to respond to his letter?"

Edith's eyes widened. "Of course. Whoever he is, I'm willing to get to know him through letters. That was the most intriguing letter I've ever read. In fact, I've already written a reply. Do you want to hear it?"

"What? Are you asking me? There's no question about it. I'm definitely interested."

Edith pulled an envelope out of her bag and handed it to her. "Tell me what you think."

Melinda unfolded the letter and began to read.

Dear Friend,

I feel that you have an unfair advantage, for you know all about me through someone else and I know nothing of you. Pray tell me more of yourself so I can know who you are as well. You know my name, my occupation, and my hobbies, but I know nothing of you.

Sincerely,

Edith, the Confused

Melinda laughed. "It's perfect. I can't wait for his answer. Do you think he'll reveal himself to you?"

"Of course not. He's doing this so we can get to know one another first. That's what I think, anyway." Then she grinned mischievously. "Besides, I don't want to know. It's more mysterious this way, don't you think?"

A deep voice came from the screen door. "What's more mysterious?"

Melinda turned and saw Gilbert peering inside at the two of them. Then he opened the door and pushed it shut behind him.

"Edith received a letter from a mysterious stranger."

Gilbert lifted his brow with surprise. "She did? What kind of letter?"

"A real nice one. He wants to get to know her. But she doesn't know who put him up to it. Was it you, Gilbert?"

"Me? Why would I do that when courting is a lot more fun?"

"Well, it wasn't me. Do you think it was Martha? She's such a matchmaker."

"I wouldn't put it past her. But then, I wouldn't put it past you, either. I'm not sure what kind of tricks you would do just to win."

Edith looked between the two of them and asked, "Win?"

Gilbert grinned. "Yup. Win! We had a little challenge going and I think she's cheating."

"Me? Cheat?" Melinda said with a shake of her head. "I wouldn't do that."

Gilbert chuckled. "You wouldn't? So, who do you think he is, Melinda?"

"It's a mystery. We have no idea who he is. He wrote to her, and it's one of the most interesting letters I've ever heard."

"Really?"

With a mischievous glint in her eyes, she said teasingly, "But I suspect its Henry."

Gilbert rolled his eyes. "Oh, Henry again. Why do you think that?"

"Because of his words. The way a person uses the English language shows what kind of person he is. This man's intelligent, educated."

Seeing the challenge in her eyes, he readily responded. "Educated? Has Martha introduced Edith to the new schoolmaster in town? He's single." Then he raised his eyebrows and grinned at Melinda. "And he's *educated*, too."

Edith laughed when she heard the emphasis on "educated" and wondered what all this was about. "Oh, I don't think Mama's going to introduce me to anyone else for a while. I might embarrass her too much. Besides, I think she knows that I need to do this myself with no pressure."

Gilbert went to the sink and began to wash up as he asked, "What do you want for supper, Melinda?"

"I can make it tonight. You've been working real hard and need a break. I'm feeling so much better since I've been taking herbs. And besides, we have the catnip tea for emergencies."

Gilbert grabbed a towel and dried his hands in silence. Then he turned to Melinda and looked at her with soberness, his eyebrows furrowed. He did not say a word but something passed between them.

Melinda had seen that look before. It was one of concern mixed with a stern look that meant more than words could say. She knew that he was not going to allow her to cook. She also knew it was fruitless to just argue about it.

Sensing what was happening between them, Edith stood up and looked down at Melinda with a serious expression. "You've got a good husband, Melinda. Listen to him. He knows best. Don't push yourself too much just because you feel better. Use wisdom in how much you do each day so you can protect this baby…and yourself. Just because you have herbs doesn't mean you can overdo."

Melinda nodded. Two against one was an overwhelming number when one of them was Gilbert. She smiled and waved as Edith walked out the door. "Good luck and let me know how it turns out, Edith."

After she left, Melinda turned to her husband. He was standing next to the sink with the towel still in his hands and he was staring at her with a worried look. She knew that he loved her beyond words and was just trying to protect her. So why wasn't she cooperating?

Melinda nodded. "Anything you say, dear."

Gilbert grinned. "At least I have Edith on my side."

Chapter 9
The Texan's Plan

The fire was crackling and popping as the men sat around a small blaze that warmed the atmosphere. The stars were bright in the dark sky above, and a coyote was heard in the distance singing a haunting melody in the desert air.

The Tall Texan looked at Gunplay and asked, "So what happened at the ranch?"

"David was hired on immediately. You were right. Mr. Roberts liked him right off and told him to stay on until the cattle drive. The rest of us are to report the last week of September. David said he'd keep me posted and tell me anything new he finds out."

The Tall Texan nodded. This was turning out better than he had planned. With a spy at the ranch, he would know more than he had expected. If Gunplay got any valuable information, he could immediately act upon it.

"There's somethin' we've got to talk about," Gunplay said with concern. "Mr. Roberts is taking his cattle from Paris to Montpelier, and then shipping 'em by train. I figured it would only be a day's job so Mr. Roberts probably wouldn't hire that many men."

"What are ya tryin' to say?"

"Well, I've talked to David already, and he said that Mr. Roberts is plannin' on taking twenty-five hundred steers to market. He's also plannin' to have more than two dozen men. That's much more than I was expectin'. I think we need more men to do this job, boss. There's only ten of us."

The Tall Texan looked at the men sitting around the fire, watching each one closely as he picked up a bottle of whiskey and took a swig. He was a good-looking man with a strong jaw, dark hair, and he was twenty-eight years of age. His name described him perfectly. He was six-foot-one inch tall and was known as the "lady-killer" of the bunch. Women fell for his debonair and rugged ways.

Gunplay was a different sort of fellow. He let everyone know that he came from the great land of Texas and had proved himself as a gunfighter by killing two men in Colton, Utah. He was known as a small-time bandit and had tried to get into Cassidy's gang for a long time.

The Tall Texan pondered Gunplay's suggestion as he took a few more sips of whiskey. He rubbed the stubble on his chin and said, "In the evening, the cattle will be settled down so Mr. Roberts won't be usin' all of his men. Gunplay, you can make sure each man on the midnight shift is quietly taken care of and gagged. I'll send a few men in to help. It shouldn't be a problem since it'll be dark. And make sure David lets the horses loose."

"The horses loose? Why?"

The Texan puffed out a breath of air with exasperation. "So no one can follow us. When all that's done, then you and David can light a cigarette to signal us that all's clear."

"But David don't smoke, boss."

"Then he'll light a match," the Texan said gruffly.

"How about the other men at camp? Won't they hear us?"

"Naw. Their camp will be too far from the steers, just in case there's a stampede." He cleared his throat, took another sip of whiskey and continued. "With twenty-five hundred cattle spread out, we'll have a good chance of getting a couple hundred head or more. We'll surround 'em at the farthest end, and quietly separate 'em and head 'em south. The steers will be mild by midnight. And if there's any problem, we'll just start a stampede. Then gather the strays and head 'em south toward Robbers Roost."

The men nodded their approval, and then grabbed their bedrolls so they could settle down for the night, leaving the Tall Texan alone.

He smiled as he stared into the fire, watching it dance brightly before him. The moon was bright and cast a few mysterious shadows upon the ground. The Texan took another swig of whiskey as he thought about his plan. It was a good one and he felt confident. Cassidy had taught him a lot about planning, and he was ready for anything that might go wrong. Besides, with David as a spy, what could possibly go wrong?

Chapter 10
An Emergency

Edith was summoned to the schoolhouse because one of the children had had an accident. Henry laid the child down on a mat in his office, awaiting her arrival. When she arrived, she noticed the door was partly open, and Henry was seated at his desk, writing. She noticed that he was intent on what he was doing. He had a crease across his brow in concentration, and he did not even notice that she was standing in the doorway.

Edith cleared her throat as she walked through the door. When Henry looked up from his work and saw her, he smiled and his eyes brightened. He was pleasantly surprised at how quickly she had come and immediately stood. Then, taking her to the corner of the room, he pointed to the young boy lying on a mat.

Edith knelt down beside him and gave him a sympathetic smile. "What happened, young man?"

The little eight-year-old boy winced as he held up his hand. It was wrapped with a piece of white cloth, and she noticed a red stain that had soaked through the bandage near his palm. She tenderly took his hand in hers and unwrapped it.

Henry watched attentively. "He was running and fell down, landing on his hands among rocks and debris."

She winced. "Ouch!"

After unwrapping the temporary cloth that Henry had used, Edith took a bottle of liquid from her bag and said, "This will sting a little."

The boy nodded and held his breath as she poured the liquid over it.

When he jerked back with pain and whimpered, Edith said, "I'm so sorry." Her voice was soothing and full of empathy. "This will kill the germs, and then I'll put on some ointment."

The young man nodded.

Edith could tell that he was trying to look brave as he blinked back tears forming in his eyes. "So, what's your name?"

"Tom."

"I have a nephew by the name of Tommy, and he's very dear to me."

"Really?"

Edith nodded. If she could keep him talking, maybe he wouldn't notice what she was doing. As she rubbed the ointment on, she asked, "Do you like music?"

Tom winced as she wiped the ointment on the wound. "I ...I play the harmonica."

"You do? That's wonderful."

"Yeah. My teacher has the superintendent come to our class, and he teaches us how to play. He plays real good, too."

Henry nodded. "Actually, I really don't do much. He's a talented young man and plays quite well. I volunteered 'cause

I thought it would be a good experience for the children. I bought a bunch of inexpensive harmonicas for them. I believe that music helps a child's brain grow, and it improves the mind."

Edith was surprised by this information, so surprised that she didn't even dare turn her head to face Henry. *He played the harmonica*, she thought to herself, wondering if he could be the mysterious stranger. No, he couldn't be.

Quickly, she took out a strip of cloth and wrapped it around the young boy's palm and secured it. "There, young man, I'm done. You were quite brave."

Tom smiled up at Edith. "Thank you, Ma'am. Can I go out to play now?"

"I don't see why not. You're as good as new."

After the young man skipped out the door, Henry smiled appreciatively. "You have a way with children."

Edith glanced up, feeling uneasy and apprehensive for some reason. He liked her and she knew it. This always happened when she knew that someone liked her. She would back off, not allowing any man to get close to her.

With a slight smile, she answered, "I love children."

"Me, too. That's why I accepted this position. I moved here from the other side of the mountain, and I really love it here."

Edith swallowed nervously. "From the other side of the mountain?"

"Yes. That's where I grew up."

Edith's head was swimming with all this new information. He played the harmonica, and he was from the other side of the mountain. No! He couldn't be the mysterious stranger. The man in the letter spoke with eloquence.

Then it dawned on her. If he were, then why would he be telling her all this information? She knew that he wanted to remain anonymous. Surely, Henry could not be the one. This whole mystery was too obvious, too easy to solve. He had told her too much. Or was he telling her all this information to throw her off guard?

Henry sensed something was wrong as he watched her stuff her medicine and bandages into her bag. He nervously bit his lip and asked, "Are you all right, Miss Edith? You're not very talkative and you look a little pale."

Edith shook her head. "No, I'm all right. I've just got a few things on my mind."

"You know, you and I started off on the wrong foot. I guess that I was trying too hard to impress you. I tend to jabber away when I'm nervous and say the wrong things. Can we start again?"

When she looked up, Edith could see that he was smiling at her in a charming manner, and his eyes had a twinkle about them.

"Don't worry about it, Henry."

"May I see you to your buggy, Miss Edith?"

She nodded. "Yes, I'd like that."

Henry smiled, took her bag in one hand, and took her by the arm. After helping her into the buggy and handing her the bag, he smiled sweetly once again, his eyes never leaving hers.

"May I call on you some time, Miss Edith?"

Edith was about to say she was too busy, but changed her mind and nodded. "Of course, I'd like that."

Edith waved, whipped the reins, and the horse took off in a trot.

It was about time she gave men a chance. She had been too judgmental and she wanted to change all that. Edith had

78

noticed the way Henry watched her and had not taken his eyes off her the whole time. He had a gentle voice and loved children as she did. He believed in the importance of music for children. And she realized that he was trying harder to be a real gentleman by escorting her to the buggy. In fact, he seemed more humble since the last time she saw him. Perhaps she had misjudged him and had been too hard on him.

She nodded to herself. She really should give him another chance, get to know the inner person, his heart. If he called on her, she would not mind. But...

She shook her head in confusion. But he was lacking something. What he was lacking, she was not sure. But...

There it was again. There was always a "but" in her courtship experiences. No man had ever lived up to her qualifications.

Why that was, she was not sure. Perhaps she was looking for a man that didn't exist? Perhaps she put the perfect man on too high of a pedestal that no man could ever live up to? If the ideal man didn't exist, then what? Was she supposed to reevaluate her life and priorities? Was she expecting too much in a man, as her friends had once accused her of doing? What was she afraid of?

Whatever the problem was, she was waiting to fall in love, and it had not happened as of yet. Although, if she was constantly turning men away after their first or second call, maybe she would never fall in love.

Chapter 11
Melancholy Music

It was dusk, and the evening was peaceful and pleasant. Edith bid farewell to Melinda and Gilbert, and headed for the buggy. A couple days had passed since she had given her mother the letter to deliver to the mysterious stranger, and she was wondering what he looked like, who he was, and what he did for a living.

As she stepped into the buggy, she heard the soft melodic sound of music in the distance. The music was mingled with the sounds of a soft breeze and a Meadow Lark singing in the background. Whatever it was drew her in the direction from whence it came.

Edith immediately stepped down from the buggy and listened. It was a soft melancholy sound, so beautiful that it took her breath away. The melody was one of longing and full of emotion. She had heard melodies such as this in the Celtic folk songs of long ago.

As she approached the bunkhouse, she recognized the delicate strumming of a guitar and the faint sound of the harmonica. The music was played in perfect harmony, but yet each instrument carried something special of its own. The music was coming straight from the soul of the person playing. The sweet notes were elusive and sweet, and it held her spellbound.

She was tempted to enter the bunkhouse, but at the same time, she didn't want to disturb those who were creating this lovely music. But curiosity overtook her, and she tiptoed into the doorway of the rustic-looking building where a dozen bunk beds were strewn across the open room. She stood as silently as possible, for she did not want to startle anyone by her presence.

At the far end of the room was a lean handsome young man in his teens, sitting on a bed playing the harmonica. His eyes were closed, and he was gently swaying with the music. The person playing the guitar was sitting on another bed opposite the young man. He was in his thirties with wavy brown hair. He was a rugged-looking fellow with broad shoulders. His eyes seemed to be far away in a dreamland, as he carefully listened to the harmony of the music.

For a few minutes, she stood in awe and watched, loving every note that drifted toward her. The sound caressed every fiber of her being, and she was completely relaxed. Edith closed her eyes and could imagine singing to this haunting melody. It had touched her heart. When it came to an end, she opened her eyes, and the two men were staring at her.

Startled that she had been caught eavesdropping, her face flushed a rosy color and she quickly dropped her eyes to the floor.

David immediately recognized her and stood. "Can I help you, Miss Edith?"

Edith looked up, feeling embarrassed. She tried her best to blurt out an apology. "I...I'm so sorry."

"For what, Miss Edith?"

"For disturbing you. You see, I heard your music and…Well, I couldn't help it. I had to see who was playing such lovely music."

She looked at the other man who acted amused by her nervousness. He had a grin on his face as if enjoying her flustered look.

She took a deep breath and continued. "The music was so relaxing. It sounds familiar. Is it a Celtic melody?"

The man nodded. "Irish. My grandparents are from Ireland. I've been teaching it to David."

"It was lovely. Simply lovely. In fact, I was touched by the way you played it. You know what I mean, from your heart."

David turned toward his partner and introduced him. "Miss Edith, this is Joseph. We all call him Joe around here. Joe, this is Miss Edith. She's a cousin to Mrs. Roberts."

Joseph nodded. "Glad to meet you, Miss Edith."

Joseph strummed a few chords as he watched her. His eyes swept over her, looking her up and down as if he were appraising her, judging the nature or value of her. This made Edith feel uneasy.

Then he turned to his music, ignoring her and looking down at his guitar as he strummed one chord after another, as if searching for the right melody. After a moment, he began to play the sweet melodic notes of "Beautiful Dreamer" by Stephen Foster.

Just as she turned to leave, he asked, "Where are you from?"

Edith turned to face him. She was caught by surprise, both by his question and his change of mood. One moment he looked her up and down as if judging the value of her, making her feel uncomfortable, and the next he acted disinterested in her all together and turned to his music. He was one of the rudest men she had ever met.

Edith stood in the doorway, watching him play one of her favorite songs, wondering if he were more interested in knowing where she was from or more interested in what he was playing.

Joseph looked up from his strumming and asked, "Well?"

"I'm from Salt Lake City."

"Oh."

It came out as if he really didn't care at all, as if he were just making conversation. He continued playing, looking at his fingers as the melody drifted throughout the room. Then he looked up again and their eyes met. His eyes steadily held hers but he remained silent.

When she turned to leave once again, Joseph abruptly said, "So, Miss Edith, do you know much about music?"

Edith's eyes widened. Did she know much about music?

She pondered the question for a moment and then turned around and answered, "A little."

Joseph nodded. "Can you play the guitar?"

She slowly shook her head, noticing that he was changing the melody once again.

"Can you play the harmonica like David?"

She shook her head again.

"Hmmm, too bad. So, what *can* you do?"

This sort of question amused Edith.

"What can I do?" Suppressing a smile, she very quietly replied, "I can play the piano a little."

She was not lying. She did play the piano. She just left out the fact that she had played since childhood and that her mother had given her many a lesson.

"That's nice. Can you sing?"

Edith suppressed a grin. "A little."

"Do you know 'I Dream of Jeanie' by Stephen Foster?"

"Yes. Doesn't everybody know Stephen Foster?"

Joseph smiled as he played one of the sweetest melodies that Stephen Foster had ever composed.

Then he raised his eyebrows and asked, "Do you want to sing it while I play, or would you be too self-conscious or embarrassed? If you're too shy, you don't have to."

Edith's eyes widened at such a question. She had performed in many concerts, and here he was asking her if she would be embarrassed.

"You don't have to if you don't want to," he said nonchalantly.

With confidence in her voice, she answered, "No, I wouldn't be embarrassed."

"All right. How's this key?"

Edith listened carefully. "Could you bring it down a couple steps?"

"Sure. How's this?"

As she listened to the melody, she nodded. "That's fine."

As Joseph began playing, he said, "This is just an introduction. Do you know what an introduction is?"

Edith nodded, trying very hard to suppress a smile.

"I'll nod when it's time for you to come in."

Joseph strummed a few chords, and then after a while he looked up at her and smiled, giving her a nod. Then Edith began to sing.

I dream of Jeanie with the light brown hair,
Borne, like a vapor, on the summer air;
I see her tripping where the bright streams play,
Happy as the daisies that dance on her way.

Edith's voice was rich and beautiful. Her tone was exquisite. And her technique was one of complete emotion as each word was sung. She closed her eyes and sang with fervor, with great warmth and earnest feeling.

Many were the wild notes her merry voice would pour,
Many were the blithe birds that warbled them o'er:
Oh! I dream of Jeanie with the light brown hair,
Floating, like a vapor, on the soft summer air.

As she held the last sustained note, she gradually opened her eyes and noticed that both Joseph and David had their eyes transfixed upon her. David's expression was one of wonderment. But Joseph's was completely different. His was one of reverence and as their eyes met, he could not release his gaze.

After a few seconds, Joseph realized that he was staring, and instantly broke the spell that he seemed to be under. He cleared his throat nonchalantly, as if the song had not affected him one bit.

Then he smiled and said in a disinterested matter-of-fact tone, "That was nice, Miss Edith."

Edith stared at him and softly asked, "Nice?"

Joseph nodded. "Yup. That was nice. Well, I've got to go. Got a lot to do tomorrow."

Edith could not believe her ears as she repeated, "Nice?"

"Yup. Nice."

She shook her head in amazement. She had sung with deep feeling, and for an instant she thought that she had touched their hearts just as they had done to her with their music. And all he said was, "It was nice."

She felt irritated toward his attitude. Immediately she turned on her heels and strode toward her buggy, feeling unappreciated and unwanted. What was she doing singing to an unappreciative audience in the first place? What did this uneducated farmer know about music, anyway? His attitude annoyed her to no end.

She could not hear David and Joseph's last comments as she walked away, but it did not matter to her one iota. They could keep their comments to themselves for all she cared.

Joseph and David walked toward the door and stood at the entrance, watching her walk gracefully toward the buggy in a brisk manner. Her skirt swayed back and forth in agitation as she walked, and that made Joseph grin with amusement. She seemed a bit aggravated with him, he noticed.

As Joseph watched her intently, he softly said, "David, wasn't that the most beautiful voice you've ever heard in your life?"

"It sure was, Joe. I was speechless. I couldn't think of a thing to say."

"The words that came to my mind were angelic, lovely, exquisite, beautiful. And I'm not just talking about her voice, either."

David grinned at Joseph. "She is that, I agree."

Then they turned around and walked back inside the bunkhouse.

"By the way, Joe, thanks for lending me your harmonica. I bought my own today so you can have yours back."

Chapter 12
Gilbert's Wrath

Melinda walked slowly down the hall toward the kitchen. As she entered, she saw Jenny setting the table for supper, Gilbert was stirring the beef stew, and David was sitting on the floor playing with John. She headed for the cupboard and took out a small jar of honey and comfrey oats-straw.

Gilbert looked at the herbs on the counter. With a questioning look, he asked, "Your legs aching again?"

Melinda nodded. "What was it that Edith said? Was it one teaspoon mixed with a little honey?"

"Yup. And within twenty minutes it should be gone." He tapped the spoon on the edge of the pan and laid it down. As he wiped his hands with a towel, he walked over to Melinda and took the honey from her. "I'll make it for you. Go sit down."

Melinda looked up and said with independence, "I can do it. You're making the stew. It won't hurt me to be on my feet for a few minutes."

Gilbert shook his head. "Melinda, that's what you said when I came in this afternoon and found you picking up the living room floor and dusting and whatever else you got away with. Edith has already said these herbs will help you, but don't overdo just because you feel better. You've got to …"

"Gilbert!" Melinda said firmly. "I'm tired of lying around. You wait on me all the time. I'm starting to feel like an invalid, like I'm useless, like I'm not doing my wifely duties."

Gilbert let out a puff of air in exasperation. "Wifely duties?" he exploded with a stern look.

Nothing made his blood boil more or bring his wrath to the surface than the labeling of duties between husband and wife. He believed this was a union where duties were shared.

He threw the towel on the cabinet with frustration as he said, "Don't talk to me about these so-called wifely duties. If a man can't help with the household chores, then what kind of husband is he, anyway? I tell you this, I enjoy helping and serving whenever I can. A man who comes in the house after his job is done and then sits down to read a newspaper while his wife is fixing the meal is no example of a husband who truly loves his wife. Why can't a husband help? Is there a written law that wives should wait on their husbands? I don't think so."

Melinda was in shock at Gilbert's stern voice. What had she said to bring on such a change in attitude? She stared at him, waiting for him to calm down.

"Don't speak to me about wifely duties, Melinda. Aren't we both here to help and serve one another? Aren't these the quiet ways we show our love, with our actions?"

Melinda listened with disbelief. She noticed that Gilbert's voice was full of exasperation.

As he slowly shook his head, Gilbert saw her shocked look and tried his best to calm down before he continued.

Taking a deep breath, he said, "When I came home from work yesterday, I was tired. I collapsed on the sofa. When you saw me sitting relaxed, you walked up to me and asked if I needed anything. You weren't feeling good. I could see it in your face. But you asked what you could do for me. I simply asked you to unlace my shoes and pull them off. You sat down on the floor next to me and lovingly unlaced my shoes and slipped them off. You could have gone to the bedroom to lie down, but instead, you wanted to see if I needed something. And you wanted to make me comfortable."

All was silent. No one said a word. Melinda looked down at her hands, thinking, trying to figure out why he was so upset. She had hit a very delicate subject without even knowing it. She had sparked something inside of Gilbert by using those two words: wifely duties.

When he saw Melinda's sorrowful expression, he realized that he had been awfully stern. He gently lifted her chin with his fingers, looked into her eyes with gentleness, and said softly, "Melinda, I didn't mean to hurt your feelings, but marriage is all about serving, sharing, and caring."

Gilbert noticed that David had been watching them intently during his outburst, and had listened to their conversation. David looked surprised at what he had just heard.

Gilbert rubbed his chin as he looked at him and then said, "David, you look a little confused. What's wrong?"

David stood and tucked his hands in his pockets as he asked shyly, "Sir? I don't understand. Isn't it a woman's duty and responsibility to wait on her husband? To unlace his shoes, so to speak?"

Gilbert chuckled. He had heard this before by many a man who felt his wife's duties were to wait on him hand and foot.

He smiled and said softly, "A wife is your most precious, eternal helpmate. A helpmate is your companion, your equal partner, not someone that you expect to wait on you. She's not someone to take for granted. David, what does it mean to love someone with all your heart?"

David pondered the question and then said, "It means to love with your emotional feelings."

Gilbert nodded. "That's right. But it's much more than that. When you love your wife with all your heart, you don't criticize her or find fault with her. You must communicate with her, express your love to her, and be sensitive to her needs. You have to make sure that she knows she's attractive to you. Not only that, a man should be grateful she's the mother of his children. This is a noble calling...to bear and train your children."

David was surprised as he said, "This is a new concept. I haven't heard this before."

"No, David. It's an old one. Nobody seems to spread the word."

David cleared his throat. "Mr. Roberts, my pa is the head of the house, he makes all the decisions. No one crosses him, not even ma. You have to know, though, there was never a question that he loved her, but an equal partnership was not what they had. He was the boss, and everyone knew it. That's why I left home. I couldn't stand it any longer."

David looked at Melinda and said humbly, "I...Well, I like your family. I'm impressed. Mr. Roberts lets you argue with him but Pa would never allow it. Never! And another thing, I never saw Pa look at Ma the way Mr. Roberts looks at you. It's sort of like he...Well, sort of like he adores you. That's all I have to say."

David turned on his heels and strode outside, heading for the bunkhouse.

Melinda turned toward her husband and realized that David was right. Gilbert was looking at her with adoration and it was something he had done since the first time he had kissed her. His love could be seen through his eyes and his actions. There was no mistake that he found Melinda attractive.

At that moment she handed him the herbs, looked into his eyes and said softly, "Thank you. I would appreciate a little help."

Then she reached up on her toes, placed her hands on each side of his cheeks, leaned toward him, and placed a warm and tender kiss on his lips, lingering a bit. Then she turned around and walked to a chair, and sat next to the table to wait.

Chapter 13
Edith, the Strong Minded

A rap at the door brought Melinda to her feet. She was sitting on the sofa quietly reading a book. As she opened the door, she smiled when she saw Edith. They embraced one another and then walked over to the sofa arm in arm.

"How are you feeling today, Melinda?"

"Just fine. I felt movement for the first time and I was so excited. Not to mention how excited Gilbert was. How have you been lately? It's been a week now. Have you heard from your mysterious stranger?"

Edith nodded as they sat down side by side.

A lovely smile formed on her lips as she said, "I brought the letter with me to read to you. Want to hear?"

"Of course."

"Well, when I asked him about revealing who he was, he had a very good answer."

Edith pulled two letters from her bag, opened one, and softly read it to Melinda.

Dear Edith, the Confused,

The Lord said to the Prophet Samuel in the Old Testament, "Look not on his countenance or on the height of his stature." Then he said, "Man looketh on the outward appearance, but the Lord looketh on the heart."

I prefer that you get to know my heart first. I want you to get to know what kind of person I am inside and I want to know what you're like inside, too. Isn't it our souls that must commune first? Let's not talk of what we do as a living or boast of our exploits. Let's speak of our beliefs, our desires in life, and our goals. Let's speak from our hearts and what we love most in life and what makes us happy. Or what saddens us. But let's not talk of our everyday labors.

Sincerely,
Your Friend

Melinda looked at Edith in amazement. "Oh, my. He's romantic, isn't he?"

Edith's eyes were soft as she nodded.

"So, what are you going to do, then?"

"Well, I began to worry. What if I begin to fall for this man and he doesn't fall for me? I believe that I should show my real self, right up front. And then if he isn't afraid of me, then he'll continue writing. I'm not going to hide my true feelings. I want him to know how strong I feel about some things."

"Have you written back, yet?"

Edith nodded. "I wanted you to read my response. It's quite a strong reply, so don't get shocked by it, but at the same time I feel good about it."

Edith took the second letter and handed it to Melinda. She unfolded it and began to read.

Dear Friend,

 I understand what you mean and I agree. I won't ask you about your personal life. But I will ask you of your beliefs and dreams. This idea of sharing our thoughts enchants me and pleases me.

 First, I would like to share just a few of my feelings with you. I want you to know that I am a person with very strong opinions, and I'm not easily swayed unless I realize I'm wrong. I like people who are honest with me. I am a peace-loving person, but I don't like being dominated or intimidated by others. I tend to judge others at first glance. I am stubborn by nature and outspoken, which frustrates my mother to no end.

 I have a strong belief in God, and that is very important to me. I enjoy being with and sharing my inner most thoughts with those who have a strong faith in God.

 Now for the unimportant or minor things: I enjoy walking in warm rain, reading, picnics in the woods, and taking nature walks. I feel that I'm a romantic person by nature. If at any time you feel inclined to stop writing, I won't be offended.

 Sincerely,

 Edith, the Strong Minded

After reading the letter, Melinda was stunned, shocked, and even speechless. She looked up at Edith with an open mouth and wide eyes.

"What?" asked Edith naïvely. "Why are you looking at me that way?"

"Edith, do you realize how strong your letter sounds? It sounds as if you want to end this relationship even before it begins." She sighed. "Why were you so strong headed before getting to know this man?"

"Because I don't want to get hurt. That's why. If he knows what kind of person I am up front and continues writing to me, then I'll be pleased."

Edith looked out the window for a moment and then continued in a softer tone. "Let me put it this way, what if he finds out what I'm really like after many months of writing, and then he stops writing to me. Understand?"

"Yes, I do. I see your reasoning. It's best to be honest up front before it's too late. But, if a man truly falls in love with a woman, wouldn't he accept her strong feelings just because of his love for her?"

Edith hesitated before answering. "I don't really know. I just don't want to take a chance. That's all. Now, all I have to do is wait and see what his response is." She paused and then looked down at her fidgety hands. "I'm not going to hold my breath, if you're wondering."

Melinda took Edith's hand in hers, caressing it tenderly, and smiled. She agreed, but in another way, she was worried that Edith's letter was too strong.

During courtship, a person doesn't usually come right out and tell someone his or her strongest feelings. At first, anyway. Usually it's a gradual process, but then writing letters wasn't the usual courtship process, either.

Chapter 14
Just Resting My Eyes

Gilbert grasped Melinda's hand firmly in his so he could help her out of the buggy. After stepping to the ground, she took him by the arm and walked toward the tabernacle for church services.

They were five minutes late for church. Each Sunday Gilbert always had to wait patiently for the womenfolk, especially because of all the primping that Jenny had to do. Melinda was slower nowadays and that accounted for her excuse. As for young John, his mother was walking way too slow for him, so he ran past her toward the building.

"Hey, John," Gilbert called out to him. "Save us a place to sit."

"All right, Pa."

When Gilbert and Melinda arrived, they saw John standing by the bench where Uncle William, Aunt Martha, and Edith sat. Jenny walked between the benches and sat down beside Uncle William. Melinda was next, followed by Gilbert.

John looked up at David and said, "You can sit by me, David."

As John slid in beside his father, he grinned as David sat down beside him. Gilbert noticed that his son was elated because his buddy David had decided to go to church with the family. Gilbert knew that David treated him like a young man, and that made John feel good inside.

After an hour and a half, the bishop announced that the choir would sing the closing song.

Jenny looked at Uncle William, who was breathing deeply with his eyes closed, "just resting his eyes."

Uncle William was a member of the church choir and sang tenor. He enjoyed singing in the choir and was a devoted member who supported the choir by attending every practice.

Uncle William was a short, round, heavy man with a gray mustache and thin gray hair. He was in his late sixties and had a jovial laugh that would make the most sober person break into a smile.

Jenny looked at her uncle and noticed that he was "resting his eyes." In the past, when Jenny accused him of sleeping in church, he would defend himself adamantly by saying to her, "I'm not sleeping. I'm just resting my eyes. I can hear everything that's being said."

No one, except for Jenny, ever questioned the fact, but everyone knew otherwise. The only problem was they could never prove it.

As Jenny watched the choir walk behind the pulpit toward their seats, she nudged her uncle and said, "Uncle William, the choir's going up. See?"

When Jenny nudged him, he was a little startled, but he quickly opened his eyes, grabbed a hymnbook, and stood up. Jenny watched Uncle William as he slowly edged himself out from between the benches and proceeded to walk up to the choir seats.

Melinda's eyes widened as she asked, "Why is Uncle William going up to the choir seats?"

Jenny giggled. "Don't know, Mama. I just told him that the women's choir was going up because I thought he might want to open his eyes and listen. Next thing I knew, he was standing up and making his way to the pulpit."

Uncle William stood among the women with his hymnbook in hand. After a moment, he quickly scanned the choir and noticed there was not a man among this bunch of women...and then it dawned on him. Blood rushed to his face as it instantly reddened with embarrassment. It spread from his face down to his neck.

He took the edge of his shirt collar with two fingers and gently pulled on it to let the heat escape from his neck. Humiliated beyond words, he bowed his head and quickly walked back to the bench where his family was seated. His face was flushed and he said nothing as he sat down beside Jenny.

She giggled and leaned over to her uncle and whispered, "Uncle William, why did you go up to the women's choir?"

"I'm not ever coming back to church again," he said firmly.

"What?"

"Never, never, never." Uncle William was sober and he was not in the mood to talk.

Jenny knew he was not serious, and she giggled as she looked at her mother. Melinda suppressed a smile, and Gilbert held back a chuckle.

John looked up at his father and asked, "What's wrong?" He was oblivious to the whole situation.

When church was excused, Uncle William and Aunt Martha disappeared quickly and headed for home, with the encouragement of William. He said he was not in the mood to stick around and they needed to get dinner ready for their guests, the Roberts family.

After everyone arrived, Uncle William hoped no one would mention the incident that happened at church. He already felt humiliated enough when a few people walked up to him and teased him about sleeping in church or being the only male soloist in the women's choir, but he took it good-naturedly.

William cleared his throat, leaned forward, and said, "Gilbert, I really don't believe you have to hire so many men for the roundup this year. I've heard that Butch Cassidy and his gang have split up, and he and Sundance left for South America. I don't think you have to worry about rustlers this year. It's really slowed down. Besides, I read that Kid Curry was killed in June."

"Who?"

"Kid Curry. He's known as the most feared killer in the West. When he was cornered in a canyon in Colorado, he committed suicide, rather than give himself up to the law. His cattle rustling days are over, I believe. I don't think there's anything to worry about."

"I know, William. But I have a gut feeling that I should have more men this year. Boulder, Utah was hit bad one year, and I want to be ready for anything. You don't mind taking the cattle to market on the train, do you? I hate to leave Melinda at this time."

William smiled, "Not at all. It's a pleasure to help out."

John burst into the living room from the kitchen and hopped up on William's lap. William hugged him tight and chuckled, his eyes brimming with joy. "Well, well. How's my lad this fine day?"

"I'm good, Uncle William. And you?"

"Couldn't be better."

"Good, because I was worried about you."

"Worried about me?" William ruffled John's hair and chuckled, "Why on earth would you worry about me?"

"Well, 'cause I figured out what happened at church when I heard all the whisperings."

William furrowed his eyebrows and frowned. "What whisperings?"

"Oh, that you're the newest member of the women's choir."

Gilbert and David let out a burst of laughter that could be heard all through the house and down the road for a block or two. Suddenly, William jerked his head around and stared at both of them with a sober expression. His lips were in a thin tight line, and his brows had a deep crease.

Gilbert slapped his leg and guffawed once again.

"It's not funny!" William said gruffly. "Not funny at all!"

Chapter 15
A Prima Donna

As Edith headed down the road in her buggy, she noticed Joseph standing next to some pastureland mending a fence. She reined in the horse and came to a stop. As she watched Joseph work, she noticed how tall he was. He wasn't as muscular as Gilbert and had narrow hips with rugged features. There was something about this man that intrigued her. Perhaps it was the way he caressed the strings of his guitar and filled the air with pleasant sultry music. She believed that music could bring joy to the soul. That was why she loved singing.

When she remembered Joseph's words, her brows furrowed. He had simply told her that she sang "nice." His comment came matter-of-factly as if he were uninterested. She might as well have sung to the cattle in the field. They would have at least appreciated it more than he did. And another thing, it infuriated her the way he was looking her up and down, appraising her value like a head of cattle being taken to market. Why was she even sitting here watching him in the first place? The thought of the other evening aggravated her to no end.

Just as she took the reins firmly in her hands, Joseph turned around and noticed her. A broad pleasant smile came to his face, and he waved to her in a friendly manner. His smile was charming and her irritation began to subside. She waved back out of politeness and smiled.

Joseph motioned for her to come toward him. She looked at the tall field grass and then down at her dress and shoes. She didn't see any dirt or mud where he was working, so perhaps she would see what he wanted. She lifted her skirts and carefully stepped down from the buggy.

As Joseph watched her, he noticed how graceful she was. She had such poise and elegance, not to mention beauty. Her song the other night was breathtakingly beautiful, as he remembered. The feeling she had put into each note had touched him greatly.

As she approached him, Joseph found he could not take his eyes off her. Not only because of her loveliness, but she had touched his heart the other night. He didn't know her, but there was something about her that captivated him. Was it the way she had sung so sweetly, caressing each note with emotion and tenderness? Whatever it was, he was willing to get to know her…if she gave him a chance, that is.

Joseph smiled as she approached. "It's nice to see you again."

"Thank you, Joseph. What are you doing?"

Edith knew very well what he was doing. He was fixing the fence, but her mind was blank and that was all that came to her mind.

"I'm making sure the cattle won't escape in the night. I wanted to show you something."

"Oh?"

"Do you know much about herbs?"

Edith smiled. His questions were so amusing, just like the other night. Did she know much about music? Could she sing?

With a twinkle in her eyes, she answered, "A little."

"Hmmm. Do you have a tough time relaxing in the evenings?"

"Sometimes. Why?"

Joseph knelt down and picked a few weeds with tiny yellow and white blossoms and then handed them to her. "This is chamomile. Steep the leaves and blossoms for ten minutes. It'll help you relax in the evenings and sleep better. Some people have an allergic reaction to it, though."

Edith raised her eyebrows as she looked at the handful of herbs in her hand. So many times she had passed a field with these herbs growing to the side of a fence, but she had not stopped to pick herself some. She knew all about chamomile, but this rugged farmer was sweet enough to give her a bunch and educate her on its effect. Perhaps she shouldn't have been so hard on him.

Edith's beautiful chocolate brown eyes lit up as she smiled. "Why, thank you, Joseph."

His eyes held hers for a moment, transfixed by her sincerity, and then he took a deep breath and let it out slowly.

He instantly became businesslike and turned back to his work, and said soberly, "Well, I've got to finish this job. Gilbert needs help milking this afternoon."

His sudden change of mood was so perplexing to Edith as she stood watching him. He grabbed a wire and wrapped it securely around a post and connected it to the loose fence.

As he twisted the wire firmly with his gloved hand, he asked, "Do you like city life better...or the country?"

She thought for a moment and answered, "They both have advantages."

"Oh? Like what?"

"In the city I don't have to travel ten miles just to get groceries or a yard of cloth."

"True."

"But here, I can sit beside a brook and listen to nature and completely relax. To listen to the soft bubbling water and a song of a bird is so pleasant. I can quietly read, ponder, or even sing, with no interruptions."

Joseph turned from his work and looked into her eyes, wondering what kind of person she was. He could see softness and goodness in them, someone who loved nature and cared for people. It was as if he could see into her soul just for an instant, and then it left. Joseph smiled at what he saw.

Then he turned back to his work and asked matter-of-factly, "Have you ever been to Paris Springs?"

Just as Edith saw a hint of tenderness in his face, it quickly left and soberness took over once again. He was the most perplexing man she had ever met.

"What did you say?"

"Have you been to Paris Springs where the water pours out of the mountain?"

"Yes, I have."

"Now that's not such a relaxing sound, nothing quiet about it. It's not one of those soft bubbling brooks you were talking about. The water gushes out of the mountain so rapidly and with such force that it would drown out any quiet thoughts a person might have. In fact, it would easily drown out the singing of a prima donna."

Edith was startled. "A prima donna?"

A prima donna, she knew, was a high-strung, vain, demanding, and temperamental person. She had been unfairly accused of being a prima donna once and she had been greatly offended. She hoped he was not referring to her, but nonetheless, for some reason she felt offended by his example as if he were hinting that she was.

"A prima donna?" she repeated with an edge in her voice, not even hiding the irritation she felt.

"Yup. It's pretty loud when it pours out of the mountain like that. It bubbles over the rocks and creates quite a noise."

"Are you insinuating that I am?"

"What?" Joseph said with confusion.

Edith knew she was being overly sensitive, but she could not help it. She was fed up with his sudden mood changes and off-hand comments, so she immediately turned around and stomped away.

Her frustration had made her forget the small stream of water between the road and the pasture. When she stepped on the edge of the ditch with her heel, she lost her balance and slid down into the water with a splash, bottom end first.

She gasped as the cold water splashed in her face. As she sat sprawled out in the ditch, soaking wet, water dripping from her face, she heard chuckling. When she turned toward Joseph, he was standing by the fence, smiling.

When Joseph saw her stomp away, he knew she was not happy with his comment about the prima donna. He had not meant to insinuate that she was. He had to suppress a chuckle when he saw her frown and stomp away. But when he saw her land right smack dab in the middle of the ditch, he let it out. He could not hold it in any longer. The sight of her in the ditch was humorous, and he could not help but laugh. Now she was looking up at him with frustration and helplessness in her eyes. All of her spunk had left.

Joseph pulled off his gloves, stuffed them in his pocket, and then strode quickly toward her. He stooped down, offered his hand to her, and pulled her to her feet. She stood in the ditch, looking down at her sopping wet dress.

As Joseph watched her, he noticed how lovely she was, even soaking wet and with a smudge of mud that had splashed on her cheek. As she looked up at Joseph, she wiped the water from her face, smearing the mud across her chin. Noticing what a mess she had made of herself, he took a handkerchief from his back pocket and wiped the mud from her face with short gentle strokes.

As Edith looked into his eyes, all frustration began to fade. She saw a gentle side to Joseph. The corners of his mouth turned up, and he smiled as he gently wiped away the mud. This man puzzled her greatly. One moment he was laughing at her situation, and in the next he was gently wiping the mud from her face with true tenderness.

When he was finished, his eyes held hers for a few seconds, and then his hand gently touched her cheek as he wiped a loose curl from her face. She noticed the tenderness in his touch and in his eyes, and she did not even notice she was still standing ankle deep in the ditch.

When Joseph realized what he was doing, he quickly stuffed the handkerchief in his back pocket and cleared his throat.

Looking at her dilemma, he chuckled once again. "That was quite a fall you had."

When Edith saw the tenderness instantly leave and change to humor, she wondered what he was afraid of. It was as if he were trying to hide his feelings, his gentle ways.

"You know, Miss Edith, if you wouldn't have stomped away like you did, you would have noticed the ditch."

"I didn't stomp," she said with a tinge of irritation. "I don't know what you're talking about."

"Oh?"

When she saw the humor in his face, she defended herself once again. "I didn't stomp. I was walking quickly."

"Is that what they call it in the city?"

He was so infuriating. Edith frowned. "I don't like your attitude. You frustrate me, and I don't know why."

"Perhaps it's because I don't dish out lavish compliments like you're used to. Perhaps you're a little spoiled."

Edith was taken aback by his frankness and was upset at his insinuation.

"I admit that I may be a little spoiled. But I'm not a prima donna. I'm not vain and temperamental. I'm not demanding."

"I didn't say you were. I only said that you probably expect lavish compliments. I never once accused you of being a prima donna."

Edith was stunned. She loved singing but was she actually expecting lavish compliments? Was this really true? Had she forgotten to be humble and grateful for her God-given talent?

Instantly a scripture came to mind as clear and distinct as if she were reading it. "For they loved the praise of men more than the praise of God."

Then it dawned on her. Joseph was right. She had been offended the other night simply because he had not lavished her with praises. He was not comparing her to a prima donna at all, and she knew it. She was touchy because of what had happened to her years ago, and she was taking it out on Joseph. It was not his fault that she fell in the ditch, but she acted as if it were. Then he helped her up and wiped off her face. Were these the actions of a callous man? No, they were not.

Edith felt ashamed of her behavior and lack of humility. Was it pride that was standing in her way? How had she allowed it to happen, caring more for the praise of man than of God?

Edith slowly shook her head and looked down at her feet. She was still standing in the ditch, dripping wet. She looked up at Joseph, smiled, and realized the humor in her situation.

That was all it took for her to burst into a fit of uncontrollable laughter, releasing every tension and stress that had built up during the past few months.

Joseph was amused at her sudden change of attitude and chuckled, his shoulders and chest shaking with laughter. He held out his hand to her and helped her out of the ditch.

"My, you're a sight! I sure hope you haven't ruined your dress."

He picked a piece of mud from her hair and tossed it into the ditch with a grin.

She looked down at her soaking, muddy dress and laughed once again. She had not laughed like this for months. What had happened to her sense of humor? Had she been so wrapped up in her duties that she forgot to laugh? Why had she become so serious lately? Why had she allowed pride to sneak into her life?

Joseph took Edith's arm and said, "I'll walk you to your buggy, Miss Edith."

"Thank you. I'd like that."

As they walked, Edith said, "Thanks for the chamomile. It's too bad it landed in the water."

"I'll pick you some more and send it to your house."

"Thanks. I didn't know farmers knew so much about herbs."

"Did you think we were an uneducated lot?"

Edith refrained from answering that question because inside she had thought that very thing. She had been too judgmental, and she knew it.

Joseph was able to perceive her thoughts, perhaps by her actions. But he let it lie.

Edith lifted her heavy wet skirt and petticoats, and stepped into the buggy.

As she took the reins in hand, she turned toward him and smiled. "I hope you have a nice day, Joseph."

He gave a curt nod. "Thank you."

"I needed a good laugh today. I've been much too serious."

"Me, too, Miss Edith. Me, too."

Chapter 16
Jenny's Book of Life

David was enjoying his work immensely. He had made friends, and everyone accepted him as part of the family, which was unusual to him. They had treated him with respect, and that impressed him a lot. Supper had ended, and everyone went his or her own way for the evening. When he watched Jenny walk outside, he decided to lay his book aside and follow. As he walked outside, he saw Jenny sitting on the porch steps, looking up at the stars.

As he approached, Jenny said, "Isn't it a beautiful night, David?"

He cleared his throat before speaking. "Yes. Very beautiful. The stars seem brighter than usual. How'd you know it was me?"

Jenny smiled at his question. "I know the sound of papa's boots and his sureness of step. Yours is softer, completely different." She patted the steps beside her and asked, "So, do you like it here in Idaho?"

David accepted the invitation and sat down. "Yes, I do. It's different from Colorado, but I like it a lot. The people are different, too."

Jenny turned and looked at David. "How?"

"Well, you seem more laid back around here."

"Laid back? Are you referring to us not being on time for church last Sunday?"

"Well, yes, among other things. I haven't been to a church service since I was sixteen. Ma was a religious woman and we all went to church, but we were never late."

Jenny giggled. "Well, I guess we should work on that, shouldn't we?"

David grinned as her laughter filled the air. It was like music to his ears, and it brought a smile to his lips each time he heard it. Jenny acted as if she loved life, and that was refreshing to him.

"David, why don't you ever talk about your father?"

He stared off into the distance. "We didn't get along. I know that sounds lame, but I was fed up with being told what to do with my life. So, I set off on my own."

"Is it hard to be on your own?"

"No. I like making my own decisions. Wouldn't you like to be more independent?"

"I am. My folks let me do pretty much what I like. You saw our little conversation about going on the cattle drive. We compromised."

David turned toward her and looked at her silhouette in the light of the moon. "You compromised?"

"Yes. Didn't you ever compromise with your family?"

David's tone was a little sarcastic. "Pa never knew what the word meant. It was either his way or not at all."

Jenny turned to face him. "I'm sorry. It sounds as if you weren't happy at home."

"Don't get me wrong, I love my family and I miss them. I just needed to make my own decisions in life. I was fed up with my pa making the decisions for me."

Jenny nodded. "I understand. By the way, Papa told me that he really likes you. He said you're a hard worker."

"Thanks. I do my best. I notice sometimes you're out doing some of the work alongside your pa. At home, it's different."

"How is it different?"

"Well, my sisters don't do that sort of work. They clean the house and all those chores that women are supposed to do."

Jenny laughed out loud. "Did you say chores that women are supposed to do?"

"Yeah, and I heard what your pa said."

"Does your pa go home and sit down in his soft chair and read the newspaper while waiting for supper?"

David grinned. He knew what she was referring to. "Yup. He even complains if it's not ready on time. He doesn't raise a finger to help, though. He said that women have their chores and men have theirs."

"Do you agree with him?"

"Well, at first I did because I was raised with that sort of thinking. But since I've been here and since I've been watching your pa, I'm changing my opinion. Your pa is smart and he cares about his womenfolk."

Jenny smiled with approval. "David, I like you."

David's eyes widened with wonder. This young woman sitting beside him was not afraid to say what was on her mind. She was uninhibited and had an innocence that he admired. She also had the trust of a child.

David smiled. "I like you, too, Jenny. You know what?"

"What?"

"You shouldn't trust strangers so much. You never know what sort of people they are."

"What do you mean?" Jenny smiled in a teasing manner. "Are you referring to yourself?"

"Yup. I'm a real culprit."

Jenny giggled softly. "You're funny. Why wouldn't I trust someone who is kind to my little brother and treats him with respect? Why wouldn't I trust someone who treats my parents with respect? Respect goes a long way in my book, David."

"And what book is that, Jenny?"

"The book of life."

"Oh, and what's written in this book of life?"

"Things that are important to me. My code, so to speak."

"Your code?" David chuckled. "You have a code?"

"Yes. My code is a collection of rules and beliefs that I go by. Like a gentleman's code of behavior, I have my code of behavior. My book has quotes and ideas that help me to be a better person. It guides me."

David scratched his head with puzzlement. "You're serious, aren't you, Jenny?"

"Yes, I am. In my small Book of Life, I write my own thoughts, but I also collect those I like. I have some quotes by Abraham Lincoln and George Washington. Susan B. Anthony has really worked hard for women's rights, and I have a few of her quotes, along with Eliza R. Snow, who is a great poet."

"Can you give me an example?"

Her eyes brightened as she grinned. "Cicero said, 'A room without books is like a body without a soul.'"

"That's a good one, Jen."

"My pa used to quote this one to me whenever I didn't want to read or study. President George Washington said, 'A knowledge of books is the basis upon which other knowledge is to be built.'"

"I like that one, too."

"Washington also said…" Jenny looked up at the stars, and her voice was soft as she quoted, "'It is the duty of nations to acknowledge the providence of Almighty God, to obey His will, to be grateful for His benefits, and humbly to implore His protection and favor.'"

David was silent, staring off into space, thinking, pondering his life. He didn't know what to say after that quote. He hadn't gone to church in ages and couldn't remember the last time he had even prayed. The last thing on his mind was God, let alone thanking him for "benefits," as Washington put it.

"Do you want to hear my favorite one, David?"

He blinked and turned toward Jenny. "Yes, I would."

Jenny closed her eyes as if concentrating and remembering her memorized code. "'If I can stop one heart from breaking, I shall not live in vain. If I can ease one life the aching or cool one pain, or help one fainting robin unto his nest again, I shall not live in vain.'"

As David listened to the sincerity and expression of her voice, he knew it meant a lot to her. After she finished, she opened her eyes, smiled, and looked at the stars above.

"Who wrote that one?"

Jenny turned to face him. "Emily Dickinson. I liked it so much that I memorized it and put it in my Book of Life. I also like the way George Eliot put it. 'What do we live for, if it is not to make life less difficult for each other.' What she said is so true."

"She?"

"Uh-huh. George Eliot is her pen name. She's a woman."

David said nothing more but sat in silence, just watching the stars and listening to the evening noises. A symphony of crickets was heard, and there was an occasional lowing of cattle in the distance. They were soothing sounds to David.

After a few minutes, he turned to Jenny and watched her for a long time. She was a beautiful young woman, not only on the outside but on the inside as well. And she was stirring feelings within him that he never knew he had. He noticed that his heart would flutter more than usual when he was in the same room as Jenny. The way she looked at him, the way she walked, the way she smiled when he would speak to her, and her vulnerability!

He took a deep breath and let it out slowly, hoping to calm his fluttering heart. "Jenny, you're an unusual person, I must say."

She turned and faced David directly with a coy smile. "Thank you, David. I appreciate the compliment."

David laughed. "Why would you take that as a compliment?"

"Because I could tell it was, by the tone of your voice."

David nodded and grinned. "You're right."

She hopped up and walked toward the door with David's eyes following her every move. "See you tomorrow, David. Sleep well."

David was now alone with his own thoughts. As he sat in silence, he wondered if he had taken the right road or destination. Had he chosen wisely when he decided to turn into an outlaw? He thought he had...until he met the Roberts family and saw the happiness that abounded there.

And Jenny! That was another subject all together. He was attracted to her more than he ought to be.

David shook his head and decided not to think about it any longer. This was the road he had chosen, and he had a job to do. The Tall Texan was his friend and had trusted him to do his part. He would not let him down.

David looked at the moon above. It was late. He stood and strode off toward the bunkhouse to get some sleep.

Chapter 17
Edith Dines with Henry

Edith sat at Aunt Sarah's Café, chatting with Henry. He had made a point to make the evening extra special. He had given her some flowers and taken her to a nice restaurant. He had been treating her with great respect, and that impressed her greatly. It was as if he was trying to make up for his boldness and outspoken ways the first two times they met.

They had discussed music and teaching, and agreed on every subject. In fact, he was so congenial that she felt sorry for being so hard on him. She knew the man of her "dreams" would have many things in common with her, but would Henry support her in her decisions as a companion and mate? She had to know his true feelings so she decided to test the waters.

Edith took a deep breath and said with soberness, "I'm sorry that I bit your head off at the house. You know . . . about equality. But that's very important to me."

She could see his discomfort with the subject as he answered, "I know, Miss Edith. But you completely misunderstood me that night. Men can never take a woman's place no matter how hard they try. I have always felt that women have a certain mother's intuition and tenderness that men don't have. Therefore, children should have the influence of their fathers, but mothers are the ones that will make the difference in their lives. If a small child needs help, whom do they run to?"

Edith nodded. "I see what you're getting at. They go to their mothers first."

"That's right. When children get hurt at school or if they're sad, I've never had them beg for their father. They always call for their mother. Why is that?"

Edith shrugged. "I'm not really sure. I suppose there's something comforting in having a mother wrap her arms around a child that's been hurt and whisper those soothing words they need to hear."

Henry smiled and gave a nod. "Did you ever have an experience in which you called for your mother before your father?"

Edith thought for a moment and then leaned toward Henry and said softly, "I remember when I was a child, and when I walked in the door from school, the first name I called out was my mother's, not my father's. I just needed to know if she was available or even around in case I needed her."

Henry smiled congenially. "Edith, I know that men should be a part of raising their children, but their main responsibility is to provide for their family and protect them. Now do you understand what I meant the other night?"

Edith nodded. He was good. He was so diplomatic, knew the right questions to ask, and had a way with words. He should be a politician, she giggled to herself. She smiled as she pictured him giving diplomatic talks and kissing babies in mothers' arms.

When Henry noticed the cheerfulness in Edith's countenance, he smiled. "Edith, I bet it's wonderful to perform for people and bring joy into their lives through music, traveling around and meeting people, meeting the great musicians."

"In a way, yes. In another, no. That's why I quit."

"What do you mean?"

"Well, I enjoyed meeting people, but a lot of the musicians are quite temperamental. I had had enough and decided it wasn't the life for me. I would just sing in my own hometown and take care of people."

"Temperamental? What happened?"

"Well, a few years ago someone once accused me of being a prima donna, simply because I refused his intentions. I wouldn't allow him to call on me. He was a demanding person, a director of an orchestra, and was used to having his way. When I wasn't interested, he saw to it that I didn't get a part in Handel's *Messiah*. He made life miserable for me because I wouldn't allow him to call on me."

"Why not?"

"Because he had a reputation. I didn't want to be compromised."

"You know he was just saying that out of spite. He must have been some kind of high and mighty person to accuse you of such a thing."

"Yes, he was."

Henry smiled and said with a honey-coated voice, "Besides, if you were considered a prima donna, then I believe being a prima donna would not be such a bad thing after all."

Edith laughed. Henry was so supportive. He was a charmer and he was sincere. He was a kind and sweet person, and she felt she had misjudged him. She decided that it was about time to get to know him better. So, why did she think that he was just too nice to be anything more than a friend?

When she saw Henry grinning from ear to ear, she smiled back and said, "You're very sweet, Henry, and say the nicest things. Why hasn't some girl grabbed you up by now?"

"Hmmm, I'm not sure. I'm quite busy as you know. I don't have a lot of time for courting."

"Henry?" Edith looked into his eyes and said sincerely, "I appreciate your friendship. I've had a great evening and I want to thank you."

They continued talking, enjoying one another's company. Edith had finally made her decision. She would see him again if he asked. Her mother was right. He did have a good heart.

Later that night, as she lay in bed, she could not help but wonder why it was so difficult for her to accept a man at face value. Why did she find fault with every man she came upon?

Well, no matter what sort of sweetness came from any man's lips, she was determined not to give her heart to anyone too easily. No matter what! Her shield was up, and she would protect her heart. The man she chose had to endure to the end for her. He would never give up on her.

Was she expecting too much?

Chapter 18
The Third Letter

"Well? Tell me what he said," Melinda whispered. "You've finally got your third letter. I can't wait."

Edith watched Melinda as she began to clean up the picnic they had had in the meadow. The meadow was not too far from their home, and according to Edith, the little jaunt should not have caused any cramping. Melinda sat near the tablecloth gathering up the leftovers and the plates, putting them into the basket.

Gilbert lay on the grass with his hands under his head for support. His eyes were closed, and he was resting with his hat tipped toward his eyes for shade. John was chasing after their mongrel dog Shep, and David had asked Jenny to take a walk with him. So they were all alone except for the sleeping man lying beside Melinda.

Edith looked over at Gilbert and saw his chest rising and falling with each breath he took. He was probably asleep and would not hear much. So, she took a chance.

With excitement rising from every fiber of her being, she whispered, "Oh Melinda, I got the most wonderful letter. Do you remember what I wrote to my friend?"

"Of course. I was absolutely shocked at your letter. I felt you were being too headstrong. So how did he respond to it?"

"I brought the letter with me. Here, let me read it to you."

Edith looked over at Gilbert, and he had not budged. She pulled the letter from her pocket and smoothed it out on her lap.

Then she said softly, "My Dear Charming Friend."

Melinda immediately held her hand up in front of Edith. "Whoa! Stop! What did you just say?"

"Charming friend."

"Charming? Wow, how romantic! I'd like to be called charming." Then with an accusatory tone, she said, "But I thought you didn't like gushy words."

"Don't get me wrong, Melinda. I love a compliment just like any other woman. I hate flattery. There's a difference, you know."

Melinda nodded. "Well, I would still like to be called charming."

Edith grinned, then turned to the letter and continued:

My Dear Charming Friend,

After reading your letter, I presumed that you wanted me to know how "strong" your opinions were before we continued our friendship. This amused me quite a bit. It was as if you wanted to make sure I still wanted to write after you told me how strong-minded you were. For example, it would either chase me away or I would be captivated by your personality. To let you know, I felt it was quite refreshing. I'm glad that you have definite opinions. I get tired of flirtatious women with no opinions of their own who hide their feelings behind a facade and never show their true selves until after marriage.

I, too, have definite opinions. My personality is not domineering, though. In fact, quite the opposite. I allow others to have their opinions and usually try to respect them. In fact, I believe that respect is very important in a relationship, especially between a man and a woman.

From now on, I will call you my "Charming Friend" for that is what you are. You fascinate me with your opinions and I would enjoy continuing our friendship.

Sincerely,
Your Friend

Melinda swallowed before talking. She was in awe. Then she whispered, "You fascinate me with your opinions? Oh, my. I like him already. I didn't know that a man could talk so romantic."

A deep, low chuckle startled the two of them. Gilbert lay with a grin on his face, tipping his hat back with his fingers so he could look at Melinda.

"That sounds like he's sweet-talking her, if you ask me. I wouldn't trust a sweet-talking man. He's got too much honey in his letter. I say, dump him and I'll introduce you to a real man, someone that's mighty fine, a down-to-earth man."

Melinda looked at Gilbert with feigned disgust. "Ha! You don't understand. Women like sweet talk."

Gilbert chuckled once again. "Melinda, do you really like sweet talk?"

"Of course, Gilbert. What woman doesn't?"

"Hmmm, how would you react if I told you that you bewitch me? That you have me under your spell? Would you swoon?" His eyes had a bit of mischief in them as he looked up into her eyes. "What would you say if I told you that you had the 'bear's ethereal grace' or the 'bland hyena's laugh' or the 'neck of the giraffe'? By the way, those aren't my words. They're Lewis Carroll's. But I think they're a little romantic. Don't you?"

Melinda narrowed her eyes at Gilbert. He was making fun of her, and she knew it. She quickly reached under the shrub next to her and gathered a bunch of grass and leaves. With both hands filled, she leaned over and dropped them on Gilbert's face.

He was ready for her and immediately grabbed her arms and carefully pulled her on top of his chest, chuckling the whole time. Then he wrapped his arms around her and held her tight as he shook the leaves off his head.

"Hey, woman! What are you trying to do to me? Didn't my sweet talking work?"

Melinda struggled, trying to get loose, but his hold was too strong. She laughed as she struggled for freedom. "Let go of me, you old sweet talker, you!"

"I will if you tell me something."

Melinda gradually relaxed in his arms and asked, "What?"

"Would you like me better if I sweet-talked you? Tell me honestly now."

Melinda thought for a moment. "I guess not. I love you just the way you are. I wouldn't want you to change."

Gilbert grinned. "I thought so."

"But a little sweet talk wouldn't hurt."

Gilbert slid one hand up to her neck and pulled her close to him. Raising his head up, he kissed her firmly on the lips and said, "I love you, too. That's all the sweet talk I have inside of me. Sorry."

Melinda looked into his eyes and smiled. "That's all I need, Gilbert. No more, no less."

Gilbert smiled as he enfolded her in his arms, but this time he kissed her gently and lovingly with a lingering kiss. Then he allowed her to roll out of his arms and lie down beside him. Melinda gazed at the delicate puffy clouds floating in the sky. Unconsciously, she placed her hand upon the roundness of her belly and sighed.

Chapter 19
Melinda, Self-Willed Woman

The sound of the rooster in the background awoke Gilbert from his sleep, but Melinda did not stir. She was breathing evenly and was in a deep sleep. He rolled over on his side and watched her as she slept. As he gazed upon her, marveling at her beauty, he thought how lucky he was to have her. His eyes studied every curve of her face.

He thought of the love he had for his wife and tried to put it into words, but found it difficult to describe his deepest feelings for her. Irresistible? That was it. She was overwhelmingly irresistible to him.

With an impulse of tenderness, he touched her cheek with the tips of his fingers. As he traced his finger across her cheek and over the curves of her chin, he told her of his love.

Melinda sighed and stretched her arms and legs. Then she opened her eyes and smiled. "Were you talking to me?"

"Uh-huh."

"What did you say?"

"I was telling you that I loved you beyond words and that I was grateful you chose me as your husband. I would be nothing without you, Sweetheart. You make life worth living."

Melinda smiled at his confessions. "But I thought you weren't a sweet talker."

"Well, I fibbed so I could sound tough in front of Edith."

Melinda laughed, then cuddled up into his arms, nestling her head under his chin, and closed her eyes. She felt his arm wrap around her waist. It was such a safe feeling to be snuggled in his arms, like there was nothing to worry about.

After a few seconds, she felt the movement of a tiny infant exploring the small world inside of her. When the definite thump of an infant's foot punched against her ribs with great force, she quickly opened her eyes.

"Oh, my."

Gilbert looked down at her. "What?"

"This baby is going to be an active one when it's born, I can tell you that."

"Did the baby kick again?"

Melinda nodded.

Gilbert furrowed his eyebrows and said in a tone of disappointment, "Melinda, I just can't believe it. Every time it happens, I miss it."

Melinda smiled at his downcast expression and rolled on her back. Then she took Gilbert's hand and gently placed it on top of her round belly.

"Just wait."

Gilbert rose up on his elbow and watched intently. Melinda was almost six months along, and he still had not felt the baby's movement. Each night, he would cuddle up to his wife and lay his hand on her belly, waiting for some sort of movement, but after a while he would fall asleep.

One minute passed and there was nothing. Two minutes passed and still nothing. After three minutes, he gave up.

"Well, I've got to get up and get started for the day. It's getting late. Maybe the little rascal will do something later on in the day."

Just as Gilbert pulled his hand away, the baby gave two large thumps that even he could see by looking down at her. His eyes widened and a grin pulled at the corners of his mouth. "The little rascal! Just as I take my hand away, she gives a kick. But at least I was able to see her do it this time. All the other times, she would wait until I wasn't looking."

"She?"

"Yup. It has to be a girl."

"Why?"

"Because she's a stubborn little thing, not allowing her Papa to feel a kick or two."

Melinda burst into laughter, which brought another grin to Gilbert's face. He enjoyed making her laugh. Her eyes would light up, and her cheeks would turn a rosy color. He realized that she hadn't laughed for a long time, ever since her morning sickness and cramps began, and he was getting worried about it. He had made her laugh now and that cheered him up.

Gilbert's eyes held hers for a long moment as he watched the joy in her expression. "You know, I would like to see what you were like when you were a little girl."

"I'll see if I can arrange it," she said with a wink.

Realizing the time, he sat up, and swung his feet to the floor. He walked over to the washstand and looked in the mirror that hung from the wall. He pulled his fingers through his unruly hair a couple times, and then poured water from the white china pitcher into the matching basin.

As he lathered his face with shaving soap, his wife watched intently. Shaving was a part of getting ready that Melinda always enjoyed watching. She was not sure why, but it always intrigued her.

"I'm taking David to Montpelier today to pick up a shipment. Jenny will be here if you need her, and Edith said she was stopping off to check up on you and see how things are going."

Melinda smiled. "You like David, don't you?"

After he took a few swipes across his face with the razor, he answered. "Yup. I've gotten to know him quite well. He's a good kid. Sometimes I wonder if something is bothering him, though. I can't put my finger on it. It seems as if he's struggling with something deep down inside, and I'm not sure what it is. Maybe we can have a talk on the way to Montpelier."

Then he turned and smiled at Melinda. "Do you realize that you only have three and a half more months to go?"

Melinda nodded. "If I could live a more normal life and clean the house and do my usual routine, then it would go by quicker. But as it is, each day I try to think of something new to do that doesn't bring on any serious cramps."

Gilbert stopped shaving and grinned. "Or you try to get away with more than you're supposed to."

Melinda frowned. "What do you mean by that, Mister Roberts?"

There was a hint of indignation in her voice, and he could hear it. Gilbert drew his razor over the curves of his chin and then answered, "Well, simply that you won't listen to doctor's orders or *mine*. You're so self-willed that it's exasperating at times."

Melinda's eyes widened. "Self-willed?"

136

Melinda could see the twinkle in his eyes as he pulled the razor across his neck. He was having fun with her and awaiting her reaction, which he knew he had triggered. That was one word she had hated since childhood and he knew it. How she hated that word!

She slowly and awkwardly pushed herself up to a sitting position, folded her arms indignantly, and waited for an apology.

Gilbert finished shaving and wiped his face clean with the towel lying next to the basin.

When he turned and saw her offended expression, he asked with feigned innocence, "What?"

"Self-willed, you say?"

Gilbert chuckled. "Melinda, you know very well that was one of the first things that drew me to you. You were so darned independent and self-willed that I couldn't resist you. Being self-willed isn't all bad, Sweetheart. I like your independent nature but when it comes to endangering my wife and baby, then I draw the line."

This softened her for the time being, and she relaxed her hands in her lap. He was so exasperating at times, but he was also honest. She was self-willed and she knew it.

Gilbert sat down on the bed, pulled his pants on, and buttoned his shirt. Then he leaned toward Melinda and grinned. He liked her spunk. He wished he had more time with her, but David was waiting.

He took her by the shoulders, pulled her close to him, and planted a warm lingering kiss firmly upon her lips. "I love you, Sweetheart. Take care. I'll be back this afternoon."

His tender kiss and sweet voice warmed Melinda's soul as she smiled lovingly and said, "Don't worry about me, you 'ole sweet talker, you. I'll be just fine."

"Now don't you tell a soul about that, or I'll have to quit my sweet talking ways." He grinned and added, "Don't want to ruin my reputation for being a tough guy, ya know."

She felt the mattress relax slightly as he stood. "Of course not."

Melinda smiled and waved as he slipped out the door.

***

As Gilbert rode toward Montpelier, he felt a cool breeze touch his cheeks. He noticed the fluffy cumulous clouds forming in the sky, creating shadows upon the ground. A small hawk soared overhead, looking for its dinner, and the wild lush grassland gently waved in the distance.

Most of Gilbert's horses were roans simply because he loved the varied colors and temperament of the animal. His goal was to some day own a field full of roans. The horse he was riding was a beautiful animal: chestnut color with gray and white sprinkled across his back and rump.

As the men rode northward, Gilbert asked David a few questions to see if he could find out what was eating at him. So far, David acted just fine and answered his questions with the utmost respect.

A new idea came to Gilbert. Perhaps he could find out David's goals and talk about them. Maybe that was a good direction to go.

He turned toward David and said, "You know, David. There must be purpose in our lives. We are here to accomplish something and we must have a goal to work towards. Of course, there are great risks that we must take in life. A goal can determine the choices that we make from day to day. Do you have any goals or dreams in life that you're working towards?"

David shook his head. "I once did. But it's not obtainable any longer."

"Why not? Any dream is worth working for."

"It's too late."

"It's never too late to turn your direction around. What was it that you wanted to do?"

David gave a bitter laugh. "I wanted to own my own freight business. When I told Pa, he said that he would support me if I gave up my so-called undesirable friends. My friends didn't mean that much to me, but I didn't like being bossed around, being told what to do. We had a fight about it, and he said that I wouldn't amount to much as long as I hung out with those kinds of friends. So I took off." David sighed. "We both said words we didn't mean."

Gilbert was taken aback by what he heard. To actually tell a child that he wouldn't amount to much could destroy this boy's hope and faith for a better future. That must have been some humdinger of a fight. But at the same time, he understood the worry of a parent and how peers can lead a child astray.

Without any thought of what he was saying, Gilbert blurted out, "David, if you're interested in a freight business, I'll be glad to help you. You get it started, and I'll fund it for you. You can pay me back after the business gets a good start, plus you can even work some of it off by helping me on weekends. You wouldn't have to worry about paying me back right away until you had the money. I'd trust you." When he noticed the surprised look on David's face, he grinned. "Just think about it."

David didn't know what to say. He was stunned, to say the least, and all he could say was a mumbled, "I'll think about it."

Gilbert chuckled at David's expression and then changed the subject. "I'll need you to get my order at the freight yard when we get to Montpelier. I've got some business to attend to in town and will pick you up within the hour."

For the rest of the ride, Gilbert remained silent. He wanted David to think about his proposition. He trusted David. He could see goodness in him and knew he would pay him back.

As David rode in silence, he began to think about the Robert's family. There was something about this family that was so different, but what was it? Was it the "trust" they had for one another? Was it "compromise," as Jenny had mentioned? Or was it "service" that Gilbert had mentioned once before, the service we owe one another?

Chapter 20
More Letters

Edith continued seeing Henry and Joseph, but only as friends. And the letters continued to flow between her and this mysterious stranger. Each letter brought her great satisfaction. Since Edith had been so bold in her second letter, they had become more like friends than strangers.

Her letters were much more relaxed, without fear of any commitment whatsoever. Each letter that he wrote began with "My Dear Charming Friend" and Edith warmed up to the sweet words he wrote. She would fondly place each letter in her upper drawer along with the others, all tied together with a pink ribbon. And consequently their friendship blossomed:

Dear Friend,

I love sitting in a peaceful meadow with the sound of bubbling streams. While I'm there, I enjoy opening a book and relaxing into a world of my own. I just finished "Little Women" by Louisa May Alcott. I wept, I laughed, and I felt the love of this family as I read. I found myself realizing how strong a family unit should be. That's what I want in my life. What kind of books do you enjoy?

Sincerely,
Edith

My Dear Charming Friend,

I enjoy adventure books, mostly. Also, I love progress. Did you know that 11,200 cars were sold in the year of 1903? I can't afford one, but wish to some day. Also, they're opening the New York subway this year. It's completely underground. Ever since the blizzard of 1888, when it put everyone out of commission and many people froze to death, they decided to build this underground subway. They hope this will save more lives the next time they have such a terrible blizzard. I surely wish I could go and see it some day. It would be an incredible thing to see.

I was curious about something. I know that you sing very well. How do you feel when you sing for others? Do you sing simply to lift people's spirits and bring joy into their lives?

Sincerely,
Your Friend

Edith was elated when she received his letter. This was the first time he had mentioned her singing, and she was excited to answer his questions. Music was a part of her life, and she was glad that he realized it. She had not mentioned it to him, but he knew about her love of music.

Dear Friend,

It sounds like someone has told you an awful lot about me. To answer your question, singing has always been a part of my life. At first, it wasn't easy. I found myself quite nervous standing in front of others. I could never figure out why, because I loved singing. And, yes, I wanted to bring joy into people's lives.

Why did I become so nervous when I was doing what I loved most? It finally dawned on me. I was actually pouring out my heart and soul to these people, in the form of song. In fact, I was vulnerable and I knew it. When I would sing a sad song, I felt it deep inside my soul. When I sang the praises of God, then my soul would rejoice in what I was singing. You see, I was actually bearing my soul to these people.

Just before each concert, after months of preparation and memorization, and feeling prepared and good about my repertoire, then something would happen the day before. I would get cold feet. I would actually think about canceling the concert each time. So, I decided I had to do something about these feelings. I couldn't go on like this. I prayed about it, asking God to help me so I could relax and enjoy the concert. That was when a scripture came to mind that has comforted me ever since.

It's found in Matthew 5:14–16. "Let your light so shine before this people, that they may see your good works and glorify your Father who is in heaven."

I realized that the Lord wanted my light to shine, which was my talent of singing. I would not be doing what the Lord wanted me to do if I canceled my concert. So, just before each performance, I would read this verse and all my fears and frustrations would dissipate. It comforted me.

I hope this answers all your questions.

Sincerely,

Edith

My Dear Charming Friend,

Thank you for the reply to my letter. I think I understand you much better now.

Have you ever stood on the top of the Rocky Mountains in the early fall and looked down into the valley below? It's a magnificent sight to behold.

Last fall I went hunting with a friend when the leaves had turned color. We hiked to the top of the Rocky Mountains near Logan Canyon, almost forgetting the purpose for our little adventure. The hike was not only exhilarating, but it was so peaceful that my friend and I were able to talk and speak of our innermost thoughts and desires.

As we stood there, I could see other mountains before us that were even taller than the one we were on. Then when I looked down into the valley, I saw the most spectacular view before me. The valley below looked like a patchwork quilt, with a variety of colors before my very eyes: red, yellow, orange, green. It was beautiful.

Sincerely,
Your Friend

Edith realized that her mysterious friend loved the beauties around him. He acted like a sensitive person. She knew she was taking a chance by pouring out her feelings, but she needed a little help with a problem, and he was the only one she could turn to. She had tried talking to her mother, but she did not understand her discouragement at all. Perhaps her new friend had an answer and could help her, so she made up her mind to ask for help.

Dear Friend,

Have you ever gotten discouraged with life and wondered if you were progressing or standing still? Sometimes I feel so discouraged with myself. I feel that I'm not making headway, not progressing in life. Then I look up at the clouds and see them moving across the sky, passing me by. What's wrong with me? Why do I feel so restless?

Don't get me wrong. I believe my Father in Heaven loves me and has a purpose for me. It's just that I don't know what my purpose is at times. Sometimes I ask myself, "What would God like me to do with my life?"

Sincerely,
Edith, a Discouraged Friend

As Edith put the letter in an envelope for her mother to deliver, she pondered her feelings. Her discouragement was real, and many times she struggled with it. She needed advice and perhaps her friend could help.

When she talked to her mother about it, she would tell her that it would pass and perhaps it was depression. But she needed something more than that kind of advice. Would her friend have anything new or different to say? Could he help her?

After sealing the envelope, she walked into the kitchen where her mother was peeling potatoes and handed her the envelope.

Martha smiled. "Another letter?"

Edith nodded.

"Do you like him?"

"Yes, but only as a friend. Nothing more. I've enjoyed our communication and it's been fun. After Melinda has her baby, I'll be heading back to Salt Lake."

Martha nodded. "It's been grand having you here. I've missed having you around."

Edith smiled. "Me, too, Mama. I'm real sorry for snapping at you when I first arrived. I didn't mean it. I guess I was going through a bad time. With the stress of everyday life, I was beginning to feel a little ornery."

"I noticed, but I understand completely."

She kissed her mother on the cheek, picked up a knife, and began peeling potatoes.

Edith gave her mother a sidelong glance and decided to test the waters. She really didn't know who her mysterious friend was, but she thought she could worm it out of her mother by asking various questions.

"I've got it narrowed down to someone."

"Who?"

"The man I've been writing to."

"Oh?"

"I think it might be Henry."

She carefully watched her mother's eyes and actions to see if anything would give her a clue. She didn't believe for a second that it was Henry. She was trying her old tricks by watching her mother's reaction.

Martha smiled. "How do you know that?"

"Well, he's from over the mountain and plays the harmonica."

"You don't think it could be someone you haven't met?"

Edith's eyes widened. "I hadn't thought of that."

"There are plenty of single men in the county."

"County? That covers a lot of territory."

Martha smiled knowingly. "It sure does."

Edith narrowed her eyes as she looked at her mother. "Did you tell him to write to me?"

Martha smiled with humor dancing in her eyes. "Oh my. Sweetie, I can't answer any questions. He asked me as a favor, including that one."

"So, someone else told him to write me?"

Martha hesitated and then slightly nodded her head in the affirmative. "I can't tell you a thing. So, don't ask any more questions."

Edith grinned. "You're so easy to get information out of, Mama. Just like Christmas, you always let the cat out of the bag, so to speak, and I would figure out what you were giving me each time." She touched her mother's hand. "I understand. I won't ask any more questions because he trusts you. At least I now know that you didn't put him up to it."

"Thank you, my dear. I really appreciate it."

"How about papa? Is it papa?"

All was silent. There was no answer to that question.

Chapter 21
The Greatest Gift

It was Saturday morning and Gilbert sat next to John, watching him eat his breakfast. Since Melinda had been in a "family way," he had not been eating very well and no one could figure out why.

"All right, son, now all you have left is five more bites and you'll be done."

"Pa? Where is Mama?"

"She didn't have a very good night last night. The baby was kicking too much and kept her awake. So, if you need anything this morning, come to me or Jenny, and we'll help you."

John took another bite of egg and looked up at his father. "I'm done."

Gilbert looked at John and smiled. "Hmmm, I don't know. Let me feel your arm first and see if you're strong enough yet. I need a strong helper today."

John pulled up his sleeve and flexed his arm for his father.

Gilbert felt his tiny muscle with two fingers and his eyebrows shot up. "John, it's growing. You're getting stronger. Only four more bites."

John took another bite of scrambled eggs and buttered whole wheat bread, and then looked up at his father. "Pa?"

"Yes, son?"

"When is the baby going to be born?"

"In December."

"When's December?"

"In three and a half months."

"Oh. Is that very long?"

Gilbert chuckled. "For your ma, it's real long. For us, it's not too far off."

"Oh."

"Take another bite. You just have three bites left to go."

"I'm full, Pa."

"Let me see your muscle again and see if it's big enough."

John smiled and flexed his arm once again with all his might. As he did, Gilbert gasped.

"What, Pa?"

"It's much bigger, John."

"Really?"

"Just three more bites and it'll be big enough to help me lift a bag of feed."

John smiled, took three more bites, chewed them quickly and swallowed. "Now, check it out, Pa."

Gilbert felt John's skinny little arm and smiled. "Wow! Those last three bites did it, John. Now you can help me feed the horses."

John hopped from his chair and skipped out the door. Gilbert followed his son outside as he chattered away, asking his father question after question. He was quite the "question box," full of unanswered questions, needing to know the whys and what fors about everything.

"Pa?"

"Yes, son."

"Last night when I was in bed, I heard some crickets by the window. Pa, how do crickets sing?"

"They rub their legs together and that makes the music."

"Why do they sing only at night?"

"Because they sleep in the daytime."

"Do grasshoppers sing, too?"

"No. They're just a menace."

"What's a menace, Pa?"

"Something that's a nuisance."

"What do they do to be a nuisance?"

"They eat our crops and destroy them."

"Do crickets eat our crops, too?"

"Yup."

"How do we stop 'em, Pa?"

"We don't. The seagulls do."

"What else do seagulls eat?"

"Nice fat worms."

John thought about all this new information and then said, "So do we have seagulls in Idaho because we have so many fat worms, crickets, and pesky grasshoppers?"

"I suppose so."

"Oh."

David was listening to the chattering as Gilbert hefted the sack of feed over his shoulder. "Sir, I've never heard anyone ask so many non-stop questions."

Gilbert chuckled. "You know when we become adults, we can't think fast enough. Just try it. It's hard to come up with so many questions one after another."

David laughed. "I believe it, sir."

Gilbert headed for the corral with John trailing behind him. "Pa? Can I help?"

"Sure. Bring that small bag over and meet me at the corral."

John smiled from ear to ear. "All right, Pa."

David watched as John hefted the small bag on his shoulder just like his father had done.

David could not help but admire the determination of this young boy as he asked him, "Do you think you can do it, John?"

"Yup. I ate all my breakfast this morning. I'd show you my muscle, but I'm busy. So, I'll show you later."

It took all of David's strength to suppress a chuckle so John wouldn't think he was laughing at him. He stooped down, hefted a sack upon his shoulder, and followed John and Gilbert to the corral.

After dumping the feed into the feeding trough, David looked over at Gilbert with great respect. "Do you always have your children work beside you and help you? I've noticed that every now and then Jenny's out here working beside you, too."

"Yup. Children need to learn responsibility and independence. I remember when I first worked alongside my pa. I was probably more of a hindrance than a help. But the memories are wonderful, and I'll never forget them. We need to spend special time with our children and help create happy memories for them. We should give them unconditional love and a sense of belonging."

Gilbert grabbed a fork, jabbed it into a pile of hay, and tossed it into the corral.

"A sense of belonging?" asked David.

Gilbert stopped and turned toward David. "Yes. If for any reason our children stray away and tread a thorny path just like the prodigal son, they'll know they're welcome to return home. In other words, we should show unfailing love to them. I believe the greatest work a man can ever do is raising a family."

"The greatest work?"

"Yup. To be a father is a most important and sacred responsibility, and I take it most seriously. I believe that no matter how much success a man has in life, it will never compensate for failure in his own family."

"I never thought of it that way before, sir."

"Pa? I need help," said John as he struggled with the bag of feed.

David watched as Gilbert laid the fork aside, stooped over and helped John dump the small bag out into the trough.

Then David said quietly, "Sir? What do you think is the greatest gift a father can give to his son? Save up a good inheritance for him so he'll never be wanting? Send him to college? Or perhaps help him financially get started in a business of his own? What's your opinion?"

Gilbert turned toward David and smiled. "Do you really want to know?"

"Yes, sir, I do."

Gilbert straightened to his full height and answered. "It's simple. Very simple, indeed." He looked down at his son and ruffled his hair and smiled. "The greatest gift a father can ever give his children is to love their mother with all of his heart."

Gilbert turned and strode toward the barn with John following close behind, running as fast as his little legs would go.

David stood in silence and thought about what Gilbert had said. His answer was the last thing he would have ever guessed. He was thinking more of monetary things. It was a new concept that he had never thought of before. His own father had placed his career and making money before his family. Maybe that was why their relationship deteriorated.

Chapter 22
Eavesdropping

Edith froze in her tracks as she rounded the corner. Henry was standing at the steps of her home. He had just kissed Martha on the cheek, and was holding a piece of paper in his hand. She quickly ducked behind the lilac bush, watching and listening.

"Thanks, Martha. I'm forever in your debt," he said as he waved the stationary in the air.

"It's my pleasure, Henry. Let me know if there's anything else I can do."

What was that all about? What was he holding, and why was he thanking her mother? The paper was decorative like the ones she had written to her secret friend. Was Henry the mysterious stranger? Had her mother given Edith's reply to him? No, he just couldn't be. She and Henry had become good friends but nothing more. It could never be more.

"Oh, by the way, Martha. How long do I bake them?"

"About twelve minutes. When you smell the cookies baking, that's a sign they're done."

"Thanks. I really appreciate this recipe," Henry said as he stuffed the instructions in his pocket and headed for the road.

Edith breathed a sigh of relief. Her mother had given Henry one of her favorite cookie recipes. She now remembered that he had once asked for it when he came by to visit.

She stealthily inched her way around the bush so Henry couldn't see her and then stood very still, not making a sound. She wasn't in the mood for chatter, and Henry was the biggest gossip in town.

Edith felt a hand touch her shoulder. She gasped. Her heart flip-flopped as she jumped a few inches from the ground. Turning quickly, she found Joseph standing behind her, grinning and chuckling.

"Joseph!" she said with exasperation. "What are you doing here?"

He held a basket of vegetables in his hand as he replied, "Delivering red potatoes, zucchini, Hubbard squash, and delicious red tomatoes to your mother. She told me that you've been eating her out of house and home. So, I'm replenishing her stock." Joseph grinned. "So, what were you doing? Spying on your mother?"

Edith's eyes widened as she realized that he had been watching her. Not only that, he was right. But she couldn't admit it.

So she blurted out, "Of course not. I'm just…uh…just…"

"Waiting for Henry to leave?"

Involuntarily, Edith drew a sharp breath at his truthful question. How *long* had he been standing behind her, and why hadn't she heard him walk towards her? She was speechless and couldn't think of a decent reply in her defense. She felt like a willful child caught with her hand in the cookie jar.

When Joseph noticed her startled look, he realized that he had embarrassed her, so he changed the subject. "Hey! Do you like fried zucchini?"

"Fried zucchini?" she asked, bewildered.

"Yup. Fried. I don't much care for it steamed. I just slice a zucchini up, dip it in a beaten egg and then dip it in some finely crushed breadcrumbs and fry it. You need to put salt on the breadcrumbs or in the egg for flavor. I tell ya, you've got yourself the most delectable meal ever. Try it."

Edith was relieved by the change of subject and at the same time was impressed by Joseph's knowledge. Of course, he was a bachelor, so why wouldn't he know how to cook?

"Thanks, Joseph. I think I'll try it." As she waved her hand toward home, she said, "Shall we?"

Joseph smiled and gave a nod. As they meandered toward home, he talked about the vegetables he had raised that summer and how huge the banana squash had grown.

"Edith, it was really a sight. You should have seen them. The vines began climbing up the apple trees and were hanging over the branches. They blossomed and turned into the largest banana squash I've ever seen. The largest one measured just over six feet long. I've never seen anything like it. They're dangling over the branches, dozens of long golden squash."

"No! Are you exaggerating?"

"Nope!"

"You measured them?"

"Sure did. I wanted to know how long they'd grown so I could brag a little."

Edith laughed. "Brag a little?"

"Of course. Men need a little something to brag about. It's in our nature. You know what I mean? We brag about how

157

big a fish we caught, how large a buck we shot, how many head of steer Gilbert raised this fall, not to mention the shooting competition we men have between us. Then we brag about how many times we got a bull's-eye."

Edith grinned and said, "Women brag a little differently. We brag about a bargain we got at the store, a fantastic meal we cooked, and about our children and their accomplishments." Then she giggled. "We even brag about how big a baby is when it's born and then afterwards how fast he's growing. And it doesn't even matter if you're the mother doing all this bragging. A woman will still brag about her nieces and nephews and grandchildren, and so on and so forth."

Joseph burst into laughter. "Women are so…so…." He threw his hands in the air and blurted out, "What do you call it when women discuss babies all the time? Even little girls do it. They carry around this dolly and treat it like a real baby, mothering it, feeding it, and changing its diaper. The other day I was at a friend's home and his little five-year-old girl was burping her dolly after nursing it."

"Maternal."

"What?"

"Maternal. That's what it's called."

Joseph smiled as he stopped at the doorstep. "For the lack of a better word, I think maternal fits just fine."

Edith opened the door and called, "Mother! You've got company. Joseph is here to replenish your stock of food that I've been eating since I arrived."

Martha peeked around the corner from the kitchen and smiled. "Come on in, Joseph. I was expecting you."

Martha took the basket from his hand with a sly smile. "I'll give it right back. Just wait for a moment while I empty it."

Martha walked into the kitchen while Edith headed up the stairs, calling over her shoulder, "Thanks for the recipe on zucchini, Joseph. I'll try it tonight."

When Martha returned, she handed him the basket as she winked. "Thanks, Joseph. I really appreciate it."

Joseph grinned. "Me, too, Martha. Me, too."

Then he turned and meandered out the door, feeling lighter on his feet than usual. Being with Edith always brightened his day and made his heart flutter with joy. Whether or not she felt anything for him, he definitely knew he was becoming quite fond of her. In fact, he knew that his relationship toward her was changing to something deeper than friendship. But how did she feel about him?

After closing the door, Martha went to Edith's bedroom and stood beside her door. "Want a tomato sandwich? We have some fresh ones just waiting to be cut."

Edith was cleaning and arranging her room, as she said, "I'm trying a new recipe tonight, one that I got from Joseph."

Martha smiled knowingly. "You like him, don't you?"

Edith turned toward her mother and shook her head in denial. "We're just friends, Mama. Don't make something out of nothing."

"But I see something in your eyes that's new, Edith. I've never seen you like this before. You seem to be happier lately."

Edith smiled with a twinkle in her eyes. "I know. But it's not because of Joseph. Did you send my letter off?"

She nodded. "Yes, I did. Yesterday." Then she held up a letter and grinned. "But I received this sometime today."

Edith's heart skipped a beat when she saw the envelope. Before Martha could blink, Edith had it in her hand and was sitting on the bed opening it. Edith's heart was racing, and her countenance was glowing with undeniable joy.

Then she glanced up at her mother and said, "I'll tell you what he said later. I need just a little privacy right now, Mama."

Martha couldn't help but notice the brilliance in her daughter's smile. She had a lilt in each step and her attitude was more positive than the day she arrived. She even found Edith humming as she did the dishes and folded the clothes. This man, who was writing to Edith, was gradually changing her daughter's outlook on life. She was much happier. She was her old self again.

This change was refreshing, but she hoped it would last once she found out who the mysterious stranger was. Edith was sticking to her guns about what kind of man she wanted to marry, and that worried Martha. She wondered if her daughter would ever listen to her heart.

Chapter 23
Gored by a Bull

Edith heard a rap at her bedroom door and slowly rolled over on her side, groaning. Wearily, she answered, "Yes? What do you want?"

William opened the door and peeked in. "Hey, sleepyhead, you're wanted for an emergency."

"Emergency?" she moaned slightly, her voice barely audible.

William's voice was sober as he answered, "Yes. Emergencies even happen early in the mornings before the sun is up. One of Gilbert's ranch hands is hurt. An angry bull gored him this morning, and the doctor is out of town. He's gone fishing for the weekend."

Edith's eyes widened as she sat up in bed. "I'll be downstairs in a few minutes, Papa."

William smiled, "That's my girl. I'll have a buggy ready and waiting for you."

"Thanks. I'll hurry."

Just as he began to shut the door, Edith asked, "Oh, Papa?"

"Yes?"

"Do you know who was gored?"

"No, dear. I didn't ask. Why?"

"Oh, just wondering."

After William left, Edith kicked off the blankets, hopped out of bed and washed her face. The cool water quickly woke her up. As she patted her face dry, anxiety grabbed at her heart as her thoughts strayed to Joseph and David, hoping neither of them had been gored.

She pulled on a lavender print dress, and quickly secured her hair into a soft chignon. After brushing her teeth, she grabbed her black medicine bag and headed downstairs.

Waiting in the living room was a lean, tall man standing motionless with his back toward her, looking out the window.

When he heard Edith enter, he turned around. His eyes were creased with worry as he asked, "Are you ready?"

"Joseph!" she blurted out, relief spreading through her as she looked into his eyes. "I was so worried it might have been you that was hurt…" she stopped, feeling embarrassed by admitting her feelings.

Joseph saw the relief in her face and smiled. "No, I'm fine. It was Sam. Gilbert sent me to get you. He's hurt bad…in the stomach."

Joseph quickly strode toward the door and held it open. As he led her to the buggy, he explained, "All of us were herding the cattle to another pasture this morning, and an ornery old bull took his anger out on Sam. He didn't even know what hit him. Gilbert took him home and sent me to get you."

Joseph took the medicine bag from Edith's hand and helped her into the buggy. After handing her the bag, he climbed in. "I'll leave my horse here and get him later."

Joseph whipped the reins and yelled, "Hee-ya!"

The horse responded instantly and galloped toward the outskirts of town. Anxious about Sam's condition, Joseph whipped the reins once again, ignoring the rough road as the buggy jolted from side to side.

Edith was thrown against him repeatedly but she said nothing as the wind rushed into her face and sifted through her hair. She knew they had to hurry.

When she bumped into him once again, Joseph turned to face her and said, "Edith, I'm sorry for such a bumpy ride, but I'm worried about Sam."

Seeing the concern on his face, she answered, "That's all right, as long as we get there on time."

As they traveled through town, Edith felt the wind tugging at her hair. She put her hand on the side of her head to hold it in place, but it was to no avail. She had arranged her hair so quickly that she had not secured it well enough. The wind did a dandy job on her hair and she regretted not wrapping a scarf around her head before leaving.

When they pulled into Sam's yard, Joseph climbed down from the buggy and tied the horse to a hitching post. Edith quickly tucked the loose strands of hair into place the best she could, but she still felt frumpy.

As she blew a loose curl from her eyes, Joseph looked up and smiled. "You look nice. Don't worry so much."

Then he took her bag and held his hand out to help her down from the buggy. She gathered her skirts together in her hand and carefully stepped down. As they approached the porch, Sam's wife opened the door and welcomed them inside.

With an unsteady and shaky voice, Judy said, "Thanks for coming. Gilbert just arrived. He put Sam in the bedroom. He's still unconscious."

Joseph took Judy into his arms and held her tight. She burst into tears, sobbing on his shoulder, and letting her fears out in the arms of a friend. Edith noticed his tenderness toward Judy, and she was impressed with his gentle and caring attitude.

Joseph spoke softly, "It'll be all right, Judy. He's a stubborn man. He'll get better. He has to."

She nodded, and between sobs, she said softly, "Thank you, Joseph. And thank you for coming."

Judy calmed down enough to lead them into the bedroom where Gilbert was standing beside the bed, watching over Sam.

When Gilbert heard Edith enter, he turned to her. "Thanks for coming so early in the morning. If there's anything I can do…" His voice cracked with emotion and his eyes misted over as he looked at Sam.

Edith walked toward the bed and looked down at her patient. His face was pale, with no color whatsoever. His shirt and pants were ripped, and saturated with blood. She had taken care of many wounds before and knew what to do, but none of them had been life threatening like this.

With sympathy, Edith looked at Sam's wife and said, "It's going to be all right, I promise. I'll do my very best to help your husband. First, I need sterile water, some rags, and a clean sheet that can be ripped into long strips, but go quickly because I have no time to waste. Every minute counts."

Judy left the room and did as she was told.

Gilbert inched closer and asked, "Can I do something?"

Edith shook her head. "No. There's nothing you can do. Both you and Joseph may go home now, and I'll take care of Sam. Don't worry. Right now the important thing is to work quickly so infection doesn't set in."

Gilbert nodded and walked out of the room. Joseph stayed, quietly watching and worrying, not saying a word to distract her.

Edith calmly unbuttoned Sam's bloody shirt. She gasped. His abdomen was torn open and blood was oozing from the gash. She knew she needed to work quickly.

Edith met each crisis with a calm, prayerful attitude, and as much courage as she could muster. So, she took a deep breath, said a prayer in her heart, and began working.

Looking at his shirt and pants, she realized they would be impossible to take off without disturbing his wound, so she took a pair of scissors from her bag and cut his sleeves and pant legs open.

Joseph walked to the bed and said solemnly, "I'd like to help."

Edith looked up at him with surprise. "I thought you'd gone with Gilbert." Looking at her patient, she shook her head. "Joseph, there's nothing to do here. You'll just worry and get in the way. Besides, stomach wounds aren't very easy to handle, and you might get queasy. I've seen many tough men faint at smaller injuries than this."

"I can take it. Sam's my friend and so is Judy. I want to help."

Edith was doubtful, but seeing his determination, she decided to give him a chance, expecting him not to last very long.

"All right, then help me take off his shirt and pants."

As they carefully uncovered Sam's wounds, Edith winced. His intestines were protruding from his abdomen. She had never taken care of anything like this before. She took a deep breath and then looked up at Joseph, wondering if he was able to handle it.

Noticing her inquiring eyes, he nodded, giving her the message to proceed. Carefully, she and Joseph pulled the soiled clothes loose and then laid them in the corner of the room.

"Now, what do you want me to do, Edith?"

"I need boiling water, clean rags, a sheet, and an extra pan. A small one will do. Would you mind checking on Judy for me to see if she has it ready?"

Joseph nodded and immediately left the room.

While he was gone, she sterilized her hands with alcohol and examined the gash in his abdomen. In no time, Joseph had the pan of water and rags placed beside her.

She looked up at Joseph and smiled. "Thank you." She handed him the sheet. "Could you please rip small pieces of cloth to use as a bandage? And then tear longer strips to wrap around his hips and abdomen. It'll keep the bandage in place."

"How wide?"

"About six inches wide."

Joseph nodded, sat down on a chair next to the bed, and began ripping long strips.

Edith poured some water into the small pan, took out a sterilized violin gut string from her bag, and dropped it into the boiling water to soften. Next, she took a rag and dipped it into the water, and began washing away the blood and germs from his wounds and intestines. After she was sure that every inch was clean, she very carefully relocated Sam's protruding intestines.

The violin string was ready, so she threaded it through a sterilized needle and sewed up the tear. She looked up at Joseph, who was standing beside her, watching intently. She noticed he hadn't turned blue, so she said nothing and sutured the wound shut.

When she finished, Edith went to the kitchen and fixed a liniment of arnica burrs steeped in alcohol. When the mixture was ready, she saturated the smaller strips of cloth and applied them to his wound.

As she worked, Joseph sat watching, feeling amazed at her knowledge and perseverance. She had not taken any time to rest, and she was still going. She looked weary, her hair was mussed up with several curls hanging awry, and she had small circles under her eyes. But to Joseph, she looked lovely.

They had been there for several hours and he had picked her up in the wee hours of the morning. William had told him that she even went to bed late that night because of staying over at Melinda's too long. She had such stamina. He never knew a woman quite like her.

He had to grin when he remembered his "prima donna" slip of the tongue. He didn't realize she had so much spunk, but then he should have known when she stormed off at the bunkhouse. That night she had intrigued him to no end, and he wanted to know more about her.

Gilbert had told him that she didn't give men a second chance, and that she was the pickiest woman he had ever known. Joseph figured she wouldn't give him a chance, either.

After she had finished, Joseph helped her bind the long strips around Sam's hips and abdomen, securing the liniment bandages next to the wounds. Then together they changed the bedding with fresh dry linen, carefully moving Sam's body as they tucked the sheet under him.

When they finished, Edith looked up at Joseph and smiled. "You did good. And you didn't even faint. Thank you, Joseph. Personally, I didn't expect you to last this long."

Joseph grinned. "Oh, I'm a tough ol' bird."

"Well, if you wouldn't have been here to help, then I would have been much longer. Thank you, Joseph. I appreciate it."

Edith had been sitting for several hours taking care of Sam without any rest. She could feel the tension in every muscle of her body, not to mention her aching shoulders and back while leaning over her patient. She stretched her sore muscles, rubbing her neck and arching her back.

Joseph watched with interest. Through her weariness, he could see the fortitude of a strong, determined woman, a woman who cared for others and showed it in her actions. He realized that she was an unusual person, thinking of others in spite of aching muscles.

After taking one last look at Sam, Joseph followed Edith out of the room where Judy awaited anxiously.

Edith announced, "He'll be all right, I promise. Twice a day I'll come by and wash the wound with carbolic water and apply fresh bandages and liniment. Don't worry. His heart is beating strong. He'll make it."

Judy wept with joy as Edith took her in her arms and hugged her. "Now, if anything goes wrong, send someone for me. All right?"

Joseph took Edith's arm, gently led her to the buggy, and helped her in.

After climbing beside her, he said, "You did good in there."

Edith slightly smiled, not saying a word. She was too exhausted to think or make conversation. She was too drained.

Joseph gave a gentle flick of the reins and the horse trotted down the road at an easy gate. As they slowly rode toward home, the buggy gently swayed back and forth. Joseph was aware of Edith's presence next to him.

He studied her for a few moments and finally said, "I got you up early, didn't I?"

She nodded.

"And you didn't have breakfast or lunch, did you?"

She nodded once again.

"You must be starving."

She slightly nodded.

"You look tired, too."

She vaguely nodded.

"So, how long did it take to graduate from nursing school?"

There was no answer or nod this time.

Joseph turned toward her and saw that her eyes were closed and she was unsteady in her seat, swaying a bit. Making sure to not lose his passenger, he put his arm around her and gently pulled her head against his shoulder. She didn't push away but relaxed into a semi-conscious state, too exhausted to even care.

Joseph noticed how he enjoyed the feel of her tucked under his arm and instinctively squeezed her closer to him. His attraction to her was gradually growing and he found that he was thinking of her more often every day. Just the thought of her made his heart beat more rapidly, and an inner joy that he had never felt before was worming its way into his heart.

As he thought about it, even the sight of her made him wish that he could take her in his arms and kiss all that spunkiness away. This woman, of all women, was having an effect on him, making him think of marriage, making him want to settle down. But why? Why was such an independent, spunky woman creating these thoughts within him?

Joseph watched her sleep against his shoulder and wondered if she was aware of his presence. He grinned. Well, he was well enough aware of hers, and he did not want this little journey to end.

After he reined in the horse, he softly said, "Wake up, sleepy head. We're here."

Edith straightened, blinked a couple times, and tried to get her bearings. Joseph stepped down from the buggy, walked around to Edith's side, and held his hand out to help her down. She looked unsteady on her feet as she gathered her skirts together the best she could, and took his hand.

As Edith was stepping down, she lost her footing, and tripped on her skirts. She fell right into Joseph's arms. He pulled her to her feet, but didn't release her right away. His arms lingered around her waist, his face next to hers. He smiled as he felt the softness of her in his arms. But it didn't last long. Edith quickly pulled away, her face flushed, and her eyes wide.

When he realized that she was embarrassed, he quickly joked, "Don't worry, Edith. You didn't hurt me one bit."

Noticing how gallant he was, she laughed. "That's what I get for sleeping on the job."

Joseph grabbed her bag from the floor of the buggy and handed it to her. "You're quite a trooper, Edith."

Then he turned on his heels and strode toward his horse. He untied it from the hitching post, put his feet in the stirrups, and settled into the saddle. He gave a kick to the flanks and off he sped down the road, hoping his heart would stop fluttering enough for him to think.

Chapter 24
Groveling

The Cozy J was all abuzz with the new ranch hands preparing for the cattle drive tomorrow. Gilbert had cooked up a large pot of stew and had just fed the men an early meal so they could have the rest of the afternoon getting ready. Then he gave the men their last-minute instructions and showed them the bunkhouse where they would stay for the night.

Uncle William and Gilbert were seated at the kitchen table, chatting about the responsibilities of the drive.

Gilbert gave him an envelope. "Thanks, William. I really appreciate it. Here's the train ticket and all the information. After the cattle are sold, then you know what to do with the money. I'd go with you, but with Melinda's condition I don't want to leave for that long. Her cramps seem to be less frequent now, but I don't want to take any chances in case she needs me."

William nodded and then stood, stuffing the envelope in his pocket. "It's no problem, Gilbert."

Gilbert extended his hand to William and shook his hand. "Thanks, William. I'll see you at the train station tomorrow. Hope all goes well. The price for beef has gone up this year so we should get a good deal."

Looking over at Melinda sitting on the sofa, William smiled. "Martha and Edith will check up on you while Gilbert's gone, my dear."

"I really appreciate it, Uncle William."

Melinda smiled and waved as William opened the door to leave. After he was gone, Gilbert sat down beside her.

Melinda was resting her hand on her swollen stomach. She was now six and a half months along, and the baby was quite active, more so than John had ever been. The difference made her think this baby just might be a girl, but how would her son feel about that. John wanted a companion to play with and Gilbert needed another son to help around the farm. But whatever it turned out to be, she would be happy.

Gilbert looked down at her belly and smiled.

"So, how's the little one doing tonight?"

"Oh, so-so."

"What does that mean?"

"Well, constantly kicking me in the ribs. I don't understand. There are plenty other directions this babe could kick, but why in my ribs?"

Gilbert chuckled. He had no answer to her question. "Well, be glad that our little one isn't kicking you all night long any more like before, keeping you awake most of the night." Then he grinned. "Especially in the bladder."

Laughing softly, Melinda shook her head. "How can I forget? I think this little babe must be used to my schedule by now. He seems to know when it's time for bed."

"That's good." Gilbert blinked. "He?"

"I'm not sure what to call this little one."

Melinda shifted position, trying to get comfortable. Eyeing a couple pillows lying on the sofa, she smiled. They would do the job very well.

She grabbed one and put it behind her lower back and the other one under her arm to lean on. It was not quite right, so she took the one behind her, punched it a couple times, and then placed it at the curve of her lower back. She wiggled her backside until it fit comfortably.

Gilbert was watching her every move as she maneuvered the pillows and wiggled into a new position. After a few minutes of adjusting pillows and situating her position, he grinned. It was quite a procedure.

After settling back, she sighed with relief. Looking up at Gilbert, she saw his amused expression.

She arched her brows and asked, "What?"

"Oh, nothing. I was just watching the daily ritual of getting comfortable."

"Oh, you sure sound sympathetic."

Gilbert chuckled. "Oh yes, I am. Very sympathetic! When I see how much you have to put up with, I thank God every night that I'm a man."

Melinda grabbed the pillow from under her arm and playfully punched Gilbert with it. He burst into laughter and grabbed it from her hand.

She narrowed her eyes at him. "One of these days, Mr. Roberts, you'll get yours. Men have to go through some sort of discomfort and pain, not just women."

"Oh, Melinda, we do. We definitely do."

"What discomfort do you go through?"

Melinda folded her arms on top of her round belly and waited to hear what he had to say. It was going to be very interesting to hear his explanation.

"All right, Melinda. How about watching the discomfort and pain of your wife? I worry and I fret about you all the time, wondering if you're all right. Worrying is a very plausible discomfort. Wouldn't you agree? Not to mention, all the mood swings that a woman has to go through."

He dramatically threw his arms in the air. "We men not only have to put up with these mood swings but we have to keep on our toes, hoping we won't hurt your feelings by being too insensitive. Your emotions seem to be on the surface in your condition, and you cry over the tiniest things, such as burning the roast or reading some bad news in the newspaper. I actually had to ban you from reading it because you were becoming so emotional." Gilbert slowly shook his head. "For a man, it's no picnic."

"No picnic?" Melinda's eyes widened and her mouth dropped open in surprise as she playfully punched Gilbert on the shoulder. "I can't believe you said that. No picnic?"

Gilbert laughed. "Well? Is it a picnic for you?"

Folding her arms across her belly, she answered, "Sometimes it is. How about the time you put your mouth up to my belly and began talking. Then you sang a little melody and the babe reacted to your voice. Wasn't that a picnic?"

Gilbert sobered, and a smile played at the corners of his mouth. "Yes, it was. The baby responded to me and began kicking my mouth as I was talking, and I felt her punch me on the nose." He smiled as he rubbed his nose. "I'll have to tell this babe how she slugged her papa before she was born."

"She?"

"Just hoping. But I'll be glad for whatever he or she is."

Melinda smiled and took Gilbert's hand in hers and held it lovingly. After a while, she looked up into her husband's face and began laughing.

"What?" Gilbert said cheerfully. "Tell me, so I can laugh, too."

"Well, when you first began singing ..."

"Yeah?"

"I felt the babe rolling over and stretching its little legs and arms. But after you began singing, that was when it started kicking furiously as if something was bothering it." She bit her lip playfully and smiled. "I think the babe was telling you something. Don't you?"

Gilbert furrowed his brow and groaned good-naturedly. Then he said with feigned disappointment, "Oh Melinda. That hurts. You cut me deep. I wasn't that bad."

"Well, at least you don't sing monotone."

Melinda leaned over and kissed him affectionately on the cheek.

Gilbert gave her a sidelong glance, showing his dissatisfaction. "You think that kiss will make up for what you just said about my singing?"

"Well, I hoped it would."

He shook his head. "Nope. You've got to try harder than that. You insulted my singing and hurt my ego. I think I deserve some sort of groveling."

"Groveling?"

Melinda giggled. Then she pushed herself up from her seat and stood in front of Gilbert. He looked up at her and wondered what she was preparing to do. Before he could ask what she was doing, she carefully sat upon his lap, wrapped her arms around his neck, and placed tender kisses on his cheeks, his forehead, his nose, his chin, and last of all on his soft luscious lips.

Her lingering kiss was warm and tender, and it melted his heart. If this was groveling, he approved of it immediately.

When she leaned her head on his shoulder, she asked, "Have I groveled sufficiently?"

Gilbert soberly shook his head. "No, try it again."

"It would be my pleasure, darling."

Chapter 25
Joseph's Advice

It was harvest time and the sweet autumn scent was in the air. The maple trees were turning color, creating a most beautiful atmosphere. It was the last week of September and Edith decided to take a stroll. It was dusk but still bright enough to see her way about. The evenings were cooling down and she had a wrap around her shoulders.

As Edith walked, her mind strayed to Joseph and how he had helped her with Sam. He had insisted on helping and had not weakened once. She smiled when she remembered how he had studiously made each strip of cloth just right, measuring it so it would be what she wanted. She had told him to make them six inches wide, and he had done exactly what he had been told. She grinned at the memory.

There was something about Joseph that softened her—the way he spoke, his mannerisms, the way he looked at her. She was not quite sure what it was. Edith shook the sentimental feeling away. He was not what she had imagined for a husband.

Edith had a list, and she was going to stick to it. This list helped her to know what kind of man she wanted to marry, and Joseph did not qualify. Between Henry and Joseph— Henry was closer by far because they had a lot more in common. So, why was she thinking about Joseph, instead of Henry?

As she walked slowly down the lane, she heard a horse trotting behind her. She stood off to the side to allow it to pass. But instead of passing, the horse came to a stop right beside her. Edith looked up and saw Joseph grinning down upon her.

"Well, I'll be…What are you doing out this late in the evening, Miss Edith?"

"It's not so late," she defended. "Besides, what are you doing out this late, Joseph?"

"Oh, feeling restless. We're getting ready for the cattle drive tomorrow."

"Why are you restless? You've gone on many cattle drives before."

Joseph slid off his horse and held the reins in his hand. "Can we talk?"

Edith nodded and they began walking with the horse trailing behind them.

"Well, you see, something doesn't feel right, Edith. I'm not sure what it is. It's a gut feeling." As they strolled down the lane, he turned toward her and asked, "You know what I mean?"

Edith nodded, listening intently to what he had to say.

"Well, Gilbert's getting extra men, more than usual. I think he feels it, too. This restlessness didn't come until I began packing this afternoon, and it just won't leave." He shook his head. "I don't know what it is, but I wish I did."

"Is it an uneasy feeling?"

"Yup, and something more. Like a warning, sort of. I just wish I knew what it was."

She nodded. "I've had those feelings before, usually just before an emergency, like the birth of a baby. Sometimes I'll have a hunch I should stick around home. And sure enough, someone comes knocking at the door."

When Joseph noticed they were unconsciously walking in rhythm, one step at a time, it made him grin. As he lifted his right leg, so did she, and the same with his left leg, one foot at a time. He wanted to mention it, but decided it might throw her off rhythm.

When their arms brushed together, warmth crept through him, and he wished he could tell her his true feelings. He wanted to let her know that she had found a special place in his heart. He wanted to reveal that every time he thought of her, his heart would accelerate, that every moment of the day, he seemed to be thinking about her. But it was not time. Not yet. She needed to warm up to him first.

"So, Joseph! Tell me your feelings."

Joseph stopped in mid-stride, losing their rhythm. His mouth fell open, and he stared into her eyes. Licking the dryness from his lips, he whispered, "My feelings?"

"Yes. About the cattle drive."

Joseph began to breathe again. "Oh. That."

"What did you think I meant?"

When he saw her dark eyes looking curiously into his, he wiped his brow and cleared his throat. "Well, I talked to Gilbert about it. He's going to warn all the men to be aware of every little noise, and if something isn't right, to tell him." He waved toward her home and said, "Shall we?"

Edith nodded as they strolled toward the porch. Joseph hitched his horse to the post and followed her to the door. When she came to a stop, Joseph's hand brushed against hers and he unconsciously took it in his. He held it up and examined it curiously, rubbing her hand with his thumb and feeling the softness of it in his.

"You have small hands, Edith." He shook his head. "Dr. Jones has huge ones. And they're rough, too. Yours aren't. They're smooth and small."

Edith shook her head and laughed. "No. Yours are large. Mine are really quite normal, like Mom's."

Joseph looked down at her palm and traced his finger along a small line, noticing the softness of her hand in his. When she instantly pulled her hand away, he looked up curiously. She shrugged.

"It tickled," she said timidly as she wiped it on her skirt to take away the tingling sensation.

Joseph grinned as he watched her.

"Hmmm. You're a very curious woman, Edith."

"Why do you say that?"

"Because of a few things Gilbert and your mother have told me."

Edith laughed. "And what things are you referring to?"

Joseph sobered and said, "Edith, you've had a life of unselfish service. And because of this, you've neglected yourself and your future so you can take care of others. I admire this very much, but your social life seems to come last. Just from the little bit I know about you, I feel that you're searching for something. Perhaps true happiness."

When Edith didn't say a word, he asked, "Edith, why don't you give men a chance to get to know you? And why don't you try to get to know them? If you did, you'd probably find what you're searching for."

Edith looked up curiously, staring into Joseph's eyes, and became uncomfortable.

"I've got to go, Joseph. Please excuse me."

Edith quickly turned, opened the door, and slipped inside, leaving Joseph by himself. He raised a brow, pursed his lips in thought and sighed. He had said what was on his mind. Now it was up to her. He sauntered toward his horse, unhitched it, and climbed on.

Edith leaned against the door, breathing uneasily. The words he had said were true and she knew it. Yes, she was searching for something. And yes, it was true happiness. But why did he care so much?

Then she remembered the warmth of his hand in hers and how much she enjoyed it. Was she beginning to have feelings for Joseph? She shook her head and frowned. No, that couldn't be. He was a farmer, a cowhand. She wanted more in a husband. And not only that, he wasn't her type.

Besides, she already had someone that she was growing attached to. And she couldn't wait for another letter to arrive.

Chapter 26
David's Last Chance

It was twilight and David had no chores to do. The men were given the rest of the evening to relax since they would be heading out early the next morning. So he asked Jenny to go for a walk with him. It would be their last walk together. Tomorrow they would leave on the cattle drive.

After that, the Tall Texan was going to take David to Atlanta, Georgia, and show him the ropes of being an outlaw and what it was like to live in luxury. David had never been to the East before, and he was excited.

He had just talked to Gunplay privately, and everything was going as planned. Gunplay had teased him about the boss's daughter and asked if he were going to be a "lady killer" just like the Tall Texan.

When David laughed, Gunplay reminded him, "It's best to love 'em and leave 'em. And if you're fixin' to do somethin' about it, you best do it tonight. You won't have another chance."

David was not comfortable talking to Gunplay about his relationship with Jenny. He knew he was going to miss her and the family. Sometimes he wondered if he had taken the right path or not, but then he realized that it was too late to turn back now. He had made a commitment to the Texan, and he had to go through with it.

Right now he was strolling with the most beautiful woman he had ever met and that was what mattered at this moment.

His thoughts were interrupted by the sweet laughter of Jenny as she stopped beside the clear stream. David chuckled as she sat down next to the stream, pulled her shoes and socks off, and stuck her feet in the water.

As she dangled them, he asked, "Isn't that cold?"

"Yes, but it sure feels good."

David smiled. "You're so uninhibited, Jenny."

"What?"

"Well, you're not restrained by social convention."

"Oh." Jenny giggled at his use of words. She had not considered herself uninhibited before. "I'm just a rancher's daughter, David. We don't have the same customs that you do in the city. Besides, I enjoy being free, free to choose what I want to do with my life, not what society chooses for me. Women don't usually ride bareback and shoot a gun, but I do. Society won't tell me what to do, David."

David chuckled. She was so naïve. "Jenny, society's conventions are strict. You don't seem to understand that society makes a lot of our decisions for us. Women are expected to dress a certain way, behave a certain way, get married, and have children. Men have their own set of rules, too. Then it's up to us to choose whether to obey or disobey its rules. If we obey, society smiles upon us; if we disobey, society shuns us."

"Not me!" she said adamantly.

David shook his head with wonder. She was an obstinate one. He sat down beside her and watched her splash her feet in the water. He was having fun with her, and he did not see anything wrong with a little harmless flirtation. This young woman captivated him to no end. He grinned, scooted over next to her, and then eased his hand next to hers.

When Jenny saw him slide toward her, her face flushed. She instantly pulled her feet out of the water and wiped them with the hem of her skirt. Then she grabbed her shoes and socks and hopped up.

"Let's go, David," she called as she strode down the path. "I've got other things to show you."

"Hey, wait up!"

For the past two months he had flirted shamelessly with Jenny, trying to seduce her, but to no avail. Every time he had gotten close enough to put the moves on her, she would break the romantic mood or the magical moment. He wondered if she could see right through him and knew his motives.

David jumped to his feet and caught up with her. "Jenny, you are so spontaneous. One minute you stop to dangle your feet in fresh spring water and the next you take off without warning. I can't seem to catch you in the right mood."

"Right mood for what?"

David sighed. She was oblivious of his maneuvering and his intentions. He took her by the arm. She stopped and looked into his eyes.

"Jenny, don't you know that I'm attracted to you?"

"Oh, yes. I'm aware of it."

David's eyes widened with amazement. "You are?"

"Yes. I know you like me a lot because I can see it in your eyes and your actions."

"Then why …"

David was beside himself with such honesty. This would be his last day with Jenny. With no hesitation, he slid his hands around her neck, cupped her face in the palms of his hands, and pressed his lips against hers with tenderness and longing. Her lips were soft and warm, and he was instantly aware of his feelings for her. As she responded to his kiss, his pulses raced, and his heart filled with a warm glow. He had waited a long time for this day. He had planned it out neatly.

When he pulled away, Jenny's eyes were still closed and her lips were slightly parted. He could not resist, so he wrapped his arms around her and kissed this young sixteen-year-old once again. When he felt her snuggling against him, he realized that his flirtations were not the same any longer. Something had changed.

He was beginning to care for Jenny and he realized that he could not use her as he had planned during the past couple months. He had tried to exploit her for his own selfish purposes, but in the meantime, he had fallen into a trap, one that she had set unknowingly.

When Jenny opened her eyes, David looked deeply into them and saw her trust and love for him. Guilt began to overtake him. He no longer desired to seduce her. She was innocent and pure, and he realized that he could not hurt her. Had this one kiss changed his feelings so much, or had he been falling for her all along and had not recognized it?

David gently took her by the shoulders and looked into her eyes. "What have you done to me, Jenny? I used to think I knew what I wanted in life, and now I'm not so sure any more."

Jenny looked into his face with surprise. His question was a strange one, and it came out with such anguish.

"What's wrong, David?"

He pulled her into his arms and held her tightly. What was he to do now? His future had been planned but meeting the Roberts family had changed all that.

Could he betray the Tall Texan, his mentor and friend? Besides, if he betrayed him, the men would probably shoot him down on sight.

On the other hand, he had learned to care for the Roberts family. Mr. Roberts had been good to him, befriended him, and trusted him. And what about Jenny? Could he betray her, the woman who had finally captured his heart?

Should he warn Mr. Roberts? If he warned him, someone could get hurt while defending the steers, and it could end up in a gun battle. If he let things go as planned, the Texan could escape with what cattle he wanted, and no one would get hurt. What other alternative did he have? None. He was too afraid of the outcome.

David leaned back and looked into Jenny's eyes and said, "Jenny, will you do me a favor?"

"What?"

"Jenny, please. Do me this one favor."

This time it didn't come out as a question. He had made a statement and his voice was pleading. Her eyes searched his, wondering what had caused such a change of mood.

"First," she insisted, "tell me what it is."

"Don't go on the cattle drive tomorrow."

"What?"

"A cattle drive isn't a place for a woman. Please stay home."

Jenny's eyes widened at the request. What had suddenly come over him? Was he being over protective? He had been so playful a while ago, then he turned romantic, and now he was sober. In the short time she had gotten to know him she had never seen him so serious.

"Please. Don't go," he begged.

"Why this sudden interest in what I do with my life? Remember? I don't live by social convention."

"Jenny, I just don't want any harm to come to you. That's all."

"But I've gone with my father for eight years. Why would I be in any danger now?"

David could not answer her question, but he answered as truthfully as he could. "Because I've never felt this way for a woman in all my life, and I'm worried about you."

Looking towards home, he quickly changed the subject. He kissed the tip of her nose and smiled. "Jenny, let's get back. I've got some packing to do, and so do you."

Jenny was not sure what this conversation was all about, but she was willing to change the subject. She was feeling uncomfortable and was not sure why.

Chapter 27
The Liar's Fire

The morning was chilly at the Cozy J. The sky was clear, not a cloud in sight. The sun had not yet come up to warm the day, and the men were flapping their arms against their bodies. Gilbert was ready to hit the trail. He checked the provisions in the buckboard one last time. They would set up camp near Montpelier and head the cattle to the train station the following morning. Since they wouldn't have much time to rest, the men had stuffed jerked beef in their saddlebags to snack on.

Twenty five hundred steers had been rounded up and were ready to go. Gilbert ordered a few men to ride on the fore left line, some took the rear left, and others took the right. A few rode drag while a couple took the point. As the men rode alongside the cattle, keeping them in check, Gilbert and Joseph took the rear left so they could observe and oversee what was happening.

As they rode along, their eyes warily searched the surrounding hills and trees for any problems they might encounter or anything suspicious. He had never had any problems in the past, but he didn't want to be unprepared.

The afternoon sun warmed the day considerably and it felt more like an Indian summer. The sun was pounding down on their backs and a slight breeze was drifting across their faces, which helped the drive become more bearable.

Sweat trickled down the center of Gilbert's back. He grabbed a handkerchief from his back pocket and wiped the sweat from his brow. He stood up in the stirrups and stretched the muscles in his legs. He rolled his shoulders up and down, trying to release the tension in his neck.

It was late afternoon when the cattle grew restless. A few kept breaking for the brush and had to be brought back.

When a couple steers bolted for the brush, David swore softly as he slammed his spurs into his horse. He took off after them with Joseph following close behind.

Gilbert looked at Jenny, who was riding beside him and smiled. "He's good. Real good, Jen. He knows what he's doing."

Jenny nodded. She tried not to let her father know of her fondness for David, but she suspected that he had a hunch. After tomorrow, she didn't know if she would ever see him again. David had not committed to anything in his future, and that puzzled her. Most people talked about their future, but David never did.

Gilbert watched closely as David and Joseph rounded up the steers. "Since they don't have much to do in the evenings, Joe's been spending time with David and teaching him to play the harmonica. Joe told me that he's a good kid." Gilbert slowly shook his head. "I'm glad that Joe cares about others so much, but he doesn't seem to have a life of his own. I wanted to introduce Edith to Joe but after hearing how badly it went with Martha's introduction to Henry, I thought it wasn't such a good idea after all."

"Joseph's a good man, Pa. I think he would be a good match for Aunt Edith. Why don't you introduce them, anyway? A man's introduction isn't so obvious, I'd think."

Gilbert chuckled. "You think so?"

Jenny nodded.

"But it's too late."

"Too late? Too late for what?"

"I think she's falling for this mysterious stranger of hers."

"Mysterious stranger?"

"Yup. One day this stranger just up and wrote to her. But someone set it up."

"Who?"

"Don't know. Could be Aunt Martha." Then he chuckled. "Or it could be your mother because she heard the introduction with Henry didn't turn out so well."

"Think so?"

Gilbert shook his head. "Don't know, but I wouldn't underestimate your mother. I wouldn't put it past her."

"Or he just did it on his own."

Gilbert lifted his brow. "Why, I never thought of that. Could be."

"But how can a person get to know someone in a letter? Isn't courting much better?"

"I thought so, but I've heard Melinda and Edith talk about him, and I can tell that she's quite *smitten* with him."

"Smitten?" Jenny laughed with amusement.

"Yup. I think smitten is the right word for it."

"Do you have any idea who he is?"

"Nope. But he's a sweet talker, I can tell you that much."

After a while David came out of the brush with the steers and cut them back to the herd. He glanced at Jenny and smiled, then continued on his way, riding alongside the steers. Throughout the day, a mean and temperamental steer would make a break for home, but David was on guard and cut it back to the herd.

Everyone was relieved when it was time to set up camp. They had been in the saddle all day and were looking forward to a relaxing evening by the fire. After the sun had set, the cattle settled down for the night and a new bunch of men was assigned to guard them until the next shift at midnight.

All the cowhands had eaten and most were lounging around the fire, listening to stories of the many exploits of their comrades.

A short elderly man walked toward the center and stood in front of the men. He had a long gray beard with a sober look on his face, and he was itching to tell his story.

He looked at the group before him and said in a high pitched voice, "Let me tell you an experience that would make sweat drip down your back and send a chill up your spine just by thinkin' about it."

He immediately had the men's attention and they leaned forward, waiting to hear what he had to say, including Jenny and her father. Most of the men were sitting on logs or on the ground, while Gilbert and Jenny were standing at the back.

The old-timer cleared his throat. "Several years ago, I was huntin' up on the Sow Hole, on Rock Creek in Willow Valley over in Utah. Well, I wanted to get me a big four-point buck. I had loaded my 'ole soot belcher with a double charge of powder so I would have plenty of knockdown power for that big four-point buck."

Jenny leaned toward her father and whispered, "Pa, what's a soot belcher?"

Gilbert whispered softly, "A soot belcher is a black powder rifle."

The old-timer walked toward the fire and turned around, peering into the eyes of all the men. "I had been scoutin' for hours through the willows and the thickets and the meadows. Finally I saw him, off a-ways from me, the big five-point buck I had been trackin' for the whole mornin'. I raised my thunder stick up to take a shot, and he stepped behind a big bush and disappeared. Well, I continued tracking him through the brush and the willows. Finally after several hours of trackin', I saw him again. That same big five-point buck I had seen before, and he was standin' broadside to me right across the creek."

"Papa, wasn't it a four-point buck?" whispered Jenny.

Gilbert grinned and put his finger to his lips.

"I raised up my smoke pole, and I drew a bead on that big six-point buck and squeezed the trigger. That thunder pole belched smoke and flame. Because it was backed by a double charge of powder, the ball went flyin' out of that soot belcher and headed straight for that big six-point buck."

"A six-point buck?" whispered Jenny.

Gilbert chuckled but didn't say a thing.

"Just as it crossed the stream, a five-pound brown jumped outta the water right in front of it, and the ball knocked him dead right beside the creek. And 'cause it had a double charge of powder, the ball traveled straight and true and hit that 'ole seven-point buck right in the sweet spot."

Joseph yelled to the old-timer, "A seven-point buck? This buck keeps getting bigger and bigger."

The men guffawed while the old-timer held up his hand, waiting for the laughter to subside. After a while, everyone settled down, ready to listen once again.

"Yes, a seven-point buck, he was. It knocked that 'ole buck dead, right there beside that big six-pound brown. Well, that ball had so much energy that it went right through that buck and bounced off a rock on t'other side of him and went straight up in the air just as a flock of Canadian geese came flyin' by."

The old-timer looked up and pointed to the sky and his captive audience followed his gaze.

"Well, that ball hit the lead gander, and it fell right down out of the sky and landed beside that 'ole seven-pound brown and that eight-point buck."

"Geese?" David shouted. "Now that was mighty lucky."

"It sure was, young fella. I looked up toward heaven and said, 'Thank you for providin' me with so much game with that one lucky shot.' Just as I was gettin' ready to cross the stream to gather up my eight-pound brown and my nine-point buck and my goose, I heard the most terrifyin' and blood curdlin', snarling growl behind me. It made the hair on the back of my neck stand tight at attention. I turned around and there on the trail behind me, just gettin' ready to pounce, was a huge she-mountain lion. She thought I was supper, and with all that game lyin' there, I wondered what could have been on her mind."

Jenny gasped and looked at her father. Gilbert's arms were folded across his chest, and he was smiling.

The old-timer stopped and looked around at everyone, just for effect, and waited to see the interest in everyone's eyes. When he saw Jenny's mouth agape, he smiled.

"What happened next, Old-Timer?" yelled David, who was anxious to hear more.

"I didn't have time to reload my thunder stick, and all I had to defend myself was my big eighteen-inch bowie knife. So I grabbed it and stood with my feet apart, ready to do my best fightin'."

When the old man looked up into the sky, every eye followed his. "When all of a sudden that ball—the ball that had taken out the gander—fell straight down from the sky and hit that cat right between the eyes and kilt her dead."

Each man broke into laughter, guffawing, slapping his knees, and clapping a hand on the back of someone sitting next to him.

The old-timer waited for everyone to settle down and then continued, "Again I looked up and said, 'Thank you, God.' I again got ready to cross the stream to gather up my nine-pound brown, my ten-point buck, and my two geese."

"What? Two geese?" David yelled out with glee. "Now wait a minute, Old-Timer."

The men broke into laughter once again.

The old man quickly raised his hand in the air and defended himself. "Hold it down there and let me explain. Well, everyone knows that geese mate for life and while all that monkey business with the mountain lion was goin' on, the lady goose circled down to its fallen mate and mourned itself right to death." As everyone chuckled, he finished his story. "I gathered up my game and took everything back to the cabin, and we had meat all winter long. That's for sure. And this is a true story."

The men clapped their hands and knees in approval and yelled thanks to the old-timer. Jenny stood beside her father in awe. Never had she ever heard such a whopper in her whole life before. At every cattle drive the men would sit around telling stories at the "liar's fire," but this one beat them all.

The camp settled down for the night. Crickets had already begun to make their music. As the next shift of guards took their places, a coyote howled in the distance. But the sound that brought everyone to attention was one of beauty. The soft, plaintive notes of a guitar were heard in the distance. The melody was soothing and touched the hearts of everyone listening. The camp became instantly quiet as they listened to the sweet and mellow sound of the drifting notes that filled the air. Gilbert smiled as he watched the mood change when Joseph began filling the atmosphere with music.

Chapter 28
The Cattle Rustlers

Jenny could not sleep. She tossed and turned. She was used to sleeping on the ground so she knew that wasn't the problem. When she and her father went hunting together, many times they stayed over night and slept on the ground. But this time, something was disturbing her. The night seemed to be filled with a sense of deep foreboding, and she felt it.

Jenny rose to a sitting position and scanned the camp. Everyone was asleep, and everything was quiet except for an occasional snore from one of the men or a snort from one of the horses. The cattle were quiet enough; they had taken their midnight stretch and most were settled down again. But a few of them were stirring. Some were rising and others were lying down. Others were grazing or chewing their cud. Everything looked normal, and she could find nothing wrong, so why did she feel so uneasy?

Not able to relax, she pulled herself out of her bedroll. She grabbed her coat, pulled it on and then flipped the collar up around her neck to keep herself warm. Then she placed her hat securely upon her head. She thought she would take a walk and see if that would relax her. She looked at her Winchester 30-30 rifle lying beside her bedroll and decided to take it along. Her father had taught her to take it wherever she went when they were on cattle drives.

Jenny quietly picked her way out of camp, trying not to disturb anyone. As she walked toward the herd, she noticed the full moon that was brightening the sky and giving her enough light to see where she was going.

She remembered that David was on duty that night, and she decided to search the area to see where he was. As her eyes scanned the cattle, she saw only a few men on guard. Where were the others? This did not feel right. She knew that her father had assigned more men than that to watch the cattle.

As she searched for David, she saw one of the men light a cigarette. That was not David. She knew he didn't smoke. When she saw movement out of the corner of her eye, she immediately turned toward a man who was standing near the horse corral that had been roped off to keep the horses in. He lit a match and held it up high, allowing it to flicker in the still air. What was he doing? And the horses, where were they?

When she saw another light appear from the trees in the distance, her eyes widened. Then she saw a few men riding directly toward the man holding the cigarette. When they joined the others, they chatted for a while as if they knew one another. Were these the men who were supposed to be on duty? Surely not! The men knew they were to never leave their posts. As she peered more closely, she could not figure out what they were doing. Why didn't they go back to their posts?

Jenny turned toward the man who had been standing by the roped off corral, but he was nowhere in sight. Her eyes searched among the cattle, but he had disappeared. This did not feel right.

The same ominous feeling overtook her once again, and she knew that something was wrong. She had to listen to her intuitions. That was what her father had taught her.

Right now she had to get help but she was quite a distance from camp. If she went back, it might be too late. If these men were rustlers, they could rustle what cattle they could within minutes. If she fired off a shot, then it would spook the cattle, and they might stampede.

The ache in her chest grew until she could scarcely breathe. The protest that wedged inside her made the blood rush to her face. As she felt the anxiety rising within her, she knew that she had to run and get help. That was the only answer. Before she had a chance to turn around, she felt the barrel of a pistol push up against the small of her back.

"Don't move! Drop your rifle or you'll be a dead man," came a forced harsh whisper from behind her.

Then he shoved the pistol harder into her back, warning her against any heroic deeds.

Jenny tried hard to fight the increasing panic rising inside her. What was she to do? If she dropped her rifle, then the rustlers would have their pick of the cattle, and they would be gone without her father even knowing what had happened. The horses were gone, too, so no one could even follow. As she saw it, the outlaws had thought of everything. They were helpless.

No, Jenny could not let this happen. Her pulse throbbed rapidly as her brain worked feverishly for a way out.

The outlaw nudged her with his pistol. "Drop the rifle."

She had no more time to think. As she stooped down to place her rifle on the ground, she could see the boots of the outlaw and knew he was close to her. With all the strength she could muster, she swung her rifle around and smacked the shins of the outlaw.

The outlaw yelped with pain as she took off at a dead run, leaving her rifle behind. She ran as quickly as she could toward camp. She knew that she had to get to her father in great haste.

As Jenny ran, she heard the pounding of feet behind her. She panicked. The outlaw was catching up to her. With terror building up inside her, she picked up speed and so did the outlaw.

With a great plunge, he leapt toward her, grabbed her around the chest, and threw her to the ground. Her breath was forced from her as she hit the ground with a thud. The world was spinning around in circles, and she blacked out.

The outlaw lay on top of his victim, breathing hard from the chase. His chest heaved with each breath he took as he realized the man he had been chasing was unconscious.

David had never had such an experience like this. First getting hit in the shins with a rifle and then chasing a gazelle with great speed.

Trying to get his breath back, he noticed that something was wrong. This man did not have the broad shoulders and muscled chest of a hard-working rancher. In fact, quite the opposite! This person was soft and slender with narrow shoulders.

As he pulled his hands out from under his victim, he realized this person was a woman. There was no question about it. David was stunned when he realized who she was. It had to be Jenny. There was no other woman on this drive but her.

David knelt beside her and pulled her hat from her head. His heart ached as he rolled her onto her back and saw her face powdered with dust. She moaned softly as the Tall Texan rode up beside him.

"Good job, Kid. I'll send someone with a rope and you can tie him up. Afterwards, git your horse and we'll head on out."

David nodded.

After the Tall Texan rode off, David leaned over Jenny with trepidation. He pulled a handkerchief out of his pocket and dusted the dirt off her cheeks.

"What have I done?"

His chest tightened with emotion as he gazed upon her. The dark cloud that hovered over him affected his ability to think. Mr. Roberts had treated him with respect and believed in him. Jenny had treated him with gentleness, and he had fallen for her during his stay on the ranch. They had both trusted him. What had he done with that trust?

David looked toward the outlaws and watched them separate the cattle. The Tall Texan had been good to him. He had praised him every time he did something right, which caused him to swell with pride. But where was his pride now?

David felt torn. What was he to do? Should he betray the Tall Texan who had trusted him with his life? Or should he betray Mr. Roberts and Jenny who treated him decently and befriended him?

He rubbed his aching shins and grinned. The courage Jenny had displayed had taken him by surprise. David had never met a more courageous woman in his life. This was a side of Jenny he had not expected.

She opened her eyes and recognized David kneeling beside her. She pushed herself up on her elbows and frantically scanned the range, watching helplessly as the rustlers separated the livestock and quietly drove them away.

She panicked. Pointing toward the cattle, she whispered, "David! The rustlers are stealing our cattle."

"I know," he said softly, without emotion.

"David, we've got to do something about it."

When David did not react to her concerns, she began to suspect what was happening. The oppressing feeling that came over her was frightening. Could it be true? Could David have deceived her? Was he one of them?

Her eyes narrowed. Flaming with anger, she demanded, "David! What have you done?"

As she looked at David accusingly, her eyes pierced his very soul. Quickly, he shifted his gaze to the cattle. He could not look into those accusing eyes. What was his answer? *I didn't know what I was doing.* Of course not. That was not the truth. He knew very well what he was doing. He had made a choice and this was it.

"David? Are you one of them?"

Jenny's voice was stern, tinged with bitterness, and her face was laced with pain as she waited for an answer.

David glanced at her and then down at the ground. He stuffed his handkerchief back in his pocket and said nothing.

Jenny's face reddened with anger. "You are, aren't you? How could you?"

Jenny's voice tightened with emotion as she stared into his eyes. Her frustration began to rise. He had deceived her. She had been used. He did not care for her after all. The feelings he had for her was just an act, a façade, a pretense. He felt nothing for her.

The ache in her throat was unbearable. Tears stung her eyes. She had given her heart to this young man, and he had betrayed her.

When David looked up and saw tears dripping to her checks, his heart filled with anguish. What had he done? What could he say to make things right? There was nothing he could say.

When he saw how he had broken her heart, he quickly said, "Jenny, it wasn't supposed to work out this way."

"What way?"

Her voice was hard and cold. There was nothing David could do to explain himself. He had betrayed her and her father. He had no excuse.

"Well? I'm listening. What did you mean by that?"

"I was assigned to do a job. This was my first assignment, and I wanted to make good. I wasn't supposed to be treated with such kindness by your pa. I wasn't supposed to like him so much. And I wasn't supposed to fall in love with the rancher's daughter. Now, I don't know what to do."

"Ha! Do you think I would believe that you actually loved me after what you've done? That's not love. You used me and you know it. Besides, how could you do this to pa when he treated you like a son? He believed in you."

He shrugged his shoulders in despair, and she saw the shame in his face.

"I had no other choice, Jenny."

"David, everyone has a choice in life. And apparently you have made that choice."

David was silent. He stared into her accusing eyes and said softly, "I'm sorry."

"Sorry?" The sarcastic tone in her voice made him wince. "You seem to be standing at the edge of a cliff, wondering which direction to go. You have to make a choice, David. If you're really sorry, that is."

"What do you mean by that?"

"You can't stand at the edge of a cliff. You have to make a choice. If you step forward, you'll plunge to the bottom, and you'll end up with bruises and scratches and even a few broken bones. But if you turn and step away, you can make a new life for yourself. It doesn't have to end this way, you know. Don't do this, David!"

David pondered what she had said. He was an outlaw and a no-good cattle rustler. His former intentions were now out in the open, and Jenny knew he had used her. But she would not believe he had fallen in love with her in the meantime. It was hopeless to defend himself and tell her of his love. She was not in the right frame of mind nor was this the right place to do it.

Jenny looked anxiously toward the rustlers as they drove her father's cattle toward the horizon. She had to do something and she had to do it quick. She had no time to get her father now. She needed help and David was her only choice.

As she stared at David, she could see that he was wavering and was not sure of himself. If she could nudge him a little more, then he might go the right direction.

"David? Please step away from the cliff. You can't stay on the edge for very long. You have to make up your mind. You've got a chance to turn things around."

David looked at her pleading eyes and knew that he had hurt her beyond words. This was the woman he had kissed so tenderly by the stream. Her innocence had charmed him, and he had lost his heart to her. She might never forgive him for what he had done, but now she was giving him a chance to change his mind. He knew the answer without hesitation. He wanted to turn and walk away from the cliff.

Before he could answer, he heard a pistol cock. David turned and found Gunplay riding toward them.

The outlaw looked down at them and sneered, "What a tender sight!"

As he rode up beside David, Gunplay tossed him a coil of rope and growled, "Tie her up. Don't want any loose ends. We're almost done."

When David detected a movement out of the corner of his eye, he noticed several men in the distance crouching down beside the cattle. They were stealthily making their way toward the outlaws, with rifles and pistols in hand. He knew it had to be Mr. Roberts and his men.

Gunplay had not seen them, so if David were to step away from the cliff, he would have to act immediately. David could not allow him to see them, or all pandemonium would break loose. He had to distract him. Quickly, he got to his feet.

Taking Jenny gruffly by the shoulders and pulling her to her feet, he demanded, "Turn around so I can tie your hands."

Jenny's eyes widened with disbelief. "What are you doing, David?"

"You heard me. I was just using you, Jen, so I could get the trust of your father. I'm surprised that you couldn't see through me. You women are all alike, so vulnerable."

Jenny flared with anger. Her heart beat furiously. Blood rushed to her face as she threw her hand up and smacked David with great force across his cheek. She had never had to muster such strength before, but neither had she ever been so hurt and angry, either.

David's eyes widened with shock. His jaw ached with pain and his cheek was bright red and throbbing. As he put his hand to his face, he felt guilty for what he had just said, but there was no other alternative.

He realized that he had hurt Jenny deeply. He had hurt her so badly that she struck back. This made him sick inside, but he could think of no other way to distract Gunplay. Besides, he had to have perfect timing for what he had planned.

As he heard Gunplay chuckling at the situation, David knew he had to act quickly. He clenched the coil of rope tightly, swung it around, and hit Gunplay right in the face. The outlaw howled with excruciating pain. In reflex, he squeezed the trigger of his pistol. A blast pierced the atmosphere, causing the cattle to jump and become restless.

Before David knew what was happening, his knees buckled under him. He fell to the ground, writhing in agonizing pain. He grabbed his thigh and held it. *What had just happened*, he thought to himself.

Gilbert's men were crouched behind the cattle when they heard the shot. He and his men jumped into view and stood their ground, with pistols and rifles cocked and ready, aimed at the rustlers that sat upon their horses.

The outlaws quickly turned toward the direction of the blast and saw the rancher and his men all lined up, with guns in hand and pointing in their direction. The Texan immediately knew they were a prime target upon their horses, and they had no other choice but to run. With only nine men to fight back, it was out of the question. So they kicked their horses and off they sped toward the trees for cover.

The cattle had been spooked by the pistol shot, and a few had already taken off, so Gilbert shouted for the men to round up their horses. He yelled to a few others to quiet the steers. Hopefully, the rest of the cattle would settle down. One thing Gilbert did not need and that was a stampede.

As Gunplay listened to the entire clamor in the distance, he knew the whole plan had gone awry. His face was pulsing with pain as he held his hand against the side of his head. He stared down at David, lying in a heap on the ground and groaning in pain.

He shook his head and growled, "A woman can turn a man's head, but you shouldn't have gone against me." He took one look at Jenny and smiled his approval. "You're a spunky one." Then he kicked his horse and galloped toward the trees for cover.

A few minutes passed, and all was silent. Gilbert knew the outlaws had left for good. Some of his men were surrounding the cattle and settling them down again. Others were bringing back the strays that had bolted from the pistol shot.

Meanwhile, Jenny was sitting beside David, trying to see if he was all right. When she had seen her father and his men sneaking up on the rustlers, it never dawned on her that David had seen them, too. Then when David had swung the coiled rope at the outlaw, she had finally figured out that it was part of David's plan. But his stinging words haunted her—"I was just using you, Jen." Even though she knew he was trying to distract the outlaw, his words cut deep.

As David lay twisting in pain, Jenny said curtly, "Serves you right. You should have made your choice before you came on the cattle drive."

David heard her words of disdain but saw the grief in her eyes. The pain had constricted his breath, but he needed to speak.

Taking a shaky breath, he said, "Jenny, I didn't mean what I said." He took a deep breath as pain shot through his leg. "I was trying to get his attention drawn from your pa and …"

"Don't speak David. You're in too much pain."

"But I need to explain …"

"I know what you were doing."

"Do you really know? Do you know that I didn't mean what I said? Do you know that I love you, Jen?"

Jenny shook her head. "David, don't talk to me about love."

She was not in the mood to listen, and this was not the place to discuss it. She could see the red welts on David's face where she had slapped him, and she felt sick inside.

"David, I'm sorry I hit you so hard. I should have realized what you were doing, but it didn't dawn on me at the time."

David chuckled, regardless of the pain he was feeling at the moment. "Are you asking my forgiveness? Surely you jest. I deceived you and your pa. I betrayed your trust in me, and you ask forgiveness for slapping me?"

His voice was a little sarcastic, but she ignored it and tried to move his hand from his thigh. She wanted to see where he had been wounded. He groaned in pain as she pulled his hand away.

"No, Jenny. Don't!" he moaned.

"I just want to see where you're shot. Don't be such a baby. Let me see."

David quickly gave in, knowing that he had no other choice.

As Jenny examined his leg, she saw that it was in the middle section of his thigh and knew that he could not walk. "I'll have to help you back to camp."

She became aware that David was watching her with amusement, which took her aback. There was nothing to be amused about, especially in his condition.

Jenny raised her brow questioningly. "What?"

"Oh, I was just thinking. I haven't gotten to know this side of you before. You're quite a she-cat, Jenny. How did you learn to fight like that? You hit me in the shins with the end of your rifle. Then you run faster than a mountain lion. I can't believe how fast you ran. I could barely keep up. And I was stunned when you slapped me with such force." David shook his head slowly with amazement. "Jenny, I really feel sorry for the person who crosses you next time."

As Jenny laughed under her breath, she heard a deep familiar voice come from the distance, "Oh, she's got a lot of sides to her. That's for sure. And she isn't afraid to show them, either. Are you two all right?"

Gilbert came up from behind them, looking concerned.

"He's been shot, Pa."

Gilbert knelt beside David and looked at his wound. "I'll take him to the doctor in Montpelier while the men are rounding up the strays."

Jenny turned toward her father and asked curiously, "Pa, how did you know the rustlers were here? Weren't you able to sleep, either?"

"Oh, I was asleep, all right. But I was awakened by a yelp in the distance. It was a mournful sound like a dog in pain. It startled me. I quickly got to my feet and scanned the cattle, but couldn't see anyone tending them. I got the rest of the men up so we could check things out. That was when I saw the rustlers."

"A yelp?"

Gilbert nodded.

David chuckled but instantly winced with pain, and he knew he could not laugh any longer. Trying to hold it back, he smiled at Jenny and then looked at Gilbert.

"That was me, sir. Your daughter has a powerful arm and she got me right in the shins."

Gilbert was shocked by that announcement but before he could ask any questions, Jenny cut him off. "Pa, we'll explain everything as we head for the doctor. David's got something very important to tell you."

David's expression conveyed shame and embarrassment. Gilbert noticed it right away but said nothing as he helped David to his feet. Jenny took one arm as her father held the other, and they led him toward camp.

Chapter 29
Edith's Invitation

Edith was in a pensive mood as she looked down at her hands. "Melinda, lately I've been feeling quite discouraged with my life, as if I wasn't progressing as I should be."

They were seated side by side on Melinda's sofa.

Melinda looked at the stress in her cousin's eyes and answered, "But, Edith, you have so many talents. How could you ever feel that way? You have accomplished so much. You got your nursing degree, you have a beautiful voice, and you give concerts to uplift others. What more are you asking for?"

"Melinda, don't you ever get discouraged?"

"Sure."

"Well, look at yourself. You went to college and got a degree in teaching, you married a wonderful man who adores you, and you have two adorable children with one on the way. You have what every woman desires in life—a family. Why do you get discouraged?"

Melinda patted her cousin's hand affectionately. "Oh, I see what you mean."

"So, I told my friend about my discouragement."

"Which friend?"

Edith put her hand on her hip, pursed her lips, and stared into Melinda's eyes, not saying a word.

As the seconds ticked by, a light finally went on in Melinda's brain. "Oh! That friend!"

Edith smiled. "Well, after I told him my dilemma, he wrote back this week and answered my letter. After reading it, I felt so much better. I'd like to read it to you." She looked around the room, searching for anyone who might be in hearing distance. "Where is everyone?"

"Well, the doctor said he wanted to check David's thigh after a few days, so Gilbert took him to Montpelier. And Jenny took John for a walk."

Edith slowly shook her head. "Melinda, I was so shocked when Jenny told me what had happened. I couldn't believe it. And you're still keeping the boy on?"

Melinda nodded. "Yes. Gilbert says that David had a change of heart. He helped by distracting one of the outlaws so they could sneak up on the gang. David got shot while trying to help." She shook her head in dismay. "We're lucky it didn't end up in a gun battle."

"Can David earn his keep and work?"

"Yes. This week he had to lie around in the bunkhouse until he healed enough. Today the doctor will give him a cane to use, and he'll be able to do chores, but he'll have a limp for a while. It'll take a month before he's completely healed."

"How is Jenny taking all this? I know that she liked him a lot."

"At first, I had a tough time getting Jenny to take him food while he was in bed. She flatly refused to go near the bunkhouse."

"She's taking it really hard."

Melinda nodded. "She feels that he not only betrayed Gilbert's trust, but hers as well. She's civil to him, but won't go near him if she can help it. Just before Gilbert took him to the doctor, she was going outside with John and saw him on the buckboard. I noticed that instead of walking past him, she went around him with her eyes to the ground. When I watched, I could see the hurt in his eyes. I don't know what to say to her."

"It'll just take time, Melinda."

"I know. I tried to reason with her and tell her God tells us to forgive seventy times seven."

"Easier said than done."

"That's true. Then I tried to tell her how David must have anguished about his decision because he knew the gang might start shooting and someone could get hurt. I guess she's got to work it out on her own."

Edith leaned toward Melinda and hugged her lovingly. "I feel so sorry for her. This must be hard on you."

Melinda smiled. "Let's talk about happier things. Tell me about your mysterious stranger."

Edith grinned and dug out an envelope from her bag. "Let me read you his letter. I received it before the cattle drive; but with everything that happened with David, I didn't feel it was the right timing. You were so involved with his problems and everything. I thought it was best to wait."

Melinda smiled. "Sorry, Edith. You can imagine my dismay when I found out about the whole thing. So, read me your uplifting letter. Who knows? Perhaps it'll help me as well."

Edith smiled, unfolded the letter, smoothed it on her lap, and began reading.

My Dear Charming Friend,

Yes, I have felt discouraged before, but then I remember the importance of serving others. When I lose myself in helping others, I seem to forget my troubles. I know a woman who is a perfectionist. She's a dear friend of mine. Whenever she gets depressed about her life, she goes out and visits her neighbors so she can bring a little cheer into their lives. Sometimes she takes a plate of cookies with her, and other times she doesn't. Afterwards, it seems that life is back in perspective to her. You might know her. It's your mother, Martha.

Let me put it this way: I remember a very lovely day that brought me great joy. I don't know why. The weather wasn't unusual or the sun hadn't shone any brighter that day. Perhaps it was because someone waved and smiled at me, which brought a little sunshine into my life. I'm not sure. It could be that I stopped to chat with a friend that needed a bit of cheer. I had also stopped off and helped an elderly gentleman with a few jobs. It could be possible this warm feeling came from these deeds I did, or perhaps not. I couldn't say. Nothing happened that day that was significant or unusual. But I can surely tell you that it was a lovely day. All I can say is that service not only helps others but also those who give it.

Sincerely,
Your Friend

Melinda was lost in thought. The message of the letter had touched her, and she understood what he was saying. Looking up, she said softly, "I didn't realize Aunt Martha got depressed, too."

"Me, either. We never talked about such things. Maybe I was too busy thinking about myself. I thought I was the only one in the world who got depressed."

"Me, too. No one really talks about such stuff. I remember how she would bring me delicious cookies and she'd say that she was thinking of me. Do you suppose …"

"Don't know." Edith looked into her eyes and smiled. "If I think of others and not myself from now on, that will make all the difference in the world. And helping others will have a positive effect on me. Don't you think?"

Melinda nodded and then reached out to her, wrapping her arm around Edith. "Thanks for all that you do for me. I have been wallowing in my own self-pity because I can't get up and do much of anything. In the meantime, I forgot to thank you."

"It's nothing, Sweetie," Edith said as tears welled up in her eyes.

"Oh, no. Don't say that. You didn't have to come here all the way from Salt Lake, but you did. And it's made all the difference in the world to me." Melinda squeezed Edith tightly and gave her a tender kiss on the cheek as tears began to stream down her face. "I've been feeling a bit discouraged lately and haven't told a soul about it. I didn't want anyone to feel sorry for me. So, instead of talking about it to a friend, like you, I hold it inside and whenever I feel it building up, I take it out on my poor innocent husband who loves me dearly and is only trying to help."

As Edith's tears trickled down her face, she hugged Melinda and sighed. "My poor dear."

Melinda let out a puff of air in aggravation—aggravation only for herself and no one else. "And you know what?"

"What?"

"I'm going to try harder to make my husband happy, rather than wallowing in self-pity."

Edith laughed as she wiped her tear-stained face with her white lacy handkerchief and then dabbed Melinda's cheeks as well. "I believe this mysterious stranger is helping both of us."

Melinda smiled. "Perhaps."

Giving a sly grin, Edith said, "Guess what I've done?"

When Melinda heard the excitement in Edith's voice, her eyes brightened. "What have you done?"

"I've invited my mysterious friend over for Halloween. That way we could get to know one another. I told him that we could dress up in costumes."

"You're not serious, are you?"

"Of course. I think dressing up in costumes is a wonderful tradition. I love it. Did you know that it originated from the Celtic people?"

"No. I didn't."

"Irish immigrants brought the tradition here from Ireland in the 1800s. In Ireland, Irish beggars would go to rich people's homes on Halloween night and ask for food or money? If they refused, then evil spirits would destroy their homes."

"I didn't know that. So what did you say to him?"

"Who?"

Melinda furrowed her brow. "Your friend, of course."

"Oh, yes. Here's what I wrote." Edith pulled a second letter out of her bag and read:

Dear Friend,

I just love autumn with all the colorful leaves blanketing the sides of the mountains. Cache Valley and Bear Lake Valley are so lovely with all the fall leaves turning brilliant colors. During this harvest time is my favorite holiday: Halloween. We get together with friends and family and celebrate by having delicious meals. We even bob for apples. Sometimes we dress up in festive costumes just for fun. I would like to invite you to my home so we can meet. We can dress up, of course. This year I'll be dressed as a Spanish Señorita. How would you like to come by, dressed incognito, of course? And I could at least meet you in person.

By the way, thank you for your letter. Sometimes I get caught up in everyday life and myself. I now realize the importance of service. If I can only bring a little bit of joy into the lives of others, then that can be true happiness. Don't you think?

Our communication has meant more to me than you'll ever know.

Sincerely,

Edith

"So what do you think?"

Melinda smiled and put her hand on top of Edith's, giving it an affectionate squeeze. "I hope he does come. By the way, we're having a little get-together on Halloween night, from eight to ten. We'll have chili and cider. You can come anytime you want. We've invited several people to stop by, including Uncle William, Aunt Martha, Henry and Joseph. Gilbert has invited a few of his ranch hands, also."

"I'll be there after my mysterious friend leaves. You can count on me."

As Edith tucked her damp handkerchief in her bag, she smiled. "We're a bunch of sentimental fools, if you ask me. When we get together, we laugh and cry. And then we cry and laugh."

Melinda pulled Edith into her arms and hugged her tight as she said, "And we love so deeply, don't we, Edith?"

Chapter 30
Jockwirt

Melinda was resting on the sofa while Jenny was getting the plates and silverware out. Gilbert was dishing the roast beef and baked potatoes onto platters to be served. The aroma of the succulent beef filled the air. Gilbert knew how to cook the beef just right so it would fall apart with the jab of a fork.

As he poured the gravy into a dish, Gilbert told Jenny about his success in finding a pony for John so he could learn to ride.

"Jenny, I went hunting for a horse yesterday."

"Where?"

"In Montpelier."

"Did you find a good deal?"

"Sure did."

"What did you find?"

"I saw a real nice little roan with gray speckles all over its rump. He was reddish brown, and quite a beauty."

Melinda was listening to their small talk, with a faraway look in her eyes. She looked over at Gilbert and said, "When she went to Montpelier, she found a pretty brown one with a hint of red. She said it was a good price and thought I might like it."

"What? Who?" Gilbert asked with confusion.

"Aunt Martha, of course."

"And what did she find?"

"Hats, of course. What else would she go looking for in Montpelier?"

Feeling amused by this sudden change of subject, Gilbert burst out laughing.

He turned to Jenny and said teasingly, "You'd better watch out, Jen. Any moment now this conversation might change directions. And I don't know when nor which way it's going to go."

Melinda pulled her eyebrows together and frowned. "You're making fun of me."

Gilbert chuckled. "But, Melinda, you do this to me quite often, and I can't seem to keep up with you."

He enjoyed teasing her because she responded so readily but Melinda was not amused. She didn't like being made fun of, so she ignored Gilbert. She picked up her book, pushed herself up awkwardly to her feet, and marched down the hall to her bedroom.

As he watched her march away, Gilbert grinned and said quietly to Jenny, "She's so much fun to tease. You know, she does this to me all the time."

"What, Papa?"

"Changes subject in mid-stream. She'll begin talking about something completely unrelated to the subject, and I'm utterly lost."

He chuckled as he sliced some fresh whole wheat bread into thick slices, and then placed it on the table.

When dinner was ready, Gilbert walked down the hallway to get Melinda. As he approached the bedroom, he could hear a soft melody coming from the room. He didn't want to disturb her, so he carefully tiptoed toward the door and peeked in. Melinda was seated in her rocking chair humming and smiling as she rested her hand on the roundness of her belly. He could see her face, her eyes, and her contentment.

Gilbert's heart swelled within him. He had not heard her sing since she was with child. Melinda used to always hum or sing around the house while working. But he had not heard a note for months. Between her morning sickness, the blues, cramps, and worries about their baby, she had not even felt like singing.

As he listened, he realized that Melinda was feeling better. His spirits soared as he watched her rocking back and forth with a serene look upon her face. Her clear, velvety skin, her rosy lips, and her beautiful green eyes were like fairy gifts from angels. How he loved this woman—his wife and his companion!

As he watched intently, she whispered to her infant as she caressed her belly, "Secret prayer. That's what it's all about, isn't it, sweet one? We'll get through this together, won't we? We just need a little secret prayer."

Then she began singing the melody she had been humming. Her voice was gentle and soft:

There is an hour of peace and rest,
Unmarred by earthly care;
'Tis when before the Lord I go,
And kneel in secret prayer.

May my heart be turned to pray,

Pray in secret day by day,
That this boon to mortals given
May unite my soul with heaven.

Gilbert stepped into the room with a pleasant smile on his lips. Upon hearing him enter, Melinda was startled and quickly turned toward the door.

"Gilbert! How long have you been standing there?"

"Long enough, Melinda. Long enough. It's so good to see you back to your old self again. Thank you, Sweetheart."

"For what?"

"For singing again. For relaxing again and being yourself. I've been so worried about you."

Melinda smiled and then lowered her eyes to her belly and stroked it tenderly. "I've been praying that our baby will be all right."

"Me, too."

"And you know what, Gilbert? I feel it deep down inside that this baby will be healthy and strong. We have nothing to worry about any longer, as long as I don't overdo." She looked up at Gilbert and smiled. "Have you been thinking of names lately?"

Gilbert walked to the rocking chair and knelt down beside her. He took her hand in his and held it tenderly.

Giving a mischievous grin, he answered, "Yes, I have. What do you say about Jockwirt?"

"What?"

Gilbert said slowly, "You pronounce it jock-wurt, I believe."

"Jockwirt?" Melinda's nose wrinkled up with disgust.

Gilbert chuckled. "All right. I can see you don't like it, so I'll continue thinking about it."

224

"Good. I'd really appreciate that."

He brought the palm of her hand up to his lips and kissed it tenderly. "Just for you, Melinda, I'll think of another name. But I feel bad because I really liked it. It started to grow on me, the more I thought about it. It has a certain ring to it. Jockwirt! I like the sound of it. Don't you?"

Melinda playfully slapped him on the shoulder. "Sound of it? Maybe monotone."

"Oh, Melinda. You are so hard to please."

Melinda looked down into Gilbert's dark brown eyes and could see the humor in them. She smiled and said softly, "I have faith in you, Gilbert. Just keep thinking about it. I know you can do it. Remember, you've got less than three months to come up with a decent name." She paused. "With my approval, of course."

"Of course. I wouldn't have it any other way."

Chapter 31
Jenny Forgives David

It was October and the leaves had already turned color. The mountainside was covered with splotches of red, orange, yellow, and brown. The sight was magnificent, and Jenny had decided to enjoy the afternoon by sitting beneath the willow tree near the house, and reading a book. The air was cool, so she had thrown a shawl over her shoulders.

Jenny was reading contentedly when she heard her father shut the door. She looked up from her book and smiled as she saw him stride toward the barn to do the afternoon milking. He had been checking up on her mother. Jenny was pleased that he cared so much about her condition, and he showed it, too. He was not a romantic person, but he demonstrated his love in other ways, like helping around the house.

Jenny noticed David sitting next to the barn, coiling lengths of rope and then setting them aside. It had been a week since the cattle drive, and she had not spoken a word to him in all that time. She knew that the silent treatment hurt him deeply, but she had been hurt, too. When she saw David glance at her, she quickly looked down at her book to avoid his eyes.

As she pondered her feelings for David, she remembered the first time she had seen him. He acted as if he knew what he wanted in life and went after it. He was so sure of himself. She had noticed he had a sort of wild side to him, and that had attracted her to him for some reason. She liked the way he had flirted with her and made her feel special. He had even told her that he admired her reasoning and confidence, and was impressed with her high standards.

But now she realized that if a girl was attracted to the wild side of a man, then she had to take the bumps and bruises that went along with it. And she had been hurt badly. Her heart had been bruised, and her feelings for David were in a state of confusion. She had been so sure that she was in love, and now she was not sure of anything any more.

David had changed since the cattle drive. He was quiet, and his demeanor seemed almost withdrawn. He was different, and she could see it and feel it. When she was around him, she felt uneasy, so she tried her best to avoid him. She suspected that he knew she was avoiding him. How could he not notice?

When she looked up, David was watching her. The intensity of his gaze surprised her. It was an inquisitive look. What was he thinking?

Jenny lowered her eyes once again and began to read. It was a book full of poetry and quotes. She loved Elizabeth Barrett Browning. She was her favorite poet and it was easy to get lost in her words. That was one poet that Edith and she had in common. But right now, she was in no mood for romance.

She flipped through the pages and found one that seemed to stand out from the page, written by Sydney Smith, the great English writer. As she read, her heart sank. It had a deep message that reminded her of David.

Life is to be fortified by many friendships.
To love, and to be loved, is the greatest
Happiness of existence.

Jenny huffed as she read it. "What does he know about love, anyway? If you fall in love, you just get hurt."

After a few minutes, a shadow loomed over her. She raised her head and looked up into the afternoon sun. Lifting her hand to shade her eyes, she saw the man before her.

David dropped into a crouch and looked at her intently, giving her a scrutinizing look. It was as if he were carefully examining her soul in every detail. His eyes held hers for a long moment before he broke the silence.

"How have you been doing, Jenny?"

"Fine."

"Just fine? Or hurt?"

"You should know the answer to that."

David nodded as he dropped his cane to the ground. The pain in his eyes was evident as he said, "Yes, I know the answer." He looked down at her book and smiled. "What are you reading?"

"Is that why you came over here? To ask me what I'm reading?"

David shook his head. "Will you ever forgive me?"

Jenny looked away from David, toward the mountains. "I don't know." After a moment, she turned back and met his eyes. "You hurt me, David. I gave you my heart, and what did you do? You dropped it on the ground and walked on top of it. It's bruised now, and it will take time to heal."

With anguish in his eyes, he said, "I understand. If it makes any difference to you, there's a hole in my heart. It feels empty."

With a flash of anger, she retorted, "Don't talk to me about your heart. You have none."

"How can you say that, Jenny? Just looking at you hurts me because I love you so much, and you don't even believe me."

"I think that we look at love differently. To me, love is trust and honor. You have neither."

David licked his dry lips as he stared down at the ground. This wasn't going good at all. He pulled a dandelion and began picking at it nervously as he said, "I wrote my folks."

Jenny was taken aback by the change of subject. "Oh?"

"After sitting around and not doing much for the past week, I had a lot of time to think about my life." He looked up into her face and continued. "I decided it was time to make things right with my folks. So, as the prodigal son, so to speak, I wrote and asked if I could go back home and I asked my pa to forgive my actions. I realized how wrong I've been, and I have a lot of growing up to do. I want a better relationship with pa. He's a good man. I just treated him badly."

David's voice cracked with emotion. Feeling embarrassed, he quickly cleared his throat and looked down at his trembling hands. "Ma wrote a few weeks ago and begged me to come back home, but I wasn't ready." He dropped the mangled dandelion to the ground and continued in a quieter tone. "Now I am."

When Jenny heard the sincerity in his voice, it touched her deeply. This was exactly what she had been waiting for, a repentant attitude. As he gripped his cane and was preparing to leave, Jenny quickly put her hand on top of his. When David looked up, to her astonishment, his eyes had misted over.

"David, I was too hard on you because I'd been hurt. Please stay and let's talk. I'm so sorry. I thought you were the same person, but I now realize you're not. You've changed."

David sat down in front of her and wiped his eyes with the sleeve of his shirt. He had considered himself tough, and now he was showing a side of himself that he had hidden for years, the tender and gentle side. His mother was the only one who knew this side of him. Now for the first time, he had let someone else see it. He felt a little embarrassed as he bowed his head so she would not meet his eyes.

Jenny took his hand in hers and said tenderly, "Please, don't feel uneasy. I've seen my own father weep before. I believe that it shows humility."

David raised his eyes and smiled weakly. "Humility? Me? You must be joking. I don't even know what the word means."

Jenny squeezed his hand as she scowled. "David, stop it. I don't like it when you put yourself down. Because you were humble, you wrote to your parents and asked forgiveness."

David was startled by her tartness, but he thoroughly enjoyed it. He could see how she felt, and he was amused.

"Sorry, Jen. I forgot what a she-cat you are."

Jenny giggled. She had never been told that she was a she-cat before. It pleased her. It meant she was spunky, and she liked it.

She took his hand and tenderly placed it on her lap. Then she looked into his eyes and spoke from her heart. "David? I'm sorry I didn't forgive you right away. And I'm sorry for holding a grudge. Forgiveness is one of the most important teachings and I ignored it."

"Now look here. I'm the only one who's guilty. You have done nothing, Jenny."

"Nothing but be rude to you for the past week. I wouldn't even talk to you. Then after you started walking around and doing jobs, I avoided you. Now tell me the truth. Didn't it hurt the way I treated you?"

"Deeply, but I deserved it."

Jenny shook her head. "No, I was wrong. You have changed, but I was too pigheaded to notice. Besides, who I am to judge others? You say that you have to grow up a bit, but so do I. You know what? I would like us to start all over again with our relationship, a clean slate. And this time let's start with friendship, not with all that flirting stuff."

David chuckled and she smiled self-consciously.

"David, you never got to know me. And I didn't get to know the real you, the man behind the facade."

"Façade?" he said with surprise.

"Yes. The man who was trying to be something he wasn't."

David nodded in agreement. "All right. Let's start over." He got to his knees and gave an exaggerated bow, took her hand in his, and gave a solid shake as he said, "I'm glad to meet you, young lady. I'm an old cowpoke, and I'm headed for Denver. How about a picnic this afternoon?"

Jenny giggled. "I would love to. And when you go home, I would like you to write and keep in contact."

"Do you really mean that, Jenny?"

She smiled. "Friends?"

David squeezed her hand and nodded.

For the next three weeks, they cultivated their friendship. Jenny was right. He had never gotten to know her. He was too busy trying to sweep her off her feet with flirtation, and for his own selfish reasons. He had passed up the importance of friendship because of the excitement of being an outlaw and trying to charm every woman he met just like his mentor. There was only one problem, which he had not planned on, and that was falling in love with Jenny. "To love 'em and leave 'em" had not worked out like he had planned. Now he had to start all over again and cultivate the caring and sharing that were the beginnings of friendship. And to his surprise, he found it rewarding.

David and Jenny took walks along the stream, had picnics, and he helped her with her chores when needed. Once he even surprised her by brushing her mare down. Sometimes, when he saw her coming from a distance, he would hide behind the barn and jump out, frightening the wits out of her.

Slapping him on the shoulder, she said sternly, "You do that again, and you'll be sorry."

David laughed so hard, that she vowed to get even.

The following day, she was waiting inside the barn with a bucket of water in hand. When he stepped through the door, Jenny plastered him good. He gasped as the cold water struck his face and chest. He was soaked from head to foot.

When she saw the startled look in his eyes, she quickly ran to the back end of the barn, slipped through the window, and barely got away by the skin of her teeth.

It was the end of October now and time for David to leave. When he walked his horse toward the house, the whole family was lined up outside to say their goodbyes. They were standing in a row by age and that made him chuckle.

Gilbert stretched forth his hand.

David gave him a firm handshake. "Sir, I want to thank you for believing in me. You treated me decently even after you found out what I'd done, and you never pressed charges. I want to thank you for that and for giving me another chance. I've learned a lot about family life from you, and I'll never forget it. When I have a family of my own, I'll remember what you taught me."

Gilbert instantly pulled David into his arms and hugged him, pounding his back a few times. "David, you came here as a kid, but you're leaving as a man."

David smiled, feeling a little choked up. "Thank you, sir."

He turned to Melinda, who was waiting with outstretched arms and he walked right into them as he said, "Thank you, Mrs. Roberts, for taking care of me while I was laid up. I really appreciated it."

She wrapped her hands around his neck and gave him a kiss on the cheek. "David, I was happy to, but I didn't do much."

"You cared, and that made all the difference in the world."

Saying his good-byes wasn't as easy as he thought it would be. He was becoming slightly emotional, so he cleared his throat and took a deep breath before he continued on.

As he approached Jenny, he felt awkward. He was not sure how to say goodbye. During the past three weeks, their friendship had grown, but he had never lost his love for Jenny. Now he wanted to take her in his arms and say goodbye the right way, but he didn't want to be too forward with her parents standing there. When he saw a tear trickle down her cheek, he wiped it with his thumb and smiled.

"Don't cry, Jenny."

Then he wrapped his arms around her and embraced her tenderly. As he held her, he whispered, "I'll miss you, Jenny."

"Me, too."

After a few seconds, Jenny pulled back, blinking the tears away.

David smiled and said, "I wish I could steal you away and take you to Colorado with me."

Jenny laughed. "But I'm too young to be stolen away, David."

"I know. But if you were older, I would take you without hesitation."

"Really?"

"Really."

Jenny leaned forward and kissed him tenderly on the cheek. To her amazement, he blushed. And that made her smile.

He turned to John, who was beaming all over and waiting his turn to say goodbye. David gripped his hand firmly and shook it.

"You're a good kid, John. I want you to know that you'll never go wrong if you listen to your pa. He's a good man, and when we listen to our folks, then we won't go astray. Understand?"

John nodded, even though he was still too young to understand what he meant. But he knew that David was telling him good advice, so he listened and nodded.

David ruffled John's hair and said, "I'll write, but you have to write back. All right?"

John grinned. "I will. I'll have Pa help me."

David climbed upon his horse and rode down the path that was flanked by lilac hedges. The sun was barely rising over the Rocky Mountains. The clouds made lacy designs in the sky. It was a lovely day.

David turned in his saddle and took off his hat. He waved it in the air and hollered a last goodbye.

As he rode away, Jenny realized she had learned a lesson from David that she would never forget. He had treated her with love and respect, something that the schoolboys she had known had never shown her. Now she was considered a young woman and was treated as such by David. That was something special that Jenny would always remember.

Chapter 32
Halloween

Edith finished brushing her wavy black tresses and allowed them to fall gracefully down to her shoulders rather than pinning her hair upon her head, as usual. She thought that a Spanish señorita would have her hair hang free to her shoulders. She grabbed a red flowered skirt and pulled it on. It had three gathered tiers with a wide ruffle at the bottom. Then she pulled on a simple white peasant blouse that tied at the neck. Next she hung a dangling gold earring from each ear and slipped on her black shoes.

Halloween was one of Edith's favorite times of the year because family and neighbors would get together and dress up in festive costumes, eat foods of the season, and play games. The custom of Halloween started in Europe during the harvest season. The Europeans would celebrate the end of summer by having a harvest feast the last day of October. They would build bonfires to cook the feast and also to keep the ghosts away. They were a superstitious people and believed that ghosts roamed about on the last day of October. Hallow meant "holy" and "e'en" was short for "evening."

Because this celebration was the evening before All Hallows Day or All Saints Day, they decided to call it Halloween.

Smiling in the mirror, she pinched her cheeks for color and then carefully placed a red silk flower in her dark tresses just above her ear for decoration and color. The red flower and skirt brought out the beauty in her olive complexion. She truly looked like a lovely Spanish señorita.

Edith felt pleased with her costume. Her heart beat a little faster this afternoon and her spirits were high. She was not sure if her mysterious stranger would appear, but she had high hopes.

As she walked into the kitchen, her mother turned to look at her. Martha's eyes widened, and then she smiled. "Oh my! Edith, you look radiant. I've never seen you look more beautiful."

"Why, thank you, Mama. I appreciate that."

"This young man is going to be knocked out of his shoes. I know that, for sure. He'd better be holding onto something when he sees you."

Edith laughed. Her laughter was light and cheerful, and Martha laughed along with her.

"Mama, what if he doesn't come?"

"Don't worry. I know he's coming."

"How do you know?"

"Just a feeling." Martha smiled and then held up an envelope for her to see. "I have a letter for you that was dropped by today. I'm sure it's about tonight."

Edith's eyes brightened at the sight of the envelope. "Did he tell you if he was coming?"

"Just read his response and see what he says."

She grabbed the envelope, tore it open, and pulled out the note. As she unfolded it, Edith held her breath. Staring at the

238

words on the paper, she slowly let her breath out, and read, "Seven-thirty tonight." Those were the only words on the note.

Edith swallowed and then looked up at her mother.

Martha already knew that he was coming, but she asked, just the same. "Well? Is he coming?"

Edith nodded, not able to say a word.

When it was seven o'clock, she realized that her excitement had turned to nervousness. And then she became pale as she started to question herself and her feelings for this man. Doubts were coming in all forms and directions. She was getting cold feet. The old feelings were coming back. When she doubted the man's ability to rise to her expectations, she would not give the man another chance.

As she paced the floor, questions gradually invaded her mind. What if he was not what she expected? What if he was dull in person and exciting only in his letters? What if he had a long nose and bulging eyes? What if he was way shorter than she? Heaven forbid! That would be awful. Most men she met were shorter than she was, and this dismayed her. Oh my, this was not going well!

Edith shook her head. "No, if he had a long nose, I would love it. If he had bulging eyes, I wouldn't care. The person in those letters is whom I care about, not his looks. Besides, we're only friends." Then her eyes widened as she asked herself, "But what if he doesn't like me in person?"

After grabbing a bite to eat, she brushed her hair once again so it lay smooth about her shoulders. Then she walked to the sofa and sat down with a book. She opened it and tried to read, but her mind was elsewhere. She laid it on the sofa, took a deep breath, and let it out slowly, hoping to release some tension. She could not sit still any longer, so she hopped up and ran to a mirror in the hallway and checked her hair. Then she went into the kitchen to see how her mother was doing.

When Martha looked up, she asked, "Why are you nervous?"

"Me? Nervous? Why do you ask?"

Martha slowly shook her head and pursed her lips. "Edith, you're my daughter. I can see when you're anxious and worried about something."

"Oh."

"Well?"

"What's he like, Mama?"

"Don't you know? You've been writing for several months now."

"I mean on the outside, not the inside."

"Oh. Well, I think he's good looking, but everyone has his or her own expectations."

A knock sounded at the door, and Edith's eyes widened as she gasped. "Mama, you get it."

Martha shook her head. "I think it's time for the both of you to meet. I'll be upstairs."

Then she walked out of the kitchen and out of sight.

Edith stood frozen to the spot. Another knock came from the door and she tried to move, but her feet were not obedient. Nervousness had taken over, and she tried to overcome it by taking a few deep breaths. Her hands were trembling with anticipation, and her heart pounded furiously. When she noticed that her deep breaths were making her faint, she decided that deep breathing was not such a good idea after all. After a third knock, she let out a puff of air and then walked toward the door and opened it.

Standing before her was a Spanish bandito. He looked just like a desperado, and he fit the part perfectly. He was dressed all in black. He had on black boots, pants, shirt and hat. His black mask covered part of his nose and eyebrows, and all she could see were his soft blue eyes gazing at her.

Between her uneasiness and her delight in seeing him, she was not sure how to greet him. Should she extend her hand for a handshake or what?

Edith stood back and said politely, "Won't you come in, Señor Bandito?"

The bandito walked in with a grin on his face. He shut the door behind him and then stood where he was as his eyes swept over her. She was a vision of loveliness—breathtaking with her rich, black hair hanging softly to her shoulders and a red flower next to her cheek. Her dark eyes sparkled with happiness and her olive complexion glowed. He couldn't help but notice how her dress enhanced the gentle curves of her figure.

When Edith saw how he was looking at her, she blushed and lowered her eyes. The way he was gazing at her made her feel beautiful.

Seeing that he had embarrassed her, he quickly spoke with a Spanish accent, "*Señorita, como estas?*"

Just hearing his voice sent her spirits soaring. It was low and gentle. Edith raised her eyes and smiled. She knew just a little Spanish and replied, "I'm fine. And you?"

Afraid that she would recognize his voice, he tried to avoid speaking English. If he really needed to, then he planned to whisper.

He took her hand in his and said, "*Señorita Bonita.*"

Then he bowed, tenderly lifted her hand, and pressed his lips intimately against the back of her hand, sending a tingling up her arm and to her heart.

Edith's eyes widened as she blushed. "Señor, do you kiss the hand of every señorita you meet?"

"*Solamente tu.*"

"Only me?" Edith's eyes lowered once again and she blushed a second time.

The bandito nodded. "*Sabes Español?*"

Edith shook her head. "I don't know much Spanish, Señor. Sorry."

The bandito smiled as if amused by her shy mannerisms. Still holding her hand in his, not wanting to let go, he whispered, "Señorita, you surprise me. Why are you so reserved with me? We have written to one another for several months now."

Edith shook her head and took a deep breath. "I don't know."

The bandito smiled. His blue eyes studied her intently, searching for an answer. Edith's attitude was enchanting and she looked so appealing to him. Not only that, her coy manner was refreshing. As he gazed warmly upon her, he realized this woman was very special—special to him.

A strong desire to kiss her rose within him as his eyes trailed to her rosy lips. With an impulse of tenderness, he took her by the shoulders and placed a gentle kiss on her luscious lips. He was surprised at the depth of his emotions. Her closeness and tender kiss had their effects on him, causing his heart to pick up speed and turning his senses to mush. He had not planned to be so forward, but he could not help himself. He had fallen in love with Edith.

For Edith, this was completely unexpected. She was not only unprepared for what was happening at this very moment, but she was surprised at the emotions spreading through her. She felt happier than she had ever been in her entire life. And she knew this was what it felt like to be in love and to be cherished by another. This man had magnetic charm, and she instantly responded to it. His hands were strong, and his gentle touch made her heart sing. Her spirits rose, and a warm glow filled her heart as he squeezed her shoulders tenderly. His lingering kiss had made her heart skip several beats and she realized she was falling in love.

When the bandido released her lips and gazed into her eyes, delicious warmth filled his inner soul. A rush of love spread through him. He was smitten and he knew it.

He ran his hand down the softness of her dark tresses, feeling the thick curls beneath his fingers. The scent of it smelled like rose water. She smelled so delicious. He gently touched her face longingly, feeling the smoothness of her skin beneath his palm.

Unable to help himself, he cupped her face in his hand and slightly lifted her chin, and then gently pressed his warm lips to hers once again. He slowly enfolded her in his arms and held her close, feeling the softness of her in his embrace, caressing her back, and falling deeper in love than ever before. Warmth began to envelop him as he realized his true feelings for her and his inner desires. It was definitely time to go. He had lost his heart and had overstayed his visit.

He slowly stepped backwards as he gradually slid his hands down her arms, took her hands in his and squeezed them lovingly. When he gazed into her eyes, he noticed that his touch had taken her breath away. This made the bandido grin. He quickly backed up, bowed, and then turned on his heels and walked toward the door.

He gave a wink over his shoulder and said with a charming smile, *"Adios, Señorita. Vaya con Dios."*

Then he closed the door behind him.

Edith was dazed and her breathing was shallow. She swallowed and then drew in a breath, feeling a little lightheaded. What had just happened? She knew what had happened.

That kiss had not only sent her a message of his adoring love, but it completely changed their relationship. He had actually sealed his love with one simple kiss. That was what had happened. In fact, it was more than just a simple kiss. That kiss definitely had its effects on her, causing her heart to beat erratically.

From now on, she would not think of him as just a friend. She knew that much. Not after that kiss. Not after it had made her feel wanted and needed. Their friendship had instantly changed with that one delectable kiss.

Edith collapsed upon the sofa. Her mind lingered on his words and his intimate kiss. As she tried to relive what had just happened, she realized that his voice was low and pleasant sounding. She liked it a lot. She was not disappointed in him at all.

"Vaya con Dios," she thought to herself. She knew what that meant. She smiled to herself. He had told her, "May God be with you."

That was such a nice thought. She relaxed into the comfort of the sofa with a smile playing at the corners of her mouth. Her eyes closed as she recalled the evening and the softness of his lips once again…and again…and again.

Chapter 33
The Halloween Party

The Halloween party at Gilbert and Melinda's home had been going on for an hour. The atmosphere was joyous. The laughter of excitement and friendship filled the room. Everyone was dressed in festive colorful costumes except for Joseph. When Gilbert questioned him, he claimed to be a champion bronco rider. Gilbert burst into laughter.

While Gilbert was talking to Henry and Joseph, Melinda was seated on the sofa, listening to the men's conversations. Gilbert was telling the men about the wonderful change of attitude that had come over David when Edith arrived in her Spanish Senorita costume.

As the family entered, Melinda stood and greeted them. William gave her a little hug and then joined the men to chat, while Martha and Edith sat beside Melinda and asked how she had been doing.

"Oh, I'm much better. I have a tougher time getting up from the sofa, but that's all. At least I'm not waddling like a duck, as of yet."

The women's laughter spread through the room and drew the men's attention. Edith noticed Henry watching her intently, grinning from ear to ear. And Joseph's countenance was sober and intense as his eyes met hers.

Melinda took Edith's hand in hers and they leaned toward each other, heads touching. She looked into Edith's eyes and whispered, "So, tell me about tonight. How did it go?"

"Oh." It came out breathlessly. "It was wonderful. He was wonderful. Everything was wonderful."

"Is that the only description you know?"

"Breathtaking!" she blurted out.

Melinda laughed under her breath. "Do you know who the mysterious stranger is yet?"

Edith instantly became serious. "Melinda, I don't know who he is. There's one thing that I feel certain about, though."

"And what's that?"

"I believe he's someone that I haven't even met."

"But how about Henry?"

"Henry's kind, intelligent, diplomatic, and a well-mannered gentleman. But at the same time he's so confident and sure of himself that I fear he would always be right, and I would always be wrong, no matter what subject we discuss. But on the other hand, he's just so darn sweet, wants to help me all the time, always complimenting me, treating me like a defenseless female."

Melinda giggled, covering her mouth with her hand, but Martha reacted differently.

She rested her hand upon her daughter's and said, "But Sweetie, what's wrong with that? He'd treat you good."

"I know I'm being picky, Mama. But I can't help it."

"How about Joseph?" asked Martha.

Edith rolled her eyes in dismay. "He's completely different...so exasperating at times. And he has no education to speak of. We don't have much in common, either. The man I marry must definitely have more in common with me than he does."

Melinda looked surprised. "You've gotten to know Joseph?"

"Well, a little. One minute I feel he's interested in me, and then the next he seems completely disinterested for no reason at all. Sometimes I feel he's one of the kindest men I've ever met, and then I feel insulted...oh, I don't know how I feel anymore."

Martha was surprised. "He insulted you? That doesn't sound like Joseph."

"No, Mama. He didn't insult me. I felt insulted. There's a difference. One time I sang for him, and he didn't seem to appreciate it. But that's not all. The next time I saw him I felt he was comparing me to a temperamental prima donna, and then told me I was spoiled."

"Joseph said that?"

"Well, he wasn't referring to me as a prima donna. I took it all wrong. But after much reflection, I realized that maybe I was spoiled, that he was right. Why was I expecting praise when I performed? I guess I was so used to the lavish compliments I received, that I wasn't humble enough to accept a farmer's simple compliment. I was acting like a spoiled child."

Martha smiled. "So this farmer has humbled my daughter a bit, I take it?"

Not wanting to admit it, she conceded. "I guess you could say that. I realized that when praise is given, we should acknowledge the hand of God for all our accomplishments. Because without his help, we would be nothing."

"Hmmm," Martha smiled. "Remind me to thank this simple farmer. My daughter has changed for the better. And it took a plow boy to humble her."

Melinda was eager to know more details of the evening, so she whispered softly, "Tell us about the visit with your mysterious stranger. Are you sure you don't know him?"

Edith nodded with a glow on her face. "Yes. I'm sure. Melinda, he's so special. He's more than I had expected."

Melinda said anxiously, "Edith, tell me what happened to bring on this mood of yours."

Edith looked at her mother and Melinda, and said with a dreamy expression, "I'm in love."

Melinda's eyes widened as she exclaimed, "What?"

Melinda was surprised, to say the least, but when she expressed herself at that moment, it was not a soft whisper. It was heard throughout the whole room and it immediately got the attention of everyone. When Melinda looked up, the room was silent and her husband was staring at her.

She quickly took a deep breath and held her belly, as if the baby had given a powerful kick. "Oh, it's nothing. I'll be fine."

Martha laughed and Edith suppressed a smile.

After the men began talking, Melinda turned to Edith and asked, "Are you sure?"

"Yes, I am. I feel it deep inside. I've never been more sure of anything in my entire life, nor have I felt these feelings for anyone before. I was so nervous at first, but he's just like his letters. He's very romantic."

Martha smiled. "Romantic? Did he hug you before he left to make you feel this way?"

Edith blushed. "Well, sort of."

Melinda's eyes widened and her mouth fell open when she saw her cousin redden. "Edith! He kissed you, didn't he?"

It was not a question but a statement, and Martha and Edith both knew it. She was not asking. She was stating a fact.

Martha put her hand against her mouth and said, "Oh, my."

Edith hesitated for a moment and then nodded.

Melinda raised her eyebrows. "No!"

Edith blushed even redder. "Yes!"

"Let's change the subject or we're going to draw attention to us, especially with that beautiful rosy color all over your cheeks." Melinda glanced at the men. "Especially Joseph. I've noticed how he's been watching you ever since you arrived."

Edith nodded. "I agree."

The women headed for the table and helped themselves to the delicious food.

Gilbert joined them and asked, "How are you doing, Martha?"

"Just fine, Gilbert. And you?"

"Can't complain."

Henry poured apple cider in a glass and handed it to Edith as he looked her up and down. "My, my! You're absolutely charming this evening in your costume, Edith."

"Thank you, Henry."

"When are you going back to Salt Lake?"

"After the baby's born."

He nodded. "It's good that Melinda has someone to depend on." He glanced at Joseph and gave a haughty grin. "By the way, I thoroughly enjoyed myself at the dance the other night. How about you?"

"Yes. It was nice."

He looked out of the corner of his eye at Joseph and added, "You're a great dance partner."

Then he buttered a piece of whole wheat bread and handed it to her, all the while looking smugly at Joseph.

Edith noticed how he was going out of his way to make her comfortable, so helpful in front of others. But why all this attention and why did he grin at Joseph? It was such a self-satisfied look.

With a polite smile, she said, "Why, thank you, Henry."

"You're welcome, Edith," he said, smiling affectionately. "By the way, I expect it might snow here in a couple of weeks. We always get some before Thanksgiving. Salt Lake doesn't get snow this early, does it?"

"No, not usually."

Henry glanced at Joseph, gave a smirk once again as he touched Edith's arm affectionately. "But you have to admit, Edith, there's no place lovelier to live during the Christmas season than here in Bear Lake Valley. There's no comparison. This is the best land on earth with the best people. Don't you agree?"

"Well...I don't know. I've met some wonderful people everywhere I go, Henry." Edith hesitated. "But the miles of open land here are very beautiful, indeed, filled with golden wheat and alfalfa."

Martha was so pleased by her answer. She had been expecting another spunky answer but she had curbed her tongue. Edith really had changed.

Henry continued flirting with Edith, handing her things to eat, touching her on the arm frequently, and glancing at Joseph to see if he was watching.

Gilbert and Joseph had been talking about the ranch. But after watching Henry's flirtations, Joseph was fed up with it. He had had enough. He was not interested in the way Henry was looking at Edith, the way she smiled back at him, or the way he was touching her.

He felt his chest tighten when Henry gave him an insolent smile and sidled up to Edith. Joseph took a deep breath and let it out in a huff. He abruptly excused himself and strode out the door.

Melinda looked at Gilbert questioningly and whispered, "What was that all about?"

"Don't know."

Chapter 34
The Waddling Stage

After all the guests left, Gilbert began clearing off the table while Melinda was resting on the sofa. She was always exhausted by the end of the day, a natural feeling when "her time" was so close. Gilbert stacked the bowls and glasses in the sink to be done in the morning. Everyone was too tired to wash dishes this evening. Jenny walked into the kitchen and began helping her father put away the food.

"Pa, how many showed up this year?"

"About a dozen people. Henry and Joseph came at the last minute."

"I heard Henry really likes Edith. She told me that he's taken her several times to the town socials to dance."

Melinda announced triumphantly. "Not any more."

Gilbert took a wet washcloth from the sink and wiped the table. "Why do you say that?"

"Oh, because I know something you don't."

"And what's that?" Gilbert asked, enjoying her little game of reeling him in with curiosity.

Melinda propped her arm on the back of the sofa. "She's in love."

Both Gilbert and Jenny blurted out simultaneously, "What?"

Melinda laughed at their open mouths and wide-eyed expressions.

It was Gilbert who asked the pertinent question. "With whom?"

"I don't know."

Gilbert dropped the rag on the edge of the sink and wiped his hands dry. "What do you mean?"

"Simply that I don't know. She's fallen in love with this new friend she's been writing to."

Gilbert fell into his overstuffed chair and relaxed. "Melinda, how do you fall in love when you've never met before?"

Melinda grinned. She was bursting to tell someone, and if he had not asked, she would not have been able to contain it any longer.

"Gilbert, it's simple. She has gotten to know this man deep down inside. She knows his inner soul. That's all I can say—his likes and dislikes, his beliefs, and passions in life. You name it, and they've talked about it. She knows him deeper than people who court one another."

Gilbert watched Melinda as she spoke. She rested her hands unconsciously upon the roundness of her belly and sighed. He could see that she was weary, although she had a rosy healthy glow about her face. She had never looked more beautiful to him.

"But Mama," said Jenny with confusion. "I don't understand. Why wouldn't she let Henry court her any more?"

"She doesn't want to lead him on and let him think he has a chance with her. She's going to wait until…" She hesitated. "Well, she's sort of waiting on this mysterious friend of hers, I believe."

"Waiting for what, Mama?"

"She's waiting for him to reveal who he is."

Melinda scooted to the edge of the sofa and leaned forward. With a mighty heave, she tried to push herself up with both hands, but it did not work. She tried again with a stronger push, got two inches off the sofa and collapsed back down again. This time she tried something different. She leaned forward, her hands firmly supporting herself on each side. With three quick pushes one after another, she lunged forward with all her might and almost made it…but fell back onto the sofa once again. When she heard a pleasant low-sounding chuckle, she looked up and saw Gilbert grinning.

Gilbert had been watching her the whole time. It was such an amusing sight that he could not help but laugh. She had tried so hard and each time failed to rise from the sofa.

With a little discouragement and fatigue in her voice, she chided him. "It's not funny, Gilbert. I'd like to see you have a large belly and try to get up off this sofa. I can't lean forward enough to push myself up."

Gilbert chuckled once again. "Let me help you, Melinda."

He took her hands firmly in his and slowly pulled her to her feet, grunting the whole time as if she was as heavy as a boulder.

Melinda slapped him on the shoulder. "That's not funny!"

He laughed as he embraced her. "Sorry."

Melinda leaned her head against his shoulder and sighed.

"You're tired, I can tell."

"Uh-huh."

Gilbert kissed her temple lovingly and then rested his head against hers. Jenny quietly left when she saw them snuggling.

After a few moments, Gilbert said softly, "You've only got one and a half more months to go unless this one comes early like John."

"Uh-huh."

Gilbert could hear the exhaustion in her voice. "I think we've kept this baby up past her bedtime, don't you?"

"Uh-huh."

Gilbert led her down the hall toward the bedroom. He sat on a chair to pull off his boots, but Melinda distracted him. With great delight he admired her prominent curve that protruded just below her ribs. When he saw Melinda slowly and awkwardly walk toward the wardrobe to get ready for bed, he wanted to chuckle.

When Gilbert let out a snicker, Melinda turned around and asked, "What?"

He was watching her with pleasure as he said, "Well, I was just thinking how you have finally reached the waddling stage."

Melinda looked surprised. "I just told Edith tonight that I was grateful I wasn't waddling yet. I guess I spoke too soon."

Chapter 35
Joseph and Edith

Gilbert led the young strawberry roan over to the fence and tied him securely to the post. He had bought it especially for John to ride. Its head, legs, mane, and tail were a beautiful reddish brown, but the body had shades of auburn with white and gray hairs interspersed.

The roan felt uneasy and tried to pull away from Gilbert, snorting and breathing heavily. Gilbert knew that it was important to establish a friendly and trusting relationship with the young foal before breaking him or training him for riding. He knew that generally when a cowboy would "break" a horse, it was by force, showing him who had the greater power. They believed firmly in showing the horse who was boss and in control, which caused the horse to buck and fight back until he was broke.

Gilbert did not believe in force. This was not his way. He believed that gentleness went a long way. He often said horses were like women. They responded readily to gentleness and kindness.

Gilbert slowly raised his hand and placed it on the roan's nose to let the young foal breathe the scent of his hand, all the time whispering to him. Gilbert always whispered to his animals when they were frightened, reassuring them. It always quieted them down.

After the young horse had settled down, he slowly took the reins and began to do ground work with him. Talking softly, Gilbert controlled the direction in which the roan moved. When Gilbert changed the direction of movement, the foal immediately felt like he was under a little pressure. After the horse changed direction and followed, Gilbert quickly relieved the pressure.

He was giving a message to the young horse. Gilbert needed to release the pressure of the reins at the right moment so the roan did not feel trapped. As soon as he responded to the tug, the pressure was immediately released. This told the foal that Gilbert was not unreasonable, and at the same time, he was establishing control of the animal.

As Gilbert guided the foal, he constantly spoke to him in a gentle voice, encouraging him to turn the direction he was gently tugging. When the roan became uneasy, Gilbert immediately stopped and whispered to him once again, smoothing his hand along the side of the animal's face and nose.

"Hmmm, whispering to the roan again, are we?"

Gilbert turned and smiled. "Joe. Glad you're here. I'll another five minutes, and then we'll do the morning chores."

"That was good chili last night."

"Thanks. Why did you leave so quickly? Had an appointment to keep?"

Joseph chuckled. "Not exactly."

"Well, I was going to set you up with Edith last night since you've never courted her, but you disappeared too quickly."

"Oh?"

"But it was just as well I didn't because she seems to be spoken for."

Joseph raised his eyebrows with concern. "Spoken for?"

"Yup. She seems to be head over heels in love."

"In love? With who?" he said, trying to hide the anxiety in his voice.

"That's just it. We don't even know who he is. She hadn't met him until last night."

"I don't understand."

"Well, she's been writing to this sweet-talking man. Women go for that sort of thing, I guess."

Joseph stared at Gilbert incredulously. "She's in love? How do you know this?"

"She told Melinda last night. Remember that little squeal of excitement we heard? Well, that was it."

Suppressing his joy, he asked, "How can she love someone she's only met once?"

Gilbert chuckled. "That's exactly what I told Melinda. And you know what she said? Edith has fallen for the soul of this man, the inner person."

"The soul?"

"Yup." Gilbert pounded his chest. "She's fallen for what's inside here."

"Oh." Joseph nodded. "Well, I was fixin' to see if I could call on her, but I guess she won't want to see me now, would she?"

"Nope. Not now. She's spoken for. But it's just as well, Joe. She's a very determined and outspoken woman. Very spunky, I tell you."

"I know. I met her a few times, and twice she stomped off because she got annoyed with me. Another time I took her to Sam's. Remember?"

"That's right. I forgot."

Gilbert gently pulled the harness off the roan, wrapped it around the post, and then climbed over the fence. After jumping to the ground, he looked at Joseph and shook his head.

"Annoyed, huh?"

Joseph burst into laughter. "Yup. Exasperated!"

After the milking was done, Gilbert and Joseph split logs, placing each one on a chopping block. After an hour, sweat began dripping down the small of their backs. They stopped to rest and wiped the beads of sweat from their brow.

Melinda sat in a rocking chair on the front porch with a woolen wrap around her shoulders, watching them work. The sound of a buggy got everyone's attention. As Gilbert watched Edith pulling up, he waved and then turned back to his work. When he saw Joseph watching Edith intently, it took him aback. He was in a world of his own, and Gilbert was nonexistent. And the tender look in his friend's eyes was new to him.

Joseph had been doing a lot of thinking while splitting the logs, wondering how he could get Edith's interest. It would take a lot of planning, but he felt he could do it.

"Joseph?"

He turned toward Gilbert. "Yes?"

When Gilbert saw the softness in his eyes, he realized that Joseph was quite taken by Edith. So, a quick plan began to formulate in his mind.

"Would you mind getting both of us some water? Glasses are in the cupboard to the right of the sink."

"Sure will, Gilbert."

Now that was quick, in fact, too quick for someone who was not interested in Edith. Gilbert watched closely to see what the outcome would be. Joseph marched toward the house, but instead of walking inside, he stopped on the porch and conversed with the women. What was being said was a mystery, but he noticed Edith and Melinda laughing, and so was Joseph. Edith followed him in the house, talking the whole time. Fifteen minutes later, he walked outside grinning like a cat that had caught a mouse and was satisfied.

For the next few weeks, Joseph always found an excuse to go to the house or the porch when Edith dropped by. Joseph never pushed for a relationship beyond friends and Edith enjoyed his company. She found his sense of humor and quick wit refreshing, and he never flirted with her.

One day when Edith needed to go to Montpelier to shop, Joseph volunteered to drive her to town. He did some errands for Gilbert and then met her at Aunt Sarah's Café. He bought her a scoop of ice cream, and they sat and chatted.

Joseph took a bite of ice cream and then said, "Gilbert told me all about the catnip tea and how it helped Melinda's pain go away. He was really impressed. He said it was like a miracle."

"It works every time."

"So, Edith, why didn't you tell me that you knew all about herbs? You just let me go on and on about chamomile and didn't even say a thing."

Edith laughed. "First of all, I don't know all there is about herbs. And second, I wasn't sure what to say. Besides, maybe you knew something I didn't, so I listened."

Her humble attitude was comforting. She didn't make him feel foolish. "You know that many doctors, even nurses like yourself, don't believe in herbs."

"I know. It's a shame. Chamomile is the best relaxant there is. If one has trouble sleeping, just drink some chamomile tea."

Joseph chuckled. "Or a good back massage."

Edith smiled as she poked at her ice cream. "Now that does sound good."

Joseph noticed that she acted more relaxed and happier around him since their first encounter. She even spoke more freely and seemed to enjoy his company. She laughed at his lame jokes along with the good ones. But most of all, he had noticed a more humble attitude, and this impressed him.

"Edith, may I ask you a question?"

"Of course. Ask away."

"Why have you been single for so long? You're a mighty fine-looking woman. I'm sure you've had a few offers of marriage."

"No, not really. I've never taken the time to get to know anyone."

"So, what are you waiting for?"

Edith smiled impishly as she jabbed at the ball of ice cream in the dish. "The perfect man."

Joseph chuckled with amusement. "Is there such a thing?"

"I'm sure of it," she said with confidence.

Joseph looked at her with curiosity. "What is the perfect man?"

Edith pondered the question for a few moments, gently biting at her lip, and then said, "Well, first of all, he has to be educated. That's really important to me. He'd need a good job to support a family. And he has to be romantic enough to sweep me off my feet. I'd like him to read a lot, such as poetry and the great classics…" She paused and then added, "And he has to love nature, too."

"You left out music."

"Doesn't everyone love music? That goes without saying."

Joseph was deep in thought. His brows were furrowed, and he was not sure how to respond to her description of the perfect man.

Looking into her eyes with intensity, he finally responded, "So, what if he's self-educated, the best bronco rider in town, just slightly romantic, and his favorite poems are cowboy poetry. He doesn't much care for the classics but loves nature. And his job? Well, it isn't that great but he loves it."

Edith shook her head with determination. "You listed only one thing in common. That's not enough, Joseph. It just isn't. Nature can't keep a couple together. They need a lot more in common than one thing. Don't you see? That's why I haven't married yet." With a twinkle in her eye, she said teasingly, "Now it's your turn. What are you looking for in a woman?"

Joseph was pensive, trying not to show his disappointment in her answer. He thought for a moment and then finally answered in a quiet and humble manner, "I'm looking for a woman who is loving, and would love me with all her heart. I would like her to love God as I do. If she loved me with her whole soul, with everything she's got, I would do anything for her. In fact, I would encourage her to build her talents and support her in any decision she makes. I would give her the best kind of life I could, and I'd love her with the kind of love that lasts for eternity. I would love her with all the passion I had. Edith, I would give my life to protect my wife and companion."

Joseph's words astonished Edith. His answer had taken her aback. She had expected a lot in a husband, but Joseph was only expecting love and very little else. As she thought about his answer, she began to feel quite materialistic. Everything she listed was worldly. What he had mentioned were only spiritual things: love and God. For some reason, she knew that his answer would linger in her thoughts. Most of their discussions did. She noticed that Joseph was a very wise man, and she found herself listening and understanding his point of view many times.

Feeling uncomfortable with the subject, she quickly replied, "We've been in town for several hours already, and I'm exhausted. Are you ready to go?"

Joseph nodded, stood and pulled her chair out for her, and helped her rise from her seat. He kept his thoughts to himself on the ride home and didn't say much. He felt discouraged …disheartened… depressed.

Edith's answer had twisted his heart. He felt an ache in his chest that would not go away. Was she so wrapped up in the monetary or physical things of life to ignore the spiritual side of a person? He knew one thing though—she would not be around much longer. After Melinda had her baby, then Edith would leave.

Disappointment tugged at his heart and he tried not to think about it. Edith was a good woman with great qualities. Not only that, she made him laugh and look forward to another day.

As they rode toward home, he thought, "If God holds any favor in me at all, if I have done any good in the world, just anything at all, if he would allow me to win Edith's heart before she leaves, I'll be indebted to him for the rest of my life."

Chapter 36
The Birth of a Baby

The air was crisp, and the dark clouds hovered low. The atmosphere was filled with the scent of smoke from neighboring chimneys. The day before, the temperature was below freezing, approximately ten degrees. Since the clouds had accumulated, the valley had warmed to a pleasant forty degrees.

It was the day before Thanksgiving, and Edith stopped by to check on Melinda. She had been having pains off and on during the last four days, and the catnip tea was helping a little but not like it used to. When Edith arrived, she found Joseph on the sofa strumming his guitar and Gilbert in his overstuffed chair listening to the melancholy sounds. Gilbert invited her to rest her feet, and then left to check up on Melinda.

As she sat on the sofa, Joseph turned in her direction, looking into her dark eyes. "Looks like snow."

"Think so?" Edith replied.

"I bet so."

Edith said teasingly, "Oh, so you're a betting man, are you?"

Joseph strummed a few chords and thought for a moment, contemplating whether this was a trick question or not. He knew how the womenfolk felt about betting, and he tried to suppress a smile.

Edith had been watching Joseph as he avoided her question and laughed softly when she saw him struggling for an answer.

Joseph raised his eyebrows. "What?"

"Nothing. What were you playing before I interrupted you?"

"An English folk song."

"I love the Celtic songs."

"Me, too."

"By the way, did you hear what happened to Mrs. O'Grady the other day?"

"Oh, the overalls in her soup? Isn't there an old Irish song about that?"

"I'm not sure. Is there?"

Joseph shrugged.

"I don't understand how they got in there."

"I found out," Joseph said with a grin. "At first no one seemed to know who did it. Mrs. O'Grady's husband was so upset that someone would play such a practical joke that he was ready for a fight. He said it was such a low-down Irish trick, and whoever did it should be ashamed of himself. He was getting ready to accuse a few of their neighbors when…" Joseph burst into laughter, not able to finish.

"What? What happened?"

Joseph struggled to get himself under control. "Well, when he pulled them out of the soup and showed them to everyone, he asked who had done it. And..." He snickered.

"And what?"

"His wife recognized them and clapped her hand over her mouth." Joseph used his high-pitched falsetto voice as he said, "Oh, no. I had them soaking today and forgot to take them out." He grinned. "You see, Mrs. O'Grady had absent mindedly added her vegetables without thinking."

Edith burst into laughter, filling the room with light and joy. Her countenance was bright and cheerful and when Joseph stopped laughing, he watched her. He enjoyed making her laugh. If he could think of more jokes to tell, he would do it.

But Joseph's eyes betrayed his feelings and Edith could see his gentleness and his interest in her. His blue eyes were so familiar. She was drawn to them and was not sure why. She nervously cleared her throat and stood.

"I should check on Melinda."

Gilbert walked in just as Edith stood, and said, "Melinda seems to be all right this evening, but she's been having more cramping off and on throughout the day. Nothing serious. She's not due for another three weeks."

"That's not uncommon. Two or three weeks early isn't bad. I'll check on her."

Edith found Melinda in her rocking chair, dressed in just a robe and slippers, rocking peacefully and reading. The only sound that could be heard was the soft creaking sound of the rocker against the floor.

"How are you doing, Melinda?"

Melinda looked up from her book and answered, "So, so."

"I've heard that you've been having some cramping."

"Yeah. Nothing to worry about, though. How are things with you?"

Edith knelt beside Melinda and whispered soberly, "I've got to talk to you. I've received a couple letters from my friend. We've got to meet."

"But you already have."

"No! I'm through with writing letters, Melinda. We have to meet one another."

Melinda's brow lifted. "Oh? What's happened?"

"You don't seem to understand. Because I've enjoyed this friendship, you think it's cute. But it's beyond cute. Things have changed." She shoved four letters into Melinda's hands. "The first is his letter, the second is a copy of my reply, and so on. He hasn't answered the last one, as of yet. I'm just waiting."

Melinda unfolded the first letter and began to read:

My Dear Charming Friend,

I hate to admit this, but I seem to wait impatiently for each letter, wondering what my sweet friend will say next. When I do receive a letter, my heart thumps wildly and I sit, anxiously reading what you have to say. As I sit reading your letter, I feel content and happy, and I realize that I'm grateful for our friendship and love.

Truly yours,
A Most Devoted Friend

Melinda unfolded the second letter and read:

Dear Friend,

Do you believe in dreams? I do. I believe that if you wish hard enough and work hard enough, dreams can come true. I believe that dreams are an important part of life. Dreams give us a goal to work toward. *With lots of effort, we are the only ones who can make them come true. As a child I dreamed of singing on stage, and it finally came true. Have you ever had a dream come true? Tell me about it.*

Yours truly,
Edith

She unfolded his reply and read:

My Dear Charming Friend,

We first began writing as friends, but my affection for you has grown tremendously. You asked me if I ever had a dream come true. The answer is yes. It was you. Writing to you has been a dream fulfilled. And yes, I do love you with all my heart. I wish to see you and hold you in my arms once again.

With love and affection,
Your Friend

Melinda gasped as she eagerly opened the last letter and read:

Dear Friend,

With each letter and the revealing of our thoughts, my fondness for you has grown, also. And yes, I think it's time we meet. This time with no masks.

My dearest friend, it's difficult to tell you how I feel. Many times I struggle to tell you my true feelings in each letter. But each time I try, I can't seem to do it. You see, I want a special way to tell you. I know that you appreciate only a little poetry, but not much. Inside this letter is a poem that I would like to share with you. Please read it.

Yours truly,
Edith

My letters! All dead paper, mute and white!
And yet they seem alive and quivering
Against my tremulous hands which loose the string
And let them drop down on my knee tonight.
This said, he wished to have me in his sight
Once, as a friend: this fixed a day in spring
To come and touch my hand...a simple thing,
Yet I wept for this,...the paper's light...
Said, Dear, I love thee; and I sank and quailed
As if God's future thundered on my past.
This said, I am thine—and so its ink has paled
With lying at my heart that beat too fast.
And this...O Love, thy words have ill availed
If, what this said, I dared repeat at last!

By Elizabeth Barrett Browning

After reading the letters, she handed them to Edith, amazed and touched by the tenderness of each letter, so romantic, so full of love, so sincere and genuine.

"Well?" asked Edith.

"Oh, my!"

"Is that all you can say? He signed his letter 'With love,' Melinda. Did you realize that?"

Melinda moaned.

"What, Melinda?" Edith quickly dropped the letters in her bag. "Are you all right?"

"No!" Then Melinda grabbed her belly. The anguish and discomfort were obvious as she groaned, "O-o-o-oh."

"Melinda, are you having more cramps?"

"Yes! I am! Ah-h-h-h-h-h-h!"

The words exploded from her lips with no desire to remain calm. She was in discomfort, and she did not care who heard.

"Yes! Yes! Yes!"

The bedroom door swung open, and Gilbert burst in, his eyes wide, breathing heavily.

"What's the matter?" he demanded.

He stared at Melinda as she held her belly and moaned. He strode to her and knelt on the floor beside her, placing his hand on her knee and looking up at her twisted face.

Then he turned to Edith and said, "She's ready, isn't she!" His mouth was dry as he said, "She's never had them this hard before. During the past week they've been quite bearable."

As he spoke, Jenny and Joseph entered the room. John had gone to bed early and was sound asleep.

Joseph asked softly, "Can I help?"

Edith nodded. "Yes. Gilbert, get her to bed. Joseph, I need clean sheets and sterilized water. Jenny, I need you to help me in the bedroom."

Gilbert tenderly helped Melinda to her feet and led her to the bed. After sitting her down, he knelt beside her and took off her slippers. He fluffed some pillows behind her back to give support. And then he sat beside her, holding her hand in his. His face was laced with concern, and his heart was thumping against his chest as he caressed her fingers.

The tragedy sixteen years ago was etched deeply in his memory. He had been married for only nine months, and his first wife had died during childbirth when Jenny was born. The memory of it returned as he squeezed Melinda's hand, and tears began trickling down his cheeks. How he loved this woman!

Linda Weaver Clarke

She was his life, and he felt he could not endure a life without her. She brought him greater happiness than he thought could ever exist. He felt so lucky…no, the word was blessed. He felt so blessed that she had chosen to marry him. She could have married anyone, but she fell in love with Gilbert, a rancher. It was as if God had had pity on him and gave him this most prized possession. He lifted her hand and pressed his lips lovingly against the soft flesh of her palm.

With her free hand, Melinda lovingly pushed her fingers through his thick wavy hair and smiled, "It'll be all right, Sweetheart. Don't worry."

Before she could say another word, she grimaced and moaned once again, grabbing her stomach with her hand.

"Sweetheart, lie down. Maybe it'll help."

Edith saw his furrowed brow and knew he was worried. She watched Gilbert as he tenderly helped Melinda lie down.

"Gilbert, when she gets serious cramping, I can't allow you to stay."

"Are you sure I can't help?"

Edith shook her head. "One time I gave in and let a man stay. I was telling his wife to breathe deeply so she could relax. That way the cramps wouldn't be so painful. It didn't take long before her husband started to encourage her, too. He kept saying over and over again, 'Breathe deep, Honey. Breathe deep.' After a while, she couldn't' stand it any longer. She scowled at him and yelled, 'I am! Just shut up.' Apparently she had never talked to him that way before, and he was shocked. And then, during her strongest cramp, she scowled and said, 'You did this to me!' That was the last time I allowed a husband to stay."

Gilbert chuckled. He needed a little humor at that moment to ward off the anxiety. He was worrying too much, and he knew it.

"Yup! This was all my fault, if you really think about it."

Melinda touched his brow tenderly. He was trying so hard to joke around, but she could see the anxiety in his face.

"Don't worry so much, Sweetheart. Edith knows what she's doing."

Before Melinda could utter another word, she gasped, and a gush of warm liquid soaked her thin robe and the bed around her. Gilbert's mouth dropped open at the sight of the yellowish liquid. His heart was pounding furiously, and he began to stutter as he looked at his distraught wife.

Melinda grabbed Gilbert's arm and dug her fingers into his flesh as she groaned. A shooting pain gripped her abdomen, causing her belly to stiffen into a round solid lump.

Gilbert's worry lines deepened, his chest tightened, and his voice was unusually tense as he asked, "Melinda, what can I do to help?"

When the cramp subsided, she released her powerful grip, took a few deep breaths, and closed her eyes, hoping to be ready for the next one.

Edith stepped forward and said, "There is one thing that you can do, Gilbert."

She took Gilbert's hand and led him out of the room to be with Joseph. There was no way she would allow him to stay any longer. He was fretting too much, and in his condition, anything could happen. She had seen bigger men than Gilbert faint, perhaps from holding their breath too long. This was women's work.

When she entered the bedroom, Edith sat beside her cousin and rubbed the tension out of her back. She massaged her shoulders and gently reminded her to breathe deeply. She wiped the sweat from her brow, gave her sips of water, and continued to rub her lower back. After an hour, Edith could tell that it would not be much longer.

Melinda's cramping had increased in strength and was almost unbearable. They were coming more frequently, not allowing any time to rest. Just as she thought she could have a short breather, they started up again. Why couldn't she just take a moment to catch her breath? But no, this baby was ready to come, and no one was going to stop his or her progress, not even for a moment. She had no choice in the matter. The excruciating pain would not cease. She realized that she needed to keep breathing to help relax. She closed her eyes to concentrate.

Her cousin's soothing voice reminded her, "Take deep breaths, Melinda. Breathe deep, breathe deep."

For some reason, Melinda felt so alone, as if no one understood the pain she was feeling. How could anyone comprehend it? She knew it was all up to her to get her baby into this new world, and she felt like she was not succeeding. As each contraction began to build, she became more irritated, and she knew that if anyone crossed her or said one word, they had better beware.

Just as she thought the pain could never get worse, it did. Her abdomen tightened and held for several seconds, but in her mind, it felt more like several minutes.

Melinda moaned with despair as she closed her eyes and prayed for help. She could not do this alone. She needed spiritual strength.

As she prayed, she heard Edith saying, "It's time, Melinda. You need to push now. Yes, that's it. Push some more. I can see the baby's head. Push again."

Melinda held her breath, clutched the sheet between her fingers, and pushed with all her strength. Before she realized what had happened, she heard the soft innocent cry of a newborn infant. Relief swept over her like a warm blanket.

Melinda's body was exhausted. Her breathing had slowed down as she listened to the soft cry of her newborn child. When she opened her eyes and looked at her baby, she smiled and tears of joy trickled down her face. She could not deny the hand of God in what had just happened.

Edith quickly wrapped the infant and placed the bundle in Melinda's arms. The little pink face had splotches of filmy white colostrum. Her baby's hair was strawberry blond, about an inch long, and had big gray eyes and long eyelashes. The infant was beautiful, very beautiful indeed.

The joy that swept over Melinda was indescribable. It was as if trying to describe a sunset to someone who was blind. How does one describe the ultimate joy of holding one's child, of being in charge of raising such innocence? What a humbling responsibility!

After cleaning Melinda up, putting a clean sheet on the bed, and helping her get comfortable, Edith walked out to the living room to announce the news.

As she saw the expectant look on Gilbert's face, she said, "Your wife and new daughter are waiting for you."

"Is Melinda all right?"

"Yes. Everything went well."

Gilbert smiled. "A daughter?"

Edith nodded.

Down the hall Gilbert strode at a quick pace. When he entered, tears instantly welled up in his eyes as he asked, "Melinda, are you all right?"

"Yes. Everything's fine."

"I heard we have a daughter."

Melinda looked down at the bundle in her arms and smiled. "Yes, we do."

Gilbert strode toward her and knelt beside the bed. He took her hand in his and kissed it tenderly.

"Do you want to meet your daughter?" Melinda asked.

Gilbert smiled and nodded.

She pulled the blanket down so he could see the baby's face.

"Oh, Melinda. She's beautiful. She looks like you."

Melinda handed his daughter to him, and he carefully took her in his arms.

Gilbert held her close to his chest and marveled at such a new creation as he said, "She's so little."

Melinda watched his eyes as he gazed adoringly at his new daughter, not taking his eyes off her once. She smiled as she watched him. Nothing could be more wonderful. How could her happiness ever exceed what she was now feeling?

"Gilbert?"

His eyes strayed from his daughter's to Melinda's. "Yes?"

"I named our son. What do you want to name our daughter?"

Gilbert smiled. "I've been doing a lot of thinking and have come up with a name that describes her perfectly. It's a Greek word, and it means 'pure'. I think it fits her."

"What is it?"

"Makayla. We can call her Kayla for short."

"Oh Gilbert, I love it."

Chapter 37
Joseph's Confession

While the family was gathered together in the bedroom, Edith was washing the dirty dishes that had been used that evening, and Joseph was drying them. After a while, he stopped and watched her, enjoying being beside her and talking. She was so enchanting in her apron, tied neatly around her waist, and her hair was mussed from the busy evening. It was now eleven p.m. and she looked exhausted but was still going. What a trooper! How he admired her tenacity, her perseverance and determination!

When Edith noticed that Joseph had stopped wiping, she turned and faced him with a grin, and chided him, "Get busy drying, you slacker!"

"Me? A slacker?"

"Yes. Here I am working my fingers to the bone like a slave, helping to bring a child into the world, and now I'm slaving over these dishes. And what do you do? You just stand there watching me work. Hmmm, I once heard there was no rest for the wicked. Well, I must be a very wicked woman."

Joseph chuckled. Without even thinking, he reached out and gently moved a loose curl from her cheek. Then he backed up a couple steps and his eyes swept over her, marveling at her beauty, as he said softly, "You look mighty fine for a wicked woman."

It was not so much what he said but the way he said it that warmed Edith's soul. His eyes gave her the message that she was a very beautiful woman. Here she was with loose tendrils hanging in her face, and an apron tied around her waist. She knew that she looked tired and worn, but Joseph was making her feel like one of the most beautiful women on earth.

When Joseph saw the coy look on her face, his heart picked up speed and he wondered if she was feeling the same way he was. On impulse, Joseph stepped toward her, slid his hands around her waist, and pulled her close to him.

As he enfolded her in his arms, he whispered in her ear, "Oh, Edith. I've fallen for you."

Edith was taken aback by this gesture and his sweet words. With surprise, she pushed him back and said, "But...but how could you? You don't even know me that well. We're just friends, Joseph. We're only friends and that's all it can be."

Joseph gazed upon her, his heart filling with warmth and his pulse racing. As his eyes wandered to her luscious lips, he drew her close to him once again and placed a gentle kiss upon them. It was one of longing and tenderness, and he noticed how she responded to his touch. The message he communicated in that one simple kiss was one of exquisite love.

Edith's heart was beating rapidly, and she was not sure what was happening to her. All she knew was that being in his arms was more comforting than she had ever imagined.

His arms were strong and protective, and his kiss was so familiar…

What was she thinking? Feeling dazed from his warm kiss, she tried to come to her senses and pushed Joseph back.

"Joseph, what has come over you?"

He grinned, not saying a word.

Seeing his expression, she stepped backwards against the sink to steady her wobbly legs. "Ooh, I'm so confused."

"Confused? Why?"

Trying to get her breath back, she answered, "Oh, Joseph. I should have told you this a long time ago. I have to tell you something."

"And what's that?"

"Joseph, I'm in love with another man."

"Another man? Who?"

"This may sound very strange, but I don't know his name."

"Oh? Is this common for you to fall for a nameless person?"

Joseph stepped forward, smiling, and then slipped his hands around her waist once again. He pulled her close, gazing at her, and watching her become uneasy. Then he slowly raised his hand to her cheek and softly ran his fingertips across the curves of her face, sending a tingling sensation to her addled senses.

"What's the matter, Edith? Why are you so nervous?" he said softly as he pulled her into his arms.

Savoring the closeness of her, he smoothed his hand over her hair with affection and asked, "How can you love a nameless person, Edith?"

After realizing that she was enjoying all this cuddling a little too much, Edith began to feel guilty, unfaithful to the one man she adored.

She struggled once again to explain, "No, Joseph. Listen to me. Please."

She wanted to push away, out of his embrace, but he had her cornered against the sink. She could not back up any further.

"Joseph? Listen to me. I'm in love with…"

Edith hesitated. It was difficult to finish her sentence when she felt Joseph kissing her temple and working his way down to the soft hollow of her cheek. She felt helpless and confused. But at the same time, she didn't have the will to pull away from him again. She sighed as he spread gentle whispering kisses over her face, along her brow, and towards her earlobe.

And then he said something that she wasn't expecting.

Her eyes widened as she asked, "What did you say?"

"Do you want me to repeat it?"

Edith nodded in the affirmative.

Holding her in his arms and pressing his palms against her back, once again he repeated his message in her ear, hoping that she was feeling as deeply for him as he was for her.

"To come and touch my hand…a simple thing, yet I wept for this. Dear, I love thee. And I sank and quailed as if God's future thundered on my past. This said: I am thine."

Edith stood frozen in the very spot where she stood, trying to comprehend what he had just said. She was stunned. It was so unexpected.

Joseph leaned back and looked into her face. He was not sure what her response was going to be, and he was beginning to feel nervous. Had he moved too quickly? He thought they had gotten along quite well lately, but the conversation at the café had thrown him for a loop, and he was uneasy about her true feelings for him. All he hoped for was that her love was as deep as his.

Joseph asked cautiously, "Edith? Are you all right?"

She stared at him, unprepared for a response to his question, speechless. After a few seconds, she was able to nod.

"Edith? I have fallen in love with you, my Charming Friend. Please marry me. I don't want to read about your thoughts any longer. I want you to tell me in person from now on. Do you understand what I'm saying, Señorita? I am yours, if you'll have me."

Taking a deep breath and letting it out slowly, she gradually began to understand for the first time. Within moments, every letter he had ever written came rushing back to her memory, every tender word, secrets they had shared...when she fell in the stream, he carefully wiped her face with his handkerchief...the day he had stayed beside her and helped her tend to Sam's wounds...the Halloween night he had appeared at her doorstep and his gentle kiss...the ice cream he had bought her when he told her of the perfect mate. He was talking about her. Everything began to fit into place.

When Edith did not respond, he asked with concern and uncertainty, "Are you disappointed?"

As the confusion left her eyes, she shook her head. "No, I'm not disappointed, Joseph."

"Are you sure?"

She nodded. "In fact, I feel quite the opposite."

Joseph's eyes brightened and happiness overtook him. His heart pounded furiously with excitement as he said, "Really, Edith? Is that how you truly feel?"

"Joseph?"

"What?"

"I'm glad that it's you."

Thrilled with her answer, he enfolded her in his arms once again and held her in a tight embrace. The joy he felt was overwhelming as he pressed the softness of her against him. How could life be so filled with the happiness he was feeling at that very moment?

He pulled back and looked into her face and saw the same inner joy that he was feeling himself. A longing to kiss her arose deeply within him as he felt a rush of love warm his soul.

Realizing that Gilbert was busy in the other room and would not invade this private moment, he pressed his lips to hers and felt her respond with just as much fervor. He had not realized she was such a passionate woman until now.

While holding her lovingly, giving her one kiss after another, a deep voice scolded in a teasing manner, "Joseph? Edith? What's going on here? And in my kitchen, too?"

Quickly, Edith pulled back, her face flushing a bright red, but Joseph kept his arms around her and chuckled at her dismay.

Gilbert grinned. "Hmmm, I think Melinda owes me an apology. I just won the bet, and I didn't even have to raise a finger to do so."

Edith tried to wiggle free, but Joseph kept his arm possessively around her waist. Gilbert had caught them, and she was embarrassed, but he was not about to let her go so quickly.

As she looked at Gilbert questioningly, something dawned on her. "Did you say you didn't raise a finger? You mean you didn't tell Joseph to write to me?"

Gilbert raised his brow. "You mean he's the mysterious stranger?"

Joseph's eyes twinkled, and with humor lacing his voice, he said, "I may be strange, but I'm not a stranger any longer." Then he looked into Edith's face with a tenderness that took her breath away. "Isn't that right?"

Gilbert interrupted, just to confirm what had been said. "You mean to tell me that you're the mysterious friend?"

"I sure am, but I'm not mysterious any more. I've been found out."

"You're that sweet talker Melinda and Edith have been cooing over?"

Embarrassed, Edith quickly changed the subject by asking Joseph, "Who put you up to this? Who's the friend that referred you to me?"

"Well, I'm not sure I can reveal her name without permission."

"Her?"

Joseph nodded. "Yup. She's a woman."

Edith took Joseph's shirt in both hands and pulled tightly, asking in a pleading voice, "Who is she, Joseph?"

Joseph chuckled at her persistence. "You're one insistent lady, Edith. But I'm not at liberty to say until she gives me permission."

"It was me," came a soft pleasant voice from the hallway.

Everyone turned around and stared with disbelief.

"You?" Gilbert burst out in surprise.

"What?" Edith asked, even more stunned than Gilbert.

"I couldn't help it. I just knew the two of you were meant for one another. But I knew how Aunt Edith hated being set up." Jenny smiled innocently. "So I made it easy. This way Joseph could court her without any interference and get to know her. And she wouldn't judge him unnecessarily. She could get to know his soul first."

Turning to Joseph, Edith asked, "But how did you get the letters to Mama? I was home an awful lot."

Joseph grinned. "By way of the vegetable basket."

"The vegetable basket?"

"Yup!" Joseph squeezed Edith close to him and added, "And I've never had more fun, either. Especially on Halloween night! That was when I knew I had lost my heart to you."

A hush came over the room as Joseph took Edith's hand and walked outside on the porch. They stood enfolded in each other's arms and gazed at the stars above, not saying a word but feeling content with life and its surprises.

Chapter 38
Shhh, You'll Wake the Baby

Gilbert tiptoed into the bedroom. The lamp was set low so Melinda could see when she fed the baby. All was silent except for the soft breathing of mother and child. He bent down and quietly pulled his boots off and set them beside the door. Then he silently walked toward the bassinet and gazed upon his new daughter. He smiled and then bent down and brushed his lips across her silky plump cheek. She smelled sweet and fresh, and her breath smelled of sweet mother's milk.

Gilbert could not resist, so he scooped her up into his arms and gazed upon the beauty of his newborn child. The incomprehensible joy he felt was overwhelming as he memorized every feature and curve of her face. Kayla's plump cheeks were rosy, her long eyelashes touched her cheeks, her button nose was so small, and her double chin was adorable.

Gilbert pulled the cover from her hands and noticed how slender and long her fingers were. Her hand was so small that it could wrap around his finger. Gilbert brushed his finger delicately along the velvety texture of her arm and down to her hand. Then he slid his finger under her palm, and instinctively she curled her delicate fingers around his finger.

Gilbert's heart instantly swelled with undeniable love and tenderness. He pulled his finger free and pressed his lips upon her forehead. As he cradled her in his arms, the overwhelming love he had for this infant brought tears to this rugged and tough man, and he quickly blinked back the tears. His heart was softened and his emotions were on the surface.

The incredible joy that overtook him was indescribable. He knew it was not considered "weakness" to weep, but as a man, he felt the need to be strong and hide this sort of emotion. He had once considered himself tough, but Melinda had softened him quite a bit.

Gilbert gently put her in the bassinet and covered her up. Then he unbuttoned his shirt and placed it on a chair along with his pants and socks. After undressing for bed, ever so quietly, he slid under the covers and snuggled up to his wife. She was lying on her side with her back to Gilbert.

As he wrapped his arm around her waist, he noticed the firm roundness of her belly was gone. In a way, he missed it. For six months he had laid his hand on her belly and waited for movement. Now it was gone.

The sweet memory of it was one of happiness, but now little Kayla lay asleep in her bassinet. Life was good and all was well. The relief he felt that Melinda was all right swept over him. Now he would not have to worry about her any longer.

Then it dawned on him that his worry would transfer to raising a little daughter. His worry would be a different one. When this little beauty was old enough to notice boys, he would have to get out his rifle and lay it across his lap. When the boys would come calling, he would have to lay down the ground rules: No courting until sixteen and be home by eleven.

He would let every young man know that his daughter would not be trifled with and would be treated with respect or else. Then he would tap the long barrel of his rifle with his fingers and grin at the young man.

Gilbert chuckled at the thought of it. Melinda stirred.

He couldn't help it, so he tucked his hand around her waist and softly asked, "Are you awake?"

No answer.

"Are you awake?"

Still no answer.

Gilbert squeezed her close to him and then asked again, "Are you awake, Melinda?"

She replied in a sleepy tone, "Would you believe me if I said I wasn't?"

"No."

She laughed.

"I just wanted to say thank you," said Gilbert.

"You're welcome. For what?"

"For Kayla, for John, for being my wife, for loving me."

Melinda yawned and stretched, then turned over to face him. "To be your wife and to love you is easy. For Kayla and John, now that's another matter. That was lots of hard work and very exhausting, to say the least."

"I know it's not easy. I can relate. Just watching the discomfort, the morning sickness, and the mood swings isn't easy on a man."

Gilbert chuckled as Melinda slugged him and poked him in the ribs a couple times.

When she heard him laugh, she chided him. "Shhh. You'll wake the baby."

"Sorry," he whispered with a wide grin.

Gilbert looked lovingly into her face and then he gently pulled her into his arms as he whispered, "I would not be the man I am today without you, Melinda. You're my life and my living joy. I would be nothing without you."

Then he spread a string of sweet kisses across her face.

As he nibbled at the softness of her neck, Melinda giggled, "Stop it, Gilbert. That tickles."

He suppressed a chuckle and whispered ever so softly, "Shhh, you'll wake the baby."

This novel is one of five in the Family Saga in Bear Lake, Idaho series, which includes: *Melinda and the Wild West, Edith and the Mysterious Stranger, Jenny's Dream, David and the Bear Lake Monster,* and *Elena, Woman of Courage.* Each story in this family saga has adventure, romance, history, and courage. Intertwining fact and fiction, these novels have a blend of intriguing characters and true experiences.

Author's Notes

In forming one of the major characters, Edith, I took a few experiences and parts of her personality from two people: my mother, Florence Milred Weaver, and my grandmother, Olive Clark Weaver.

The inspiration for this story came from my own mother's experience. Her girlfriend told my mother that she was being way too picky and her expectations were too high. My mother was an accomplished pianist and a spiritual person with certain standards for a husband and first impressions were important to her. Her girlfriend said that she knew a good-looking twenty-nine year-old farmer that she could write to. My mother told me that through letters she was able to get to know my father's soul, his innermost feelings. They wrote for several months and gradually fell in love. After realizing their feelings for one another, they decided it was time to meet. The second time they met, he proposed. The third time they met was on their wedding day.

My grandmother took a Nurses Training Course at the hospital in Salt Lake City and also attended the University of Utah around 1900. She helped her sister's son recover from diphtheria when other doctors had given up. She was noted for her compassion and love for her patients. She also had a beautiful alto voice and sang with great feeling. We lived next door to her and my mother often told me how she could hear my grandmother sing as she picked her raspberries and how her voice rang with beauty. Between 1904 and 1910, she sang in the famous Mormon Tabernacle Choir. In 1910, at the age of thirty, she finally found the man of her "dreams." Halloween was her favorite time of year. She had a trunk full of costumes and would dress up every year.

The experience of the bull goring a man and what Edith did to save his life was taken from a true experience of my great grandmother, Frances Davies—Olive Weaver's mother. The doctor was out of town, and it was up to her to save this man's life. Every detail was recorded in her biography, and I used it for my story. The man lived for many years afterwards.

The story about Uncle William walking up to the women's choir was taken from a true experience. I couldn't resist inserting it into my novel. Each Sunday, my daughter, Kristina, accused her father of sleeping in church. He would become indignant and say, "I'm just resting my eyes." Kristina never believed him and would nudge him every Sunday, "Wake up, Dad." Each time, he defended himself by saying, "I'm not asleep. I can hear everything that's being said. I'm just resting my eyes." One day, my husband was "resting his eyes" when my daughter, Felicia, poked him and said the choir was going up to sing. He immediately grabbed a hymnbook, walked up to the pulpit and stood in the middle of the women's choir. We have laughed about it ever since. After this incident, Kristina never let her father forget it.

When my eldest daughter Angela was pregnant, they joked around saying they just might name their baby Jockwirt. We never laughed harder the day she made that announcement, and I never forgot that name. I just had to use it in my novel.

Jane Mason was Idaho's Calamity Jane in 1899. Kittie Wilkins was the Horse Queen of Idaho. Joe Monaghan worked as a gold miner, was a cowboy, and served on many juries for thirty years without anyone knowing she was a woman. It wasn't until her death that they found out the truth. Wilbur and Orville Wright invented the world's first power-driven flying machine, which was flown at Kitty Hawk, North Carolina on December 17, 1903.

Mrs. O'Grady and the overalls in the soup was taken from the old traditional Irish song, "Who Threw the Overalls in Mistress Murphy's Chowder?"

About the Wild Bunch

In the western part of the United States, the market for cattle was lucrative. Cattle rustling was a terrible problem in the West and these bold outlaws, such as the Wild Bunch, infested the Utah, Wyoming, Colorado, and Idaho territories. Some of the larger cattlemen tried to hire gunfighters to scare the rustlers away, while others hired known rustlers, hoping they would not steal from the person that was paying them. These two ideas were not successful, probably because outlaws weren't known for being trustworthy, and there were more outlaws than gunfighters.

Robbers Roost was in the central-eastern part of Utah. The rustlers drove their cattle to this remote area for safekeeping until they could sell them. This hideout had gained a reputation for being impenetrable because it was situated between the Colorado River and the Dirty Devil River, which was a narrow stretch of land with steep-walled canyons. The law never knew for sure if they would be ambushed while entering the mouth of the canyon.

Cattle were usually stolen from the open range. If the cattle had been branded, the rustlers would alter the brand so it could not be recognized and would ship them by train out of Utah and sell them to military camps.

Even though this story with the Tall Texan and Gunplay is fictional, I chose them as an example of the rustlers of that day.

Butch Cassidy and the Wild Bunch were one of the gangs of outlaws that existed in the Utah, Wyoming, Montana, Colorado, and Idaho region. He made it well known that he was against the rich cattle barons. He and his gang referred to themselves as the "Robin Hood of the West," out to rob from the rich and give to the poor.

Of all western outlaws, there is a feeling of intrigue when the stories of Butch Cassidy and the Wild Bunch are told. Cassidy and his gang put together the "longest series of successful robberies in all of western history."

Robert LeRoy Parker, alias Butch Cassidy, was born 15 April 1866 in Beaver, Utah and was raised by religious parents. When he was a teenager, he worked on a ranch near Circleville, Utah and became good friends with an old rustler named Mike Cassidy. After Parker left home, he took on the name of his mentor. Cassidy and his gang put together the longest series of successful robberies in the West. As far as history goes, he never killed a person in a holdup.

Ben Kilpatrick, alias the Tall Texan, was from Knickerbocker, Texas. It was said that more outlaws came from Knickerbocker than any other town. The Tall Texan got his name because of his height. He was six-feet-one inch tall and was known as a "lady killer" who swept many a lady off her feet. He was jailed in 1905 at the Federal Penitentiary in Atlanta, Georgia, for passing stolen notes. He was released in 1911 and killed the following year in Texas (March 13, 1912), during a robbery of the Southern Pacific Sunset Flyer. A guard hit him over the head with a mallet and crushed Kilpatrick's skull. He was only thirty-six when he died.

Clarence L. Maxwell, alias Gunplay, came from Texas and proved himself as a gunfighter by killing two men in Colton, Utah. He was known as a small-time bandit and longed to be part of the Wild Bunch. In 1898 Gunplay was captured during a bank robbery in Springville, Utah. While Gunplay was in the Utah State Prison, he thought he would impress Cassidy by writing a letter to the Utah governor, Heber M. Wells. Gunplay told the governor that there was a gang of 200 men defending Robbers Roost with many fortifications and a large supply of ammunition. It wasn't true. In the summer of 1909, Gunplay was killed in a gunfight in Price, Utah. He had picked a fight with the wrong man, someone who was faster on the draw than he was.

William Carver, alias News Carver, robbed a bank in Sonora, Texas, after the Wild Bunch separated. He was cornered and killed unmercifully by a large posse. It was written that he was "shot to pieces."

Harvey Logan, alias Kid Curry, was known as the most feared killer in the West. When Logan was cornered in a canyon in Colorado, he committed suicide on June 8, 1904, rather than give himself up to the law.

Willard Erastus Christianson, alias Matt Warner, had an unusual life for an outlaw. He was born in 1864 in Ephraim, Utah. He was the son of a Swedish father and a German mother who had come to Utah Territory. He came from a religious background but chose the wild life of an outlaw. While in jail, he decided to go straight after hearing about the death of his wife. He settled down in Utah and ran for deputy sheriff under his birth name, but since no one had heard of him before, he was defeated. He tried once again, this time under his alias, and won by a landslide. Later he was elected justice of the peace and was hired as a night guard and detective in Price, Utah. Matt died in 1938 at the age of seventy-four which was quite rare for a former outlaw. Most outlaws died young.

The Wild Bunch scattered in 1902 when Cassidy went to Argentina and became a rancher. After Cassidy left, things tamed down a bit. Most of the rustlers in the Utah and Idaho area moved to greener pastures. But there were still a few that stayed around looking for a little excitement and to make a name for themselves.

Bibliography

Baker, Pearl. *The Wild Bunch at Robbers Roost.* Abelard-Schuman, 1971.

———, *Robbers Roost Recollections.* Western Experience Series. Utah State University Press, 1991.

Betenson, Lula Parker and Dora Flack. *Butch Cassidy, My Brother.* Penguin, 1976.

Pointer, Larry. *In Search of Butch Cassidy,* 2d ed. University of Oklahoma Press, 1988.

Warner, Matt as told to Murray King. *The Last of the Bandit Riders.* Bonanza Books, 1940.

"For they loved the praise of men more than the praise of God."
John 12:43.

Acknowledgments

I would like to give special thanks to my editor, Pamela Peterson. My special thanks also to George A. Clarke for creating a lovely book cover. I would like to give thanks to Kelvin Smith for the use of the beautiful photo. His photos are excellent. Check out www.untraveledroad.com.

About the Author

Linda Weaver Clarke was raised on a farm surrounded by the rolling hills of southern Idaho and has made her home in southern Utah among the beautiful red desert mountains. She is happily married and is the mother of six daughters and has four grandchildren.

The author earned her bachelor of arts degree at Southern Utah University and was awarded the Outstanding Non-Traditional Student Award for the College of Performing Arts in 2002. She writes articles for several newspapers and teaches a writing workshop where she encourages others to turn their family histories into a variety of interesting stories.

In addition to *Edith and the Mysterious Stranger*, Mrs. Clarke has written another historical fiction love story, *Melinda and the Wild West*. This book, the first of five in a family saga, was a semifinalist for the *Reader Views* "Reviewers Choice Award in 2007."

To learn more about this author or to schedule a speaking engagement, visit www.lindaweaverclarke.com.